Forever

An Unfortunate Fairy Tale
Book 5

Chanda Hahn

ISBN-10: 0692432620
ISBN-13: 978-0692432624
FOREVER
Copyright © 2015 by Chanda Hahn

Cover design by Steve Hahn
Edited by Bethany Kaczmarek
Photographer Tiana Meckel
Makeup Artist J.J. Hines
Model Erica Cornelison

This is a work of fiction. Names, characters, places and incidents are either the product of the author's imagination or are used fictitiously, and any resemblance to actual persons, living or dead, business establishments, events or locales is entirely coincidental.

www.chandahahn.com

For my super fans

Bethany A Bachman

Jamie Deann and Evalyn

Paola Loader

Kerry Marriott

Marsha (Critchfield) McGregor

Doris Orman

Aliseea Patricia

Sherry Ralph-Lyle

Izabela Wardzińska

Chrissy White

Will *Beauty* have to
destroy the *Beast* she created?

One

A trail of smoke still sailed into the sky like the colorful tail of a kite. It could be traced back down to the decimated remains of the Green Mill Recycling Center.

Mina sat on the hill across the river and stared down at the dark, burned wreckage that had been the Godmothers' Guild. Only a single fire rescue worker remained, and he walked among the rubble, scattering ashes with a large rod to keep flare ups from sprouting. Yellow caution tape roped off the whole area.

"Come on," she mumbled under her breath.

She tapped her closed fist against her bent knees. She'd been sitting, watching, and guarding the building—waiting to see if any of the rescue team would discover what really lay only a few stories below them. She could only hope that the Fae had covered their tracks well.

The news had called the fire a rare accident, saying the explosion was caused by a ruptured gas line, but the Fae knew otherwise. And Mina knew otherwise, but she suspected there was some Fae persuasion being used to cover up what really happened.

The cause of this tragedy was the dark prince himself. He'd sent his army to attack the Godmother's Guild like he had done over twenty years ago. Last time, the Guild had been able to fight off the attack, even trapping one of the trolls in stone. But the prince, the Story, wasn't as strong then.

Now, Teague was nearly invincible. Joined with the other half of his soul, Jared, he had fully come into his power, and he wanted vengeance—against the Guild, against the humans, against her.

She let out a long sigh and dug her fingernails into her palms as she stared past the rubble along the river to an area that the Godmothers had warded and protected from the rescue team. Even she wouldn't have known what to look for if she hadn't been there when it happened.

The river rock was slightly darker along the embankment, where Fae flame had devoured the bodies of the dead. Of those who had died in the battle and from the fire. One of them had been Mei Wong, her faithful brownie Godmother.

"Why?" Mina whispered, her voice hoarse from crying. "Why you? You were nothing but gentle and kind. You didn't deserve this. He did. It's *his* fault."

Tears burned in her eyes, but she refused to blink. She let the pain well up inside of her. Because although she tried to place the blame on Teague, Mina knew deep down, he wasn't the one who started it. She was.

She was the one who had gone back into the past and set all of this in motion. It was her. It had always been her. She was the one who created the Grimoire. She was the one who had given it to the Grimm brothers. She was the one who betrayed Teague by saving Ferah, who, in turn, stabbed the prince with an evil dagger, the tip of which remained inside him and poisoned his heart. Of course he blamed her. When she tried to dig out the tip, he saw her only as another assassin and blasted her through the tower window.

Trying to save herself, she had inadvertently opened up a gate between her world and his, and he'd been chasing her ever since. He had to wait over a century for the timelines to catch up.

But now they were on the same playing field. There were no more secrets. She knew who he was, and he knew she knew. She created the beast, and now she'd have to destroy him. She knew that now.

Jared was Teague, at least a part of him. When she'd met Teague back in time, she saw bits of Jared in him—the smile, the smirk, the cocky grin. Even the way he looked at her when he didn't think anyone was watching. It had been Jared's look, his jokes, his smile.

But that was then, before he was poisoned. Now? Now she didn't know what to make of him, of the prince, of the Story.

Who he had been and who he was now would no longer matter. Innocents were at stake. Too many had paid the price for Mina's folly. Too many had been injured; too many had died. She could only see this concluding one way. It would end with death—hers or Teague's.

He had said she might be more agreeable in the morning. Well, it was morning. Where the heck was he? Brody and Nan had forced her to go home last night to get some sleep. But that was a joke. She couldn't.

3

She'd taken off the lavender dress and thrown it onto the bed, feeling the weight of the dagger hidden inside the pocket. She'd changed into jeans and boots, and layered a plaid top over a shirt. Grabbing mittens, hat, and scarf, she snuck back outside at first light and rode her bike all the way to the Recycling Center.

Seven hours later, her rear was numb, and her legs were stiff from sitting, Most of the damage had been contained and fires put out. She had watched and counted as each of the City Gas vehicles, the police cars, and the fire trucks had pulled away one by one.

Her stomach growled from hunger. She knew this was where he'd want to meet her. So he could gloat over his handiwork, his accomplishments. He wanted to see her cower, but she knew she couldn't. She wouldn't.

Her skin prickled with the familiar sensation that she felt whenever he was near. Mina jumped up and turned around just as he stepped out from behind a large evergreen.

His dark, angry, blue eyes crinkled up in the corners with mirth, mirroring the smirk on his face. His perfectly styled dark hair accentuated his cheekbones. He wore a long patchwork jacket, made of different leathers and black textures, like a cape off of his shoulders. Both the cape and his tall, black boots gave him an animalistic ruler vibe. The only light thing about him was his stark white shirt.

"I think I prefer these clothes to your fancy dresses," he said, his voice like velvet as he stepped closer to her.

"I think I prefer your other clothes. Are you auditioning for an episode of *What Not to Wear?*"

Teague frowned and shook his head. "Again with the insults that mean nothing to me."

"How about this? You look like an animal."

His handsome head fell back, and his eyes closed in laughter. "Now that is funny."

He came up and reached out to touch her cheek, but she slapped his hand away. "Don't touch me."

His nostrils flared in anger, but he held back his biting remark. Instead, he turned away from her and placed one boot on a rock, gazing down over the smoking building in the valley. *Here come the insults.*

"Do you have it?" His voice had lost its teasing tone. He was asking for the dagger.

"Yes."

"Then give it to me, Mina." He cast a forlorn look over his shoulder at her.

"I didn't bring it."

She could see his jaw working as he clenched it. He straightened, cracking his neck as he faced her full on. "Did you not get my warning?" He pointed down below at the very spot of the burned river rock. "I'm done playing games."

"Well, the game now has new rules. It's an expanded edition."

He raised one eyebrow. "You think to outplay me?"

"Did you bring my mirror?" she shot back. "I may exchange one for the other." She wanted the mirror. With that mirror, he could always watch her. Always.

This time it was Teague who looked surprised. "May exchange?"

5

"How about: You bring me the dagger, and I'll let your friends live."

"Without my mirror, I won't even *think* about giving you the dagger."

He sighed and sat on the large rock, extending his legs in front of him. He crossed them at the ankles. "I think I'll hold onto my mirror a little longer. I've learned that women can't be trusted, and I like the idea that you know I'm watching you. It makes it harder for you to plot against me when I can watch your..." He stood up and slowly walked around her. "... every... single... move." He leaned in on the last word and inhaled the scent of her hair.

"I hate you," she seethed.

"Wrong." He grabbed her shoulders and turned her to face him. "I know how you feel about me." The corner of his mouth crooked up. "Or at least a part of me. You were in love with me."

He tapped his head. "I have his memories."

"Then you know how he felt about me?" Her voice rose in hope.

"Pity." Teague said, sending her moment of hope crashing to the ground. "He pitied you."

It was a jab in the heart. She couldn't deny that his words hurt, but Teague was a liar, and she couldn't trust anything he said.

"Mina."

She lifted her head up to look at him.

"It seems you need a lesson in obedience." Something suddenly drew his attention past her, across the river, to the woods. Mina heard a thin, eerie whistle, and she looked at Teague.

His face took on an expression of contempt. "It seems you have company. I warned you I would take away your friends one by one. You like games? Well, so do I. But I'll wait my turn. Someone has a message for you."

He turned to glance back and pointed his finger across the river to the distant woods, far behind the wreckage. "I'd get moving if I were you. And fast."

"What did you do?" She turned to watch Teague disappear into the woods. Then she looked back in worry at the forest and the remains below.

There was still a single safety worker down there. She watched in trepidation, but nothing happened. The man was satisfied with his work and threw his tools into the back of the white city truck. A few minutes later, he was gone, driving away.

The wind changed course and blew in her direction, sending the smell of burnt wood, oil, and fumes over her. She ducked to avoid the onslaught of the aroma and caught a glimpse of something moving in the woods. Across the river, on the south side, there appeared to be a large black dog the size of a German shepherd, but with huge ears and paws.

The dog followed a scent trail. It came into the open, stared at the debris, and spent a bit of time nosing around the burned lumber and scrap metal. It walked through the large puddles left by the fire hoses. Back and forth the beast went, even stopping to scratch at something in the dirt.

After a few minutes, nothing significant had happened. Mina figured she was probably making too big a deal out of the dog's presence. Teague must've been warning her about something else. Either way, there was no point in lingering. She stood and stretched.

At least she'd been able to take the time for one last goodbye. The wind whipped her hair into her face as it shifted back toward the wreckage.

The dog's hackles rose as soon as he caught her scent. Even across the river, she saw the beast change its posture from curious to killer.

The forest around the dog blurred and shifted as a large being took his place. The thick man wore a long cloak of grayish-black wool covering black leather armor. Across his chest hung a row of throwing blades. He fingered the hilt of a knife just before he turned death-like eyes, orbs of white, her way.

Could he see her? If she didn't move, maybe he wouldn't notice her.

He reached for a knife, and she knew. No matter the color of his eyes or the distance, he could see her.

Run, she commanded her legs. But they were frozen in fear. *Run!* Mina spun toward the nearby woods but slipped and fell to the ground.

Thud.

A black knife had embedded itself into the tree right in front of her. If she hadn't fallen, the knife would have impaled her, not the tree. She looked back and saw only the dog. Hackles up, abnormally large black ears flat against his head, and lips pulled back, exposing sharp canines. The hulking head flicked toward her, its death-white eyes locking onto her seconds before it let out a terrifying howl.

A shape-shifting Reaper? Mina kept low and crawled along the ground, trying to make herself a smaller target. What had she been thinking coming here by herself? Why hadn't she brought backup?

She hadn't expected to run into a Reaper here—that's why. She'd expected to see Teague. He still wanted the dagger, and he wouldn't stop until he got it. So he hadn't sent a Reaper to kill her, had he? If she died, that didn't put the knife in his hand.

As soon as she got into a denser copse of trees, she pushed herself to her feet and took off down the hill, away from the dog, as fast as she could. Sliding along the rocks, kicking up dust, she didn't stop until someone stepped in front of her. Unable to stop in time, she plowed into him.

The man grunted as he took the full force of her blow, and they both fell to the ground rolling a few feet. Brody groaned and looked up at her. But the smile fell from his face when he saw the terror on hers. "What's wrong?"

"Run," she hissed and jumped to her feet, pulling him alongside her. But she had to stop, looking around in confusion. "Where's your car?"

"This way." He ran to the left, making sure to keep pace with her. "What's wrong, Mina?"

"Reaper," she huffed.

Her heart thudded loudly in relief when she saw the car. She ran to the passenger side and lifted the handle, but the door was still locked. *Come on.*

She held on until she heard the automatic click and then jumped into the seat. Brody pulled out his keys and fumbled with the ignition. "Go, go, go! Start it up."

"I'm trying," he said between clenched teeth.

The keys fell on the floor, and Brody bent down, feeling for them on the floor mat.

Another howl filled the air.

He stilled. "What in the world is that?"

He slowly straightened to look over the dashboard. "That dog is huge! But where's the Reaper?"

Mina glanced back. Nothing. "I think the dog *is* the Reaper. Can you still see it?"

Her hand snaked forward along the arm rest until her fingers found the switch. A soft click sounded in the car as the doors locked. Childish, but she was out of options.

Crash!

"Whoa!" Brody shouted.

Mina heard claws scraping and digging at the glass. But she couldn't see anything out there. "Is it heavy enough to break through the windshield?"

Brody shifted the car into reverse and sped backwards, spinning the wheel and executing a turnaround worthy of a stunt driver. The black beast's claws clicked and screeched across the hood as it tried to stay on, but Brody's driving threw him off. They heard a thud as it slammed against the side of the car. Brody hit the gas, flying up the road.

Thirty, forty, fifty, on up to eighty miles per hour Brody sped. Mina couldn't make herself open her eyes until about thirty seconds had passed. She tried to look at her passenger mirror, but all she saw were trees whizzing by.

Brody slowed only enough to turn onto the on ramp. When they were safely speeding down the highway among other cars, he looked over to her. "That's a Reaper… as in death?"

"I think so," Mina craned her head to look between the seats. "They're the hunters and assassins, but they've been known to go rogue."

"And that beast dog *is one?*" Brody continued driving and cast a quick look over to her. "I've never seen anything that big."

Mina studied his profile. He didn't look scared at the prospect of being hunted—he looked angry. His sun-kissed blond hair accented the deep blue of his eyes, and his strong hands gripped the steering wheel with determination.

"I'm not sure what that was." She shrugged, turning in her seat to face him. "What were *you* doing there? Don't get me wrong, I'm glad you showed up when you did, because I couldn't have outridden that thing on my bike."

"Following you." He glanced at her quickly.

"What?"

Now it was Brody's turn to shrug. "Well, Ever, Nan, and I kind of promised to never let you be without a guard. And since Ever left to try and track Teague, it was between Nan and me, and I drew the short straw for today." He sighed, trying to make it sound like a huge inconvenience.

"I'm not a straw," Mina said.

"No, but you are short." He tried to hide the smile, but Mina smacked him in the arm with the back of her hand. "I followed you this morning when you took off on your bike. I almost lost you a few times, but I figured out where you were heading. You wanted to say your goodbyes."

Her gaze dropped to her folded hands. Her heart swelled with the pain of her loss. "It's not fair," she mumbled, not expecting an answer.

"No, it's not. I know you cared a lot for her."

"She was like a second mom to me."

Mina looked over her shoulder and noticed the white handle and red metal frame in the backseat this time. "You grabbed my bike."

"Yeah, it took a bit of finagling, but I got it in." Brody reached out with his right hand to hold hers and gave it a reassuring squeeze.

Mina looked at their clasped hands on the seat between them, and she was filled with mixed emotions. This was everything she wanted, but she couldn't help but feel overwhelmed with guilt. She had been forced to face her true feelings about Teague in the tower, and—given the choice—she had chosen to stay.

But she wasn't quite herself then. Right?

"What are we going to do if that thing shows up again?" Brody's mood got serious as he faced the fact that the encounter with the Reaper would not be their last.

"We have to be prepared, 'cause what you saw is only one of many Reapers. And I don't know how many are coming."

"What do you need me to do?" He pulled up her driveway and turned the car off.

Mina studied her house. It looked as if it had been pieced together from various eras, because, in fact, it had. This was the house that had traveled across an ocean with magic, the sanctuary of the Grimms. It was the safest place for her now.

But for how long? Teague's army destroyed the Godmothers' Guild, and that had been warded and guarded. Inside were her mute brother Charlie and her mom. Was the house strong enough to protect them? She felt sick to her stomach. Even Brody's question made her reel.

"You shouldn't have to do anything. It's not your fight. I'm so sorry you got dragged into this." She touched his shoulder.

Teague's warning about taking each of her friends away one by one was making her question the wisdom of getting Brody and the others involved.

He looked taken aback. "No one forced me. And this isn't just about you. I mean it is, but if there's a threat to you, my friends, and our world, then you can be sure I'm going to fight it."

Chanda Hahn

Two

She inwardly breathed a sigh of relief, but it didn't relieve the immense feeling of pressure that built around her. Instinctively, Mina looked around the car and outside. The back of her neck prickled.

"Go, get inside. Now!" She pushed Brody toward the driver's door, and she leapt from her side and ran toward the front door, as the dog howled somewhere—not far enough—behind them.

Brody raced to her front door, opened it, and beckoned her to get inside. As soon as her feet crossed the threshold, he slammed the door.

The house shook as something large slammed against it.

"I didn't even see it." Brody pressed himself against the door. "How did it get here so fast?"

"It's Fae," Mina yelled over her shoulder. She ran to the back of the house and locked the back kitchen door. She peered out the curtains and didn't see anything, but she could hear it—the terrifying howl of the beast. There was a Reaper here. On their property. All she could do was hope the wards held better than the Godmothers'.

14

Forever

Charlie came around from the side room and stood in the kitchen, his face a mask of fear.

"Get Mom!" she yelled.

He nodded and took off running up the stairs, but their mom was already on her way down.

"Mina, what's going on?" She had a laundry basket full of clothes, and her hair was pulled back and secured with a clip. She wore jeans with an oversize men's flannel shirt—Mina's father's.

"It's a Reaper who's also a giant black dog."

"A what?" she pressed her hand to her forehead with a confused look on her face.

Her gold charm bracelet dangled from her small wrist. A new charm from Pandora's box was attached to it. When and how this new charm appeared on her mom's arm was something Mina would have to worry about later.

"Charlie," she called to her brother. "The bracelet."

Her younger brother didn't need any more direction. He ran to his mom, grasped the charm bracelet, and pulled with all of his might. Her mother yelled out as the chain broke, and small golden charms scattered across the floor. Mina recognized the memory charm and the forgetting charm, and she kicked the new one that looked like an apple under the stove. It rattled as it rolled around.

In only a few seconds, the haze in her mother's eyes cleared up. The beast howled again, and her gaze snapped to the window.

She froze, her breath caught in her throat as her eyes darted between her kids and Brody and back outside, where another long howl pierced the air. The sound spurred her into action. She rushed to the cupboards and began to dig through the spices.

"Have you seen it?" Her mom rushed about her hands shaking as she pulled out pepper, flour, and sugar and slammed them down onto the counter.

"Yeah, it's a Reaper.

"No," Sara turned and gave Mina a stern look. "Did you see the dog? What's it look like?"

"Uh, it's large black beast."

"Mina. The eyes. Tell me about the Reaper's eyes."

The fear combined with resignation in her mother's voice—that tone—scared her more than the horrifying howl.

"White as death."

Her mother gripped the countertop, and her head dropped. "An omen," she exhaled.

This time, it was Mina's turn to be confused. "What?"

"An omen, a Death Reaper." Her mother's eyes lit with anger, and she reached into the back of the cupboards and grabbed a large container of salt, which she pushed into Brody's hands. "Sprinkle it in a circle. A big one."

"Charlie," she said, "get me the hand mirror from the bathroom."

His feet pounded up the stairs.

"But it can't cross the wards, right?" Mina asked, looking out the window.

"Don't count on it. Nothing can stop Death," Sara said firmly.

The howling stopped, replaced by low growling. First it sounded far away, then by the front door, and then the beast started to ram itself against the door.

16

Thump. Thump. Thump.

Mina hurried to the front of the house but saw nothing. Something invisible was ramming against the door.

"Why can't I see it anymore?"

"You won't, honey. You only see a death omen once, unless he wants you to see him. But you see where he's been in hindsight."

The beast stopped its attack on the front door, so Mina jogged back to the kitchen. Brody handed her mother the rest of the salt. Charlie ran in with a small black cosmetic mirror and handed it to his mother.

Her mom picked the largest chef's knife out of the cutting block and tested the sharpness against the edge of her thumb. She looked pleased with the results.

"How do you know this?" Mina asked accusingly. "You've met him before. Haven't you?"

Her mother stilled. Her hand wiped a loose strand of hair out of her face, and she turned to face her daughter. "You're right. This is not the first time Death has come to my door. But this is the first time I can fight back. This isn't just any Grimm Reaper. He's not just hunting Grimms. This is Death himself, and he won't leave until he's collected."

"What do you mean?"

Sara looked out the kitchen window and across the yard. "I'm sorry I couldn't protect you better. I did the best I could, but without your father, I just wasn't strong enough. I gave up so much to be with him. I could have done something back then, but I didn't. I promised him. I had to stay for you... and for Charlie. Mina, listen to me.

Find my parents. They'll help you." She paused and looked at Charlie and then Mina. "I love you both...very much."

This was the first she had ever in her life heard her mother mention her own parents. She had grown up thinking they were dead.

Mina watched in alarm as her mother's deft hands poured the salt into her right hand, picked up the knife, and cast a furtive look over her shoulder. She added a little salt to the knife-hand too.

"Whatever happens, don't let her follow me out that door. Do you hear me?" The command was directed to Brody, who nodded solemnly. "For any reason." She stepped out onto the back porch and turned to face them through the window.

"Mom!" Mina yelled and rushed for the door, but soft hands pulled at her. Mina looked down to see her brother's head against her midsection as he held onto her in a bear hug. "Charlie, let me go."

His small head shook back and forth violently, and his shoulders shook with fear. His emotions affected Mina as if they were her own.

The howl sounded again, and Mina watched her mother, whose face was grim. Sara held the mirror up and used it to see behind her. Left and right, she swayed the mirror, staring into it intently. What was she doing? She kept her back to the yard.

Mina pulled out of Charlie's grip and headed for the door, but Brody intercepted her. He picked her up around the waist and refused to let her down.

"No. Stop it, Brody. Let me help her."

"You can't. You need to stay here for Charlie." His voice was firm.

Forever

"Please, Brody, let me go." Mina cried. "I can help."

She looked back through the upper glass of the kitchen door and saw her mother's shoulders stiffen. She must have seen the beast in her mirror. She shifted her posture, and Mina knew that the beast was close. It had stopped howling and was stalking her mother.

A loud snarl ripped through the air, and her mother dropped the mirror and spun. She tossed a fist full of salt into what Mina assumed were the beast's eyes and slashed at the air.

The beast howled in pain, temporarily blinded from the salt.

Brody's arms were like a vise on her, and Mina screamed, trying to pull from his embrace. She couldn't see the beast, but she heard a loud yelp as her mother's knife struck true. A slash of red appeared midair, and her mother followed her attack with another desperate swing. Another yelp followed, and a deep voice bellowed, shaking the windows in the house.

"Enough!"

The whole world seemed to still. Then, the Reaper appeared on the sidewalk fifteen feet from the house. Close up, he was even larger than before. His white, dead eyes were the stuff of nightmares.

"I'll kill you," Sara threatened. "Then you won't be able to collect."

"Silly mortal. You can only wound me—even as an omen. Nothing can stop me from collecting." The dark-haired Reaper laughed like crackling fire.

19

Her mother gripped the bloodied knife in front of her. "You can't have my daughter."

The Reaper hissed his displeasure. "The girl has seen my omen. I am here to collect," he answered. "I cannot leave without a soul."

Though her mother's shoulders shook, she stood even taller. Her voice didn't quake as she called out loudly, "I know you don't care whose life you take, as long as it's a soul. Your omen will not hunt her again."

"I cannot guarantee that I won't be sent here again."

"You will not take her," her mother repeated. She tossed a handful of salt into the Reaper's eyes this time. He reeled back in pain, and pressed his hands against his eyes. "Yesss."

For just a moment, Mina felt like her mother had won. But then her mother tossed the chef's knife into the grass and stepped off the porch. She walked confidently toward the Reaper.

"Then take your soul." She held up her hands as if she were walking into her lover's arms. Her head fell back, and her eyes closed.

The air around the Reaper blurred until the omen stood only feet away from her mother. It snarled and growled and let out a one last long howl.

And then it lunged and disappeared.

"*Nooooo!*" A young, high-pitched voice wailed.

Mina turned. That wail was her brother's very first word. "Charlie!"

Brody released her. She wrapped her arms around her brother as he sobbed and cried out in pain.

"No, M-M-Mom." His eyes were red and filled with tears.

When Mina glanced out the door, the yard was empty.

Three

"Mom!" Mina shouted. She fled the protection of the salt-circle. Brody reached for her again, but she shoved his hands to the side. He'd held her back! He kept her from saving her mom.

Mina raced outside, ignoring the fresh blood on the back porch. It had to be from the omen. There wasn't a lot. It couldn't have been from her mom.

There was no other visible sign. She ran into the grass where the Reaper had stood only moments ago and turned full circle, scanning the woods. Nothing. Only a bit of scorched black grass.

Mina wanted to lash out and scream her pain and her loss to high heavens, but she couldn't do that. Charlie's wailing drew her gaze back toward the house. Brody held her brother as he continued to cry loudly.

What a terrible miracle. He was talking. He'd never spoken a word...until now. Until their mother died.

Everything pressed down on her, and she couldn't breathe. The world grew smaller, colder, darker. Hope was blinking out like a dying star and being swallowed into a black hole of nothingness. She couldn't survive this. Not when the war was costing the lives of her family.

Her knees collapsed beneath her, and she wanted to give in, give up. The darkness seemed to be her only peace, so she let it claim her. The cold grass pressed against her cheek, and her eyes closed.

"Stupid. How stupid could you be?" An angry feminine voice greeted her ears.

Mina opened her eyes and saw a dark head of short hair blur in and out of focus. When she tried to look beyond the shadowy form, she saw the faint outline of the familiar fireplace and bookshelves of her front living room. She was stretched out on the sofa, covered with an old woven blanket.

The girl studied her. Her short black hair with purple highlights looked even darker in the light. But the tone, the snarky tone of voice, was all Ever.

"Dumb. That's what you are," Ever snapped.

"Who? Brody?" Mina asked, for once close to agreeing with the pixie.

"Oh no. I'm not mad at him." She thrust her thumb in his direction. "He's tolerable. He actually did something smart. Kept you from doing something stupid by running after the omen and suffering the same fate as your mother. You, on the other hand, are foolish. You went back to the Guild? How stupid can you get? The final blast of exploding Fae power probably attracted a whole bunch of evil Fae. They could be sniffing out errant bits of magic hoping to scrape it up, and then you go and get spotted by an omen. I can't leave you alone for a few hours." Her hands waved in the air, and she started to speak in pixie. It was impossible to follow along, but Mina just assumed she had run out of human names to call her and had to berate her in her own language.

Mina sighed and dropped her head back onto the cushion. She let Ever's anger roll off her, ignoring it easily.

Brody sat in a high-back chair nearby, head in his hands and elbows resting on his knees. His hands rubbed his face. He looked consumed in guilt.

Charlie sat on a rug, his arms wrapped around his knees as he rocked himself, staring off into the distance. This wasn't good. How was she going to keep him safe?

Then Mina remembered what her mom had done. She shoved the hurt away and hid it behind her anger. She didn't have time to mourn her mother's death when she had her brother to look after. How could their mom do this to them? How could she abandon them so easily?

She sat up and flung the blanket off of her lap and walked over to Charlie. Kneeling beside him, she wrapped her arms round him. "I'm so sorry Charlie."

Her brother hugged her back, his shoulders shaking in silent sobs. "M-Mom," he gushed out.

She couldn't help but cry tears of relief. Her brother was speaking, and the sound of his young, unsure, and unused voice was the one glorious spot in her grim future.

"I know, sweetie. I know." She rocked him.

"Mina," Charlie whispered.

It unlocked something inside her. And then, with Charlie, she let the tears and grief overtake her. Their pain and grief poured out in loud, uncontrollable sobs.

When Charlie finally cried himself to sleep, Mina whispered, "I'll protect you, Charlie. I promise."

Brody came over and helped lift him onto the couch that she'd vacated. Mina pulled the blanket up to his chin, and her hands accidentally brushed his cheek. It was hot. She touched his forehead. Charlie was burning up.

She grabbed a digital thermometer from the bathroom. His reading was 101 degrees. She got a wet washcloth and put it over his forehead and searched for some liquid fever reducer to give him.

"Mina, can I talk to you?" Brody spoke softly over Charlie's sleeping form.

She didn't want to even look at him. He was the reason her mom was gone. He barely knew her mother, yet he listened to her mom instead of her. How could she trust him?

"I'd rather not," she said stiffly.

Brody's hands fisted, and he took a deep breath, about to say something, when they heard a knock.

All three of them turned to the door. Ever's wings started to flutter, and she hovered off of the ground. Brody reached for the fire poker, and Mina walked quietly to the window and pulled the curtain aside to see Nan's Volkswagen Beetle parked out front. They hadn't even heard it pull up.

Mina opened the door, and her best friend rushed in the door. Her blonde hair hung plaited in one long messy braid, and she wore a sparkly headband over her forehead. Her cheeks were flushed with worry as she rushed inside.

"Mina, you won't believe what I found…" Nan trailed off when she took a long look at her friend's swollen and red-rimmed eyes. "What happened? Are you okay? Is Charlie okay?"

Mina nodded her head. "Yeah, we're fine. But my mom's gone."

"What?" Nan snapped and rushed into the living room and was greeted by Brody's somber face as he stood with Ever. "How?"

Mina didn't want to relay the tale. She looked to Ever, who pulled Nan to the side and told her in hushed tones. Mina stayed near the front door. As she closed it, something rushed inside and scurried up her pant leg.

"Whoa!" She screamed and fell backward, thinking the omen had returned.

The thing scrambled up and out her collar, and her hands flew up to guard her. But she wasn't being devoured by the invisible beast. She was being nuzzled.

A second later, Anders, the Baldander, appeared as a large brown squirrel.

"Anders?" Mina let out a relieved laugh.

Nan came back to the front room and kneeled beside her. "Yeah, he showed up at my condo this morning, a little burned, but he was okay. He wouldn't stop morphing until I promised to bring him to you. "It's like he knew something bad was coming."

Mina sat on the floor with Anders cuddled up in her lap. He seemed content and unwilling to move.

"I know that a lot has happened. I can't even imagine how it feels to lose your mother, but—" Nan spoke softly.

"Nan, not now." Mina tried to stop the lecture that was sure to come.

"If not now, then when? When your brother is killed as well?" Nan's eyes burned with indignation and unshed tears. "Ever told me Charlie spoke. Mina, you saw what happened with the Godmothers' Guild. I just want you to know that—when you're ready, you're not alone. We're in this together."

"I don't think I can involve you anymore. The cost is too high."

"That's bull! And you know it. This isn't about you versus the almighty Teague. This is about us protecting ourselves from a greater evil. So grieve, sort of quickly, and then pull yourself together and fight back."

Mina nodded and hugged her friend. "We will. I will. Thank you."

A second knock on the door had all of them turning and looking at the door in distrust.

"Were you expecting anyone else?"

"No." Mina shuffled her legs, and Ander scurried off of her lap and onto the floor as she slowly stood up. She reached for the doorknob and was about to open it when Nan hissed, "Stop! What if it's Teague?"

"He wouldn't knock," Ever said. "It's not his style. He'd just blast the door in or appear in the room."

Brody positioned himself next to the front door with a baseball bat he'd pulled from the hall closet, and he gave Mina a nod of encouragement. He twisted his hands around the grip, hefted it over his shoulder, and waited.

Without questioning her, he was once again stepping in to protect them all.

Mina let out a sigh of worry and concentrated on the door, trying to let her senses feel beyond it. She didn't feel the onslaught of Fae power that she got when Teague was near, but she did feel a tingle of something or someone Fae.

She opened the door to reveal a distraught Terry Goodmother on the other side. Dressed in head-to-toe white, she rushed into the foyer. Her white hair looked disheveled, and black streaks of mascara ran down her face. Mina quickly waved for Brody to lower his weapon.

"Oh my darling, Mina. I'm so sorry." The elderly woman, who was both her mother's boss at Happy Maids and her Godmother, came into the room and wrapped her chubby arms around Mina. Terry's shoulders wouldn't stop shaking as she started to cry big, heaving sobs, which only set Mina off on another round of her own.

"I knew as soon as it happened." She held up her heavy ringed hand, and the sparkle of her diamonds almost blinded Mina as she placed her hand over her heart. "I felt it here, and it hurts so much. What happened?"

"An omen came for me. Mom saved us all by sacrificing herself," Mina said as calmly as she could.

"She always was one of the most selfless individuals I've known. Which is why I've been trying to keep her from doing what she just did. By failing your mother, I've failed you. I'm so sorry."

"You've been the one adding the charms to her bracelet," Mina stated.

Terry nodded. "Yes, I'm also the one who's made her just fearful enough to run with you and hide from the

Fae. Otherwise, she would have sacrificed herself long ago to fight the curse upon you. I couldn't let her leave the two of you orphaned. I added another one after the attacks on the Guild."

"*You* made her fearful?" Mina said in disbelief.

"She wasn't weak as you believed. In her younger days, she fought alongside your father against the Story's wrath. But when your father died and your mother was pregnant, we needed her to stop and go into hiding to protect you. So we turned all of her passion and fire into self-preservation for you and Charlie." Terry started to wring her hands and pace the room.

"But you made her forget about the curse, forget what was happening." It felt good to finally be able to confront her mother's Godmother.

"The last year has been rough on your mother. She came to me for help. She'd been running for so long, she didn't think she had it in her to fight anymore. So we did what we could to make her non-interesting to the Story, so she wouldn't become a target—so there would always be someone here to protect your brother." She looked up at Mina, her eyes pale with age. "Now that job falls to you." Terry seemed a little unstable on her legs, and she kept grabbing her heart.

"Are you okay?" Nan asked, worried.

"Oh yes, dear. I just need to sit. " Mina helped Terry into the living room, and she sat in the high-back chair by the fire. "I'm very old, you know. My joints don't work like they used to."

Mina looked Terry over with suspicion. "No, I don't quite believe that. You're hiding something." She sat in the other chair across from Terry. "Who are you really?"

Terry's eyes flicked between Ever, Brody, Nan, and then to Charlie sleeping on the couch. "I don't know what you mean."

"Yes, you do," she accused. "I know this is a glamour over your Fae self. Mei was a brownie. Constance told us you're a house elf."

Terry looked scared, and she twisted the bracelets on her wrist. She seemed like she wanted to be anywhere but in this room.

"Terry, it's safe. You can trust us." Nan piped up and smiled widely at the old Fae woman.

Terry nodded, blushing softly. She released a long sigh and glowed white before her body began to shift. The wrinkles softened but didn't quite disappear, her body became slimmer, and she started to shrink. The smaller she became, the brighter she appeared, until only someone the size of a small doll sat perched on the edge of the cushion. Her skin was a creamy opaque color, and her ears were pointed and long with a cute dip on the tip.

In her house-elf body, it was even more apparent that something was wrong with her.

"Terrylin," Mina spoke her real name, and the house elf smiled softly and shivered. "What's wrong?"

"I'm dying. Your mother's death has affected me more than I thought it would. We've been together a long time, and we've become connected. I can feel her loss, and it's tearing at my soul. It doesn't happen often, but sometimes, when we Godmothers lose our Grimm, we lose a huge part of ourselves. It's a risk, but we are all willing to take it." Her eyes scanned the room and seemed to land on Ever as the only other Fae in the room. Nothing was said between the two, but an understanding seemed to pass between them.

Ever nodded once.

"Oh, Terrylin, what can we do?"

"There's nothing you can do for me. My time is short, but I must speak to you alone, dear." She gave the others a pointed look, and they got up and went to the kitchen.

Ever stayed where she was on the arm of the couch. "I'm her acting Godmother. I should be here."

Terrylin shot Ever a condescending look. "When you've dedicated your whole life to the cause, then I'd say you've earned your place. But you've been a Godmother what? All of a day?"

Ever looked away uncomfortably.

"That's what I thought," Terrylin said smugly.

When they were alone, Terrylin leaned forward and looked over to Charlie. "He must be protected."

"He will be," Mina answered.

"Do you really think you can protect him when Teague attacks again? He will. Make no mistake about that. He wants his revenge. He wants *you* my dear."

"Then what do you want me to do?"

"I think you know what must be done," Terrylin said softly as she started to fade in and out.

Mina couldn't help but cry at the prospect of what had to happen. "I'm not ready for that yet."

"I know, dear, but you need to think about what I've told you and put a plan in place. Do you understand?"

She nodded her head.

"Good girl."

Ever popped her head in from the foyer and frowned at Mina sitting on the floor crying over Charlie.

"Hey, Gimp! Can I come in now?"

Mina looked over to Terrylin, who nodded her approval. Ever strode in and perched back on the armrest of the couch, glaring at the small house elf.

Terrylin smiled at Ever. "Are you ready to be sworn in?"

Ever stilled, only her eyes moving as she thought about what the elder Fae was asking. She didn't take long to answer. "Yes, I am."

"You know that this will bind you two together? As her Godmother, you will always be able to find her, no matter the plane you're on, but it comes at a great price."

"Ever, what's going on?" Mina asked. "I'm not so sure this is such a great idea."

Ever turned, wings fluttering. She made a shushing noise and waved her hand at Mina. "Hush, before I change my mind. Someone has to keep tabs on you, and it might as well be me."

Terrylin moved up to the top of the chair cushion and beckoned Ever to come closer. "Hurry, girl, hurry!"

Ever kneeled on the chair before the house elf, and Terrylin raised a finger up in the air and whispered a few words that only the two of them could hear. Her finger glowed brightly, and, as she touched Ever's forehead, a bright light emanated from the touch and encompassed the room. When the light dimmed, Terrylin was gone, her chair empty. Only a small silver ring sat in her place.

Ever bowed her head in respect. She reached forward and picked up the ring, sliding it onto her middle finger.

Forever

The ring was in the shape of an infinity symbol. On Terrylin, the ring had been covered with diamonds. On Ever's hand, the Godmother ring was simple silver. She had noticed a gold ring on Mei's hand, but never before had she put two and two together. Ever had just taken the Godmother oath and bound her life to Mina's.

She had just promised to guard her with her life...forever.

Four

Charlie slept through the night and into Sunday morning. Mina had taken the chair and spent an uncomfortable night curled up with a blanket, checking on her brother every few hours. Around four a.m., his fever broke.

Brody slept on the floor by the fireplace in a sleeping bag, so he could stoke the fire throughout the night. Nan lay by Charlie's couch in another sleeping bag, still snoring quietly.

Ever hadn't slept. She paced and patrolled the house.

Each time the front door opened, Mina woke up in a panic, but it was just Ever checking the wards. It was odd to see their group, all piled into the living room like lost puppies. Sometimes she felt like that's exactly what they were. They had refused to leave her and Charlie alone after just losing their mom. Mina didn't know what excuse they were giving their parents. Frankly, she didn't want to know. But there was something comforting in seeing their band. Their mini army.

When sunlight streamed through the curtains, illuminating the dust swirling in the room, Charlie finally began to stir. Nan's uber-sensors went off, and she sat up, watching him intently. Mina uncurled herself from the chair, her leg muscles cramping as she walked across the room. When she passed Brody, still on the floor, he met her gaze and gave her a sad smile.

Charlie opened his eyes and looked up at Nan and Mina's expectant faces. His alert eyes darted here and there around the room. They noticed Brody and Ever, then continued, as if searching for someone. When he didn't find what he was searching for, he closed his eyes, lay back down on the couch, and pulled the blanket over his head.

"Oh come on, little buddy," Nan coaxed gently. "It's time to rise and shine."

The blanket wiggled back and forth in a negative answer.

"Okay then," Nan continued teasingly. "You don't have to shine. How about you rise and glower or grumble and growl." Her voice became soft. "Or how about just breathe. Rise and just breathe. Like this—" Nan exhaled and was about to take another dramatic breath in when the blanket launched itself up and wrapped around her in a hug.

Charlie's little shoulders shook, and Mina crawled up on the couch next to him to rub his back. Nan had always been the best at communicating with Charlie and reading his moods. Mina didn't know what to say to comfort him. How was she going to help him cope, when she could barely cope herself?

She glanced over and noticed Brody watching her silently from his sleeping bag. He got up and started rolling it and stuffing it back into its carrying bag.

Ever came in, very somber, though her outfit was unusually bright. Little pink flowers flecked her hair, and her normal black attire had been replaced with a bright yellow sundress. "Um, can everyone come to the kitchen please?"

Charlie's curiosity at Ever had him leading the pack into the kitchen. He stopped short. Mina bumped into his back, but she was momentarily stunned as well.

Ever had transformed the country kitchen into a happy garden full of plants of all kinds. Bright paper lanterns hung from the ceiling with little tea lite candles burning. On the kitchen table in the middle of the room was a picture, framed in mint green, of her mother laughing and hugging Mina and Charlie.

Mina remembered that day. She and Charlie were thirteen and five. That windy day, they had gone to the park and were trying to fly Charlie's homemade cardboard kite. Of course it didn't fly, but that didn't stop them from trying to get the diamond shaped piece to go up in the air for more than five seconds. Just when Charlie was about to cry, the kite had taken off and hung in the air long enough to make him smile.

That had been a good day, filled with lots of laughs and memories. Mina wasn't sure where Ever found the picture, but she was glad she did. It was a great one of their mom. That's how she wanted to remember her.

"Ever, it's beautiful." Mina softly touched the edge of the frame and then ran her fingers over the blooming flowers that curled around the table. It took her a second to realize there wasn't a single vase in the room. Ever had made all of the flowers appear and bloom magically. "Thanks."

Ever blushed. "I felt it was only right to honor your mother's passing with a celebration."

"A celebration?" Nan asked. "That doesn't sound like the right kind of thing to do at the moment."

Ever looked like she was struggling to hold back a snappy retort. She took a deep breath and slowly explained. "Well, Fae live for a very, very, very long time. Deaths aren't usually sudden and unexpected. By the time we pass on, we've lived a very long and fulfilled life. The passing of Fae is usually a great honor. I know her death was sudden, but I want to give tribute to your mom with the best the Fae can offer." She gave a stern glare to Nan, and Mina knew there would be no arguing this.

Unsure what to do, Mina took a seat in one of the kitchen chairs that had been pushed to the side, and Charlie scurried up next to her. Brody and Nan sat in the row behind Mina and Charlie, while Ever stood in the middle of the kitchen next to the table and cleared her throat.

"Um, sorry. I've only been to a few of these. And I didn't have a lot of time to prepare."

"It's fine," Mina reassured her.

Ever smiled wide, and her hair moved about as her wings started to flutter in excitement. She smoothed her hands over her dress before turning to a small pearlescent seed on the table in front of the frame.

Ever waved her hand, and the seed moved to float above her fingertips. "Once upon a time, there was a seed. Small, insignificant, helpless. But Mother Earth took it into her womb and kept it warm and protected." Ever cupped her hands over the seed and continued the story. "Then, Father Sun spread forth his love from above and nourished the seed with light and sent the rain and whispered for the seed to bloom and grow."

She opened her hands slightly, and bright green vines began to stretch out of her hands. "Our path dictates how strong we will be and how tall we will grow. Will our life grow into something beautiful, or will we develop thorns for protection?" The vines bloomed into bright pink flowers with orange tints. "Each journey is different."

Mina turned to watch her younger brother get up and spin under the giant flower buds that continued to blossom and erupt. He held his hands up in the air to catch the colorful burst of Fae pollen. Nan and Brody followed suit as each they stood and stared above them in wonder.

Nan squealed as some of it touched her lips and she tasted it. "Cotton candy?" She giggled.

Charlie opened his mouth to do the same. He shook his head. He obviously didn't taste cotton candy, but whatever he tasted on his tongue, he enjoyed. He kept his mouth open.

Brody let some fall on his finger and brought it up to his mouth. "Pineapple upside down cake. How are you doing this?"

Mina smiled and laughed with everyone as they celebrated. But when she licked her lips, she tasted the distinct flavor of lemon bars, and her heart plummeted. That was her mother's favorite dessert.

Ever just shrugged her shoulders. "It's different for everyone." She licked her lips. "Mmmm." She flew up, arms wide, and made the rest of the room burst forth in colorful fireworks of flowers.

From above, Ever said, "Only when we die, are we truly reborn." When the flower had bloomed, it slowly fell and withered, and the petals fell, leaving only a single, white sparkling seed. "Because life comes from death."

Ever picked up the seed and handed it to Charlie. "When you're ready, plant this."

She dropped the pearlescent seed in his outstretched hand. "I'm not sure what kind of flower it will be, but it will be representative of your mother's life. This way, you will always have a bit of her with you."

Charlie jumped up and shoved the seed into his pant pocket.

Ever turned an apologetic face toward Mina. "Sorry, I only have one remembrance seed. I just thought that—"

"It's fine," Mina interrupted. "You did the same thing I would have done."

Throughout the morning, Mina and Nan retold various recollections about Sara. Stories of her sitting up eating ice cream sundaes till one a.m. during their slumber parties. Helping the girls with last minute book report projects.

"She really was like a mom to me. More than my own mom, and I really can't thank you enough for sharing your family with me."

Mina gave Nan's hand a big squeeze. "I can't imagine my family without you."

Brody had been quiet for most of the celebration. Obviously, something was weighing heavily on his mind. He kept looking at Charlie and frowning. He was the deep thinker of the group, so Mina figured he was also recognizing the problem at hand.

With Charlie having just turned ten and Mina not yet eighteen, without a legal guardian, they would be taken away, and their little family torn apart. It was possible a foster family would take both, but there would be no guarantee.

He finally broached the subject to Mina by pulling her into the hallway "What are you going to do about Charlie?"

Mina held up her hand and shook her head. "I'm not ready to go there just yet. I need to take it day by day."

"Mina, you can't take care of him by yourself."

"Please, Brody, I don't even know what to tell the police or social services. That my mom was taken by a death omen? Do you know how ridiculous that sounds? Well, I do. And I don't want to be sent to a mental institution."

He sighed, and she put a hand on his arm. "Just give me a few days, and I'll figure out what to do." She already knew though. Terrylin made sure Mina knew her plan. And she had to admit—it was a good plan. A little crazy... but good.

He didn't look pleased with the idea. "Okay, but I'm worried about you."

"Believe me, I'm worried too."

Ever cleared her throat, but her expressions said she felt bad about interrupting them.

"What's up?" Mina asked.

"We need some supplies. Stuff that can help us in time of need." She waved the paper in the air in front of Mina.

"I don't know." Mina hesitated, thinking it was going to be a huge list of weird items to ward off Teague.

She grabbed the paper and breathed a sigh of relief. It was just a list of food items—and tons of candy.

"What?" Ever said dryly. "Were you expecting something else?"

"Yeah, I guess things like shrunken heads or bat guano and stuff."

"Relax. You just need groceries. You've got nothing in the fridge to feed the hungry posse. I told you. This is a time of *need*. How can you not hear my stomach growling?"

Brody laughed. "It *is* almost noon."

Mina frowned. There was usually plenty of food in the fridge, but then, they always did their grocery shopping on Saturdays, and that hadn't happened.

"Besides, it might be good for Charlie to get out of the house and away from here for a bit." Ever took the paper back from Mina and fidgeted with it.

"Yeah, you're probably right."

They went back into the kitchen. Charlie was now up and smiling. Mina looked to Nan who gave the slightest head shake. Mina had hoped that Charlie would continue to talk since he did yesterday, but he seemed to have reverted back to his quiet self again.

Nan came to stand by her and gave her a quick, reassuring hug. "What's the plan?"

"Food," she answered.

"That's a good plan. I like that plan." Nan grinned.

Mina couldn't help but smile. "Of course you do. You love food."

"Hey, I'm a growing girl, and I can out-eat a boy any day. This awesome figure is totally a pizza and chocolate ice cream body."

Brody flexed his bicep. "Burgers and fries."

Ever laughed and smiled. "Lollipops and Pixy Stix."

Nan's eyes went wide. "You're serious?"

"Pixies *love* candy," Mina explained. "I mean really really love candy."

Ever pulled a lollipop out of the pocket of her dress, tore off the wrapper, and shoved it in her mouth, which had already been full with other candy. "Yep." She swirled the lollipop to her other cheek so she looked like a giant chipmunk. Then, she popped it out of her mouth and held the stick. "But we can't just live on candy. We need to get stuff for my Grimm. I'm not going to let her starve."

"I'm not going to starve," Mina argued, but Ever held up her hand.

"Nope, starve. You're worthless."

"Oh gee, Ever. Seems like you're back to your chipper self."

Ever looked down at her yellow dress. "Not yet." She waved her hand, and her dress transformed into black pants and a top. "Now I'm back to my chipper self," she said. "Let's get you some supplies."

"I don't know, is it safe to take her out, with that maniac after her?" Brody looked over to Mina for affirmation.

His question mirrored her very own fears.

"That's fine. We can stay in this house forever, but let me just say that Teague can come and go in this house as much as he wants. Since Jared has been here, Teague technically has too, and the wards won't keep him out."

"You're right," Mina said. "We can't cower from him forever. I think this will show him we're not scared of him."

Nan's hand shot straight up in the air. "I'm scared of him."

Charlie grabbed her hand, pointed to himself, and shook his head no.

"Well, if Charlie's not scared then I'm not scared," Nan amended.

"Okay, but we don't go anywhere alone. We stay in groups. You got that?" Mina said.

Nan made a salute, and Charlie copied her, slipping his hands into hers.

Brody smiled at Mina. "Aye, aye, Cap'n."

Mina laughed and turned to Ever who looked aghast.

"Nuh-uh. There's no way I'm saluting you. You can't even lead a silkie to water."

"You mean horse?" Nan corrected.

"No, I mean silkie."

Nan's face furrowed in confusion as Ever opened the door and they piled out into the driveway.

Five

M ina didn't follow them outside into the driveway
right away. She went back to the kitchen, and her
footsteps slowed. The glamour of flowers and the
celebration had disappeared. The room was back to the
way it had been right before her mom disappeared. This
was the last place she had spoken with her mom.

Moving on so soon seemed wrong. But these
weren't normal circumstances. Mina was a young girl trying
to protect her little brother in the best way possible.
Helping him heal was what was most important right now.
But they didn't have time to mourn, not when she had a
feeling there was so much more to come.

She stared at her mother's purse but couldn't open
it up to take money out of it. It felt wrong. Instead, she
went into the pantry and pulled out an old coffee tin, to
take money out of their emergency stash. Her mother was
always prepared in case they had to pick up and move
again, so even though they *felt* strapped for cash, there had
always been a couple hundred in there.

The wad of money was even larger than Mina remembered. Probably because they weren't paying rent on this place, her mom had been able to add to their fund.

Mina took three hundred dollars and shoved it into her jeans pocket. Then she placed the lid back on the tin and pushed it back up onto the top shelf.

She grabbed her jacket and locked the door before following the others. They'd apparently split themselves up into two cars instead of taking one—Nan in her Volkswagen Beetle and Brody in his SUV. Ever already sat in the front seat of Nan's car, and Mina could see Charlie strapped into the back seat. The girls were talking very animatedly, trying to keep him entertained.

Mina didn't feel like being surrounded by false joy, so she willingly jumped into the front passenger side of Brody's car. She had barely gotten her seatbelt buckled when Nan *meeped* impatiently. Nan's car horn wasn't threatening at all. It was kind of hilarious and matched her personality.

Brody gave a wave, drove down their driveway, and turned left. Sailors Grocery wasn't a long drive, and Mina was too far out to pay Brody much attention. Until she realized that he had asked her a serious question and was staring at her, waiting for her answer.

"Um, I'm sorry. What was the question?" Her cheeks heated in humiliation.

Brody's face flushed, and he stammered. "Yeah, I'm the king of asking questions at the wrong moment."

"No. I'm sorry. I'm here in the moment. Ask away."

He glanced in the rear view mirror to check his blind spot before changing lanes.

"I asked you if you got to see it."

"See what?" she mumbled and felt horrible.

He didn't make eye contact. "What was in the box I gave you two nights ago."

Oh crud. Mina blinked in disbelief. A ring? There was a ring. When? Where? Two nights ago! That would have been the night of the explosion. Then it all came rushing back to her. Brody on the balcony, holding up a small box and saying how old fashioned he was. He'd opened a box to show her a class ring. His class ring. What happened to it? She remembered the explosion, and that's it.

"Your class ring."

"Yes and…?" he trailed off.

"And…" she repeated trying to delay the answer so she could think. If he had given her the ring before the ball, she would have said yes without a doubt. But then she had gone back in time and started to fall in love with Teague, before she'd torn his life in two with the curse. Before she'd seen how ruthless he could be.

When Teague was hell bent on trying to destroy her, why would she pause? She had loved Jared—she was able to freely admit that. But a small part of her still wondered if something of him remained within Teague. Could there be a small bit of love for her within his blackened heart?

Why couldn't she just date the boy she'd had a crush on for years? It was obvious he liked her, and she really, really liked him. And this time there was no Story-funny-business messing with his feelings.

"Oh man," Brody grumbled and pulled the car over to the side of the road.

46

"What?" Mina glanced around somewhat fearfully, and they had pulled over by the school. Cars were lined up and down every street, and kids walked by with balloons and large overstuffed prizes. "Oh, the school carnival."

Brody groaned and ran his hands over his face. "Yeah, I was supposed to volunteer with the polo team in our booth today. I got out of it for Friday night, but I blew off yesterday."

"Well, you did have a lot going on, like being chased by a death omen and all." Mina tried to tease him, but it didn't help. Brody's face looked guilt stricken.

"You don't understand. This was my idea—to raise scholarship funds for underprivileged kids to go to summer camp. The team is going to kill me."

Mina understood. She had seen the banners all over school promoting the fair. Most of the clubs and teams manned a booth—it was the biggest fundraiser of the year. Luckily, Mina had been able to avoid getting roped into volunteering.

Nan pulled up beside them, and Ever rolled down the passenger window. "What's the hold up?"

Brody rolled his window down. "I'm supposed to be working today and yesterday."

"Uh oh! Somebody's in trouble," Ever taunted.

Charlie saw the balloons and the Ferris wheel and fun house in the background, and he practically crawled up between the console of the seat to point it out to Nan.

"Yeah, I see it, buddy," she answered. "So what are we going to do, Mina?" She leaned forward to ask around Ever.

Brody turned to Mina and ran his hands through his hair in frustration. "I'm sorry, but I really ought to go in

47

and work the rest of the day, or the guys will kill me. You can jump into Nan's car, and I'll swing by tonight when I'm done."

Mina looked over to Nan's car and saw Charlie jumping up and down in excitement, pleading with those big, brown eyes. It might be just what they needed.

She sighed. "I'd hate for you to get kicked off the team for shirking your duties. But I think we should all go in. It should be fine. We're surrounded by hundreds of people."

He leaned over and kissed her forehead. "You're the best."

She smiled slightly as Brody pointed out an empty spot for Nan to park in up ahead. He did a U-turn and pulled into a spot that had just been vacated.

Thankfully, he was so worried about his missed volunteer spot that he didn't ask her again about his class ring. But he did grab her hand as soon as they were out of the car and met up with the others.

With a squeeze of her fingers, he said goodbye and then ran to the volunteer line to check in before disappearing into the fair.

The group walked out by the football field and fell in line behind others waiting to pay to get into the fair. When it was their turn to pay, Mina was pleasantly surprised to see Melissa, Makaylee, and Julianne selling tickets.

"How many?" Melissa asked, opening the cash box.

Mina eyed the list of ages and ticket prices. "One student and one child," She pulled out enough money to cover hers and Charlie's entry tickets.

"How many ride tickets do you want?" Julianne piped up and pulled out a roll of pink tickets. "Everything is two tickets, and each ticket is a dollar."

"Okay then, twenty," Mina handed over the bill and paid for the tickets.

"Be sure to check out the dunk booth," Makaylee whispered to Mina. "You won't want to miss it."

"We won't miss it," she answered, unsure of the hidden message.

Ever and Nan met up with them on the other side of the ticket tables.

"Highway robbery," Ever scoffed.

"It's a fundraiser," Nan corrected. "We do this to raise funds."

"Well, the rides better be good after what I paid to get in." She held up her wad of pink tickets and made a joke of emptying out her pocket.

They started with the food vendors. Ever stopped grumbling when she got a cotton candy as big as her head. Charlie munched away happily on an elephant ear while Nan skipped joyfully and waved to each of the students working the booths.

They came upon the infamous dunk tank that Makaylee had suggested they stop by, and Mina was surprised to see how long a line it had. The cheer squad was running the dunk tank. Mina couldn't help but slow down and stare as the one and only Savannah crawled up to the seat above the tank of water and perched on the edge with her pom poms.

Mina watched in fascination as one of the basketball players, Avery Picket gave his money to take a shot at the target.

"Oh Avery, you don't really want to hit that target and get me wet, do you?" She smiled sweetly at him. "How about you give another donation, and I'll let you take me out on a date."

He paused in his throw and tossed the ball up and caught it in his hand. "How about Friday?" he asked.

She turned in her seat, and Pri held up a date book and shook her head. "How about three Fridays from now?" Savannah smiled and twirled her hair.

Avery thought about it and said, "Deal." He tossed the ball into a large bucket next to the dunk tank. Someone had plastered a big old white sign with red letters over the word "Dunk," changing it to "Date."

So instead of Dunk a Cheerleader, the squad had turned it into Date a Cheerleader. Mina watched, amazed, as almost every guy lined up booked a date with either Savannah or one of the other girls.

When a girl did make it to the line and chose to toss a ball at the target, they either didn't have enough power to make it to the target or they had terrible aim.

"You gotta admit that's pretty genius," Nan chuckled. "Wish I would've thought of it first."

"Yeah, well you didn't," Ever grumbled, following Charlie as something caught his eye.

He stopped in front of a milk-can toss and stared in awe at the large wooden popgun prize.

"Three throws for five dollars," the wiry carnival vendor coaxed. He was in his thirties and was one of the traveling fair's employees.

"There's no way we can win that, it's rigged." Mina tried to dissuade him from the game.

"Nonsense," the vendor replied. "It's easy as pie." He came over to their side of the booth and, with one easy lob, tossed the softball into the milk can.

Charlie lit up. He wasn't going to leave the booth until he had at least tried the game. So they wasted five dollars on the game to watch the ball spin around the top and roll right across the opening. Instead of falling into the hole, it rolled up and over the side. Charlie was devastated.

"Too bad. Maybe next time." The vendor smiled, showing tobacco-stained teeth.

Ever slapped five more bucks down and gave Charlie a wink. "My turn."

She grabbed the softball and tossed it underhand in a perfect arc for the milk can. It hit the edge, rolled around the rim and fell off. She frowned and tried again. This time, the ball went up and was falling in a perfect arc, right at the hole. But it changed course and bounced off the lip at the last second. Ever tossed her last throw—even more on point than the last—and it rolled into the middle, then popped out.

"That's impossible," Ever touched her finger to her lips and cast a suspicious glance at the vendor. He smiled slyly while counting out the bills in his apron.

"Oh, too bad. Better luck next time." He waved them on.

Ever rolled up her sleeves and slammed another five dollars down.

The vendor smiled. "Oh you want to try again?"

"No, I'm betting you five bucks that you can't make the shot again. If you can't do it. I get to pick a prize."

51

His eyes lit up in challenge. "Deal, and I'll only need one toss."

"Don't count on it," Ever said under her breath to Nan and Charlie.

The vendor picked up a softball and came over to stand behind the counter and toss the ball into the same milk can.

Ever stood slightly off to the side and, as soon as he tossed the ball, flicked her finger. When the ball hit the can, it rolled around and around the can but refused to go in. With another flick, Ever made it roll out.

"Oh, that's too bad," she said.

"No, wait. I get two more shots." He stormed behind the counter to grab two more softballs. Mina could see sweat beading on his forehead in concentration as he tossed the ball perfectly. It would have been a perfect toss, if Ever hadn't flicked her wings at the last second and blown it off course.

Now he was really nervous.

"One last shot, bub." Ever sat on the edge of the booth and crossed her legs. "And I've got my eye on the popgun."

"You won't be getting it," he growled.

And Mina realized suddenly what was going on.

He was Fae, and Ever knew it.

"We'll see," she smiled knowingly.

The man took his time lining up the last shot. Mina could tell he was trying to figure out what was going on. He tossed the last ball, and before it even got to the can, Ever knocked the whole milk can over, and it rolled away.

"Hey, that's cheating." The vendor turned on the girls in anger.

"So was what you were doing," Ever snapped back. "Don't even pretend you weren't doing that to us. Don't try and out-cheat a Fae." Ever glared at him, and her skin glowed a bit, making the vendor cower in fear.

"Sorry, Miss. I didn't know. I'd never intentionally cheat my own kind."

"I may be Fae, but I'm not kind—or patient. Now give me my prize." Ever pointed at the popgun.

The vendor nodded quickly, grabbed a hook, and reached up to grab the wooden gun off the display. He kept looking around nervously.

"Here. Now take your prize and scram!" He turned his back on them and went behind the booth.

"Wait, so he was Fae?" Nan asked.

"Yeah. Not a very strong one either." Ever shrugged and handed Charlie the popgun. "I wouldn't worry about it, Nan. There are lots of Fae living on the human plane now. Most of them are harmless, and you don't even know they're here."

"Most..." Nan said and waited for Ever to continue.

"Like me. I'm harmless, unless someone tries to cheat me, and then... you know."

Mina felt uneasy running into a Fae at the school fair. Still, Ever wasn't worried, so Mina told herself not to worry either. Just because there was one Fae here didn't mean there were others.

They continued walking the fair, stopping to ride the carousel and Ferris wheel and browsing the baked goods. It was easy to spot the drama club's table selling pies. The football team obviously manned the football toss game, and there was a loud ruckus from that direction.

Mina had yet to see anyone from the water polo team's booth or Brody. Until they bumped into a long line of girls.

"What's this?" Nan stood on tiptoes to try and read the banner and mumbled, "Uh-oh."

"What?" Mina asked, a sinking feeling in her stomach. She copied Nan and got up on her tiptoes to see that the white and blue banner read *Kissing Booth.*

"That's kind of disgusting." Ever made a face.

"And not sanitary," Nan said, "but look at that line. I swear we came by here earlier, and it wasn't that long."

A feeling of dread crept back into her stomach, so Mina excused herself to walk around the line and check out the front of the booth. Her fears were confirmed. None other than the water polo team hosted the booth. The boys were lined up across the back of the booth, and each girl got to pick who they wanted to kiss. It seemed like two lines had formed since almost every other girl wanted to get their five seconds with Brody Carmichael.

He even had a stool to sit on. It seemed a lot of people were upset since he hadn't been there the day before, and they had come to get their picture and kiss today. He was the town's celebrity, not to mention extremely rich. Of course everyone wanted their picture with him.

Mina had shown up just in time to watch an excited sophomore bat her eyes and lean over to give him a kiss on the lips. The chaste kiss only lasted a few seconds, so there wasn't really anything terribly wrong. Not that Mina had any official right to be jealous.

"Maybe you should get in line?" Nan suggested. "Since he *is* sort of your boyfriend."

Forever

"I don't know," Mina answered. "It's not really my thing to make a show in public."

"As far as people at school are concerned, he's your boyfriend. Show them all that you're not intimidated by this. Besides, I don't think this was his idea for the kind of booth it would be. The rest of the team outvoted him."

"Okay, you're right." Mina answered. "I should do this."

Nan and Ever took Charlie off to the zipper, so Mina could have some privacy.

The feeling of dread eased, and she was able to ignore the line of girls.

Until Mina noticed the group in front of her. It was the cheer squad. Next in line for the kiss was a petite girl with a white-blonde ponytail. Brody's ex-girlfriend, Savannah White.

Come on, Brody. Turn her away. Mina tried to send him her mental message, but it didn't really work. Savannah put her money into the donation box and pointed for Brody to step forward. She leaned forward expectantly.

Mina watched him sigh and then lean in to give her a peck, except it *wasn't* just a peck. Savannah's arms snaked around his neck and held on as she deepened the kiss.

Pull away. Pull away. Mina internally screamed, but his friends started to hoot and holler and egg them on.

"Go. Go. Go!" The guys chanted.

Savannah swung her legs over the table and got on her knees, kissing him intently. Her hands were running through his hair, and Mina still couldn't believe that Brody was letting it happen.

When he finally pulled away, his hair was tousled, and he had a confused look in his eyes. Savannah made a show of wiping the sides of her mouth and holding her hand up in the air. The cheerleading squad clapped and cheered.

"Still got it, girls," Savannah said as she stood up and jumped off the table. "Something for you to remember me by, Brody," she taunted. "Come find me later." She waved and sauntered off.

Priscilla Rose bumped her hip in congratulations.

Brody sat on his stool, a look of shock on his face.

T.J. slapped his back and said, "Man, why did you ever let her go when she could kiss like that?"

Brody chuckled and rubbed the back of his head as he scanned the crowd of girls next in line. He froze when his gaze met Mina's.

Since the squad had come to watch Savannah, that made Mina the next person in line. The five dollar bill in her hand trembled with her nerves, and she looked up at Brody. His face was flushed, and he hurriedly wiped at his mouth.

Mina took a deep breath and tried to calm her temper. It should have bothered her a lot more to see them kiss, but, frankly, it didn't. What hurt her was that he didn't pull away.

There was no way she would kiss him after Savannah. She didn't want sloppy seconds. A small part of her wanted to go away and ignore all this, but he'd just—thirty minutes ago—offered her his ring again. Who did that and then kissed their ex like *that*? She stepped forward, shoved her five dollars into the acrylic donation box and looked along the group of guys. There were quite a few she knew by name, but there were also some she didn't know. One was standing off to the side watching her intently. He had sandy brown hair, green eyes, and a hard mouth—and looked slightly out of place among the other guys. Something about the way he looked at her made up her mind.

Her hand pointed at him, and his eyes went wide. He stepped forward, and she could see confusion among the water polo team members as they all watched Brody.

"What's your name?" she whispered as the green-eyed guy came over.

He wore a gray jersey shirt and generic blue denim jeans. He smiled at her. "Whatever you want it to be," he said in a low voice.

"That's not funny," Mina chastised. Her hands went sweaty.

"It's not meant to be." He leaned on his elbows across the booth and waited expectantly.

Mina leaned forward and was about to kiss him, when her eyes glanced over at Brody. He had stood up and was being held back by T.J. He looked angry, his fist clenched. But he also seemed hurt and confused by this stranger in the booth.

As much as she wanted to try and get even, she realized that wasn't the kind of girl she wanted to be. Mina shook her head and leaned back. "I'm sorry, I can't do this. I made a mistake." A look of anger flashed in the stranger's green eyes at her change of heart.

"No, you didn't," he growled. Fast, he leaned across the table and pressed his lips to hers.

It shocked her. Literally, there was a shock as his warm mouth pressed to hers, and she froze, unable to move. There was something about that tone—that voice—she knew very well. Her heart sped up, and her hands shook. His strong hands gripped her shoulders as he kissed her. Angrily.

First she was filled with fear, then curiosity. She could feel his anger drain away during the kiss. Then it stopped being angry and turned gentle. He pulled away and tenderly nuzzled her lips with his own. If he wasn't holding her by the shoulders, she probably would have slid to the ground.

Mina couldn't open her eyes, but the strange boy didn't let go of her. Finally, when she opened them, she saw, not the green eyes of the stranger she'd picked out of a crowd, but the dark blue eyes that haunted her dreams. How in the world, out of the fifteen guys to choose from, had she picked her enemy in disguise?

He stared into her eyes, daring her to say something. He wasn't hiding who he was from her anymore, and she wondered if everyone could see what she saw. He smiled in triumph.

"Let me go," she whispered.

"Never," Teague warned under his breath just as T.J's hand gripped his shoulder. He turned in surprise, and his grip loosened just enough for her to slip out of it.

Mina realized that Brody was nowhere in sight, and she used the moment to dart into the crowd and disappear into the fair.

Six

What had she done?

Mina ran through the crowds of people and ducked behind the chipped yellow and blue house of mirrors. Her trembling hand touched her lips as she tried to process what had just happened. She'd been about to kiss a stranger to get back at Brody but decided she couldn't do that to him. And the strange boy she picked out of the group happened to be Teague, wearing a glamour. What were the chances, and what did it mean?

Why was he even at the fair, and why the kissing booth? She wracked her brain and remembered that he had been standing there for a while. He'd probably somehow instigated the whole Savannah and Brody kiss, knowing Mina was in the line and would see—his own way of tormenting her. Except that it hadn't really worked. She *didn't* feel jealous at the sight of Brody kissing the other girls.

Could it be that her heart was finally catching up with her mind? That she was outgrowing her high school crush? She needed to search for the others, but she found herself back at the Date a Cheerleader booth. The whole squad had returned from their break to resume their dating fundraisers.

The line of guys had formed again, and Mina was close enough to overhear Savannah and Pri talking.

"So do you think he'll leave her for you?" Pri asked.

Savannah had pulled out her compact and was fixing her lipstick, wiping where kissing Brody had smeared it. "He'd be dumb if he didn't. I don't get what he sees in that Grimey golddigger. But for a moment there, he really was kissing me back, just like old times."

A Grimey golddigger? Mina stormed past the dunk tank and flicked her hand at the target. Mina was so angry she didn't even realize she'd released a burst of power toward the tank. The dunk lever depressed and sent Savannah screaming into the tank. She spewed out water and started screaming at Pri to find her a towel.

Then, while Savannah was still inside the tank, a crack stretched along the clear acrylic and fanned out. Seconds later, the tank burst and water spilled out and knocked the entire squad of cheerleaders from their feet. They gasped and screamed and tried to stand, but all they could do was slip and slide in the mud.

Savannah and Pri cried about their muddy uniforms, while a crowd of onlookers pulled out their phones and snapped pictures.

Unfortunately, Mina missed all of the events that she had released onto the cheerleaders. Once Savannah screamed, something else had caught her attention. Someone who looked familiar ducked behind a red and white tent.

No. It couldn't be. I haven't seen him since... the bakery. Mina had to find out to make sure she wasn't losing her mind. She'd trapped him in the Grimoire, after all. She carefully followed the tattooed man as he entered the tent. Mina went around to the back and tried to look in through a small hole in the tarp. At first, all she saw was a bunch of blurry shapes, but then they came into focus, and she saw the man with long, greasy, black hair. He didn't bother to cover the wolf tattoo on his bare chest wearing only his black leather vest on his upper half.

It *was* Grey Tail!

He spoke quietly to an old woman wearing a bright colored dress and sash around her waist. Her white hair was covered with a shawl, and she argued quietly with the Fae wolf.

"I don't care if everyone thinks fortune telling is lame. You get people into this tent, and I don't care how. Threaten them, bribe them, or kidnap them. Just get them in this tent. I don't want to be old forever. I need to regain my strength before our next attack!" she hissed.

The woman turned with a dramatic flair to sit behind a round table that held a fortune teller's crystal ball.

"Claire," Mina breathed out the witch's name before taking a step back and tripping over a tent stake, causing it to shake.

"What was that?" Claire's voice said from inside. "Go, and deal with it."

Mina scrambled to her knees and took off running toward the middle of the fair. She bumped into someone, and a tall girl yelled at her and elbowed her in the side. She almost crashed into another person but regained her balance when she saw a large Tesla display.

The large electric coil reached high into the air, and there was warning tape that roped off the viewing area to keep spectators at a safe distance. But it was the two people she saw putting on the demonstration that made her mouth go dry. They matched this time in their black suits. Temple wore a dark suit with gold spats on his shoes and matching top hat. Reid wore a similar outfit with a bowler hat. It was unmistakably the Stiltskins, both of them.

Reid held his hand over the lever of the Tesla machine, and it started to pop as electricity ran up and down the coil. The hair on the back of her neck stood up. Not them too!

She ran from the Tesla display to check out some of the boosters' booths. She found Mr. Hamm behind the booth helping to sell Kennedy High souvenirs. There were a bunch of Kennedy High keychains, magnets, cozies, and—she quickly scanned the table and picked up a laser pointer.

She gave Mr. Hamm the money before twisting the cap to see if the pointer worked. It did. The laser pointer could cut through planes and reveal a Fae's true self through their glamour. Only Royals were strong enough to shift their shape and hold it.

Mina ran back out into the crowd and used the laser pointer, flashing it at passersby and at each of the booth vendors. Nothing morphed or changed. Maybe that was it for the rogue Fae.

She spotted Nan and Charlie on the large carousel and jogged to the metal security fence. She tried to wave at them to hurry and get off.

"Can't," Nan called from her perch on a giant brown dog before it spun out of sight. Charlie sat next to her on a smaller tan dog.

"Not till the ride is over," Nan yelled again as it went around a second time.

Mina found Ever waiting impatiently by the carousel exit.

"Ever! We have to get out of here now! Claire and the wolves are here. So are the Stiltskins."

"Wait, what?" Ever jumped to attention. "Didn't you trap them in the Grimoire?"

"Well yeah, I did, but after the Grimoire lost its guardian, it became just became a book again."

"But what about the pages... inside?"

"Blank. They were blank."

"Then they must have been freed from their prisons."

"All of them?" Mina asked, utter fear rising within her.

Ever nodded. "I'm afraid so."

Mina and Ever looked at each other, and neither one could process what was happening.

Ever turned to yell at Nan. "Nan, get off that dang wolf now!"

"Wolf?" Mina looked closer at the carousel and what she'd thought was a dog. Gold windmills and flowers were painted along the trim. In the middle stood a large colorful landscape with a castle. Instead of wooden white horses, giraffes, and swans, this carousel had wooden wolves, bears, and griffins.

Her hand trembled as the carousel slowed to a stop. She lifted the laser pointer and flicked it at a currently unoccupied golden griffin.

Chanda Hahn

The laser threw off the glamour. The griffin began to stir. A wing unfolded, and its head turned, revealing a black beady eye. It blinked right at her.

"Griffin!" Mina squealed and grabbed Ever's hand. Ever snatched the laser pointer and shone it at the closest wolf, who didn't take too kindly to her laser attack. It lost the glamour fast, shook out its fur, and howled into the sky.

People backed away in terror, not understanding how the wolf had appeared in the middle of the stopped carousel. A child stood right in front of the wolf, waiting to get on it, when it changed shape. Now the little girl was screaming.

The wolf lunged for her.

Right before it snapped its jaws around the girl, Mina saw a flash of red hair. Someone grabbed the wolf from behind and flung it back into the slowly shifting griffin. Nix handed the girl back to her mom and told her to run.

"Nix!" Ever shouted and jumped up and down.

"Run!" He pushed Nan and Charlie toward the exit as mass hysteria ensued. Everyone entering the ride tried to jump the security fence or run out the exit. The carousel creaked and groaned under the weight of all the Fae beasts as they slowly revealed themselves.

Someone in green appeared next to Nix. Ferah, knives drawn, fended off a griffin as it tried to snatch a young girl and haul her into the air.

Nan couldn't get out the exit, so she went to the fence and lifted Charlie over it and into Mina's arms. "I'm sorry! I didn't know."

She tried to swing her leg over the fence, but a bear in half-human form yanked her back. She screamed, and Mina saw her blonde head only for a second before it disappeared back toward the carousel full of monsters.

"Nan!" Mina yelled with Charlie in her arms. She tried to hand her brother to Ever, but Charlie screamed and lashed out until Mina dropped him. He wasted no time running toward the entrance to go in after Nan.

Ever was already flying over the fence to find Nan as Mina ran after her brother. Most of the Fae had scattered into the fairgrounds, and the griffins took to the air screeching a hunter's cry. Mina jumped onto the almost empty platform and saw the mangled gold bars and posts. The carousel was lopsided now, broken into two. She ran to the back and saw the bear running away, Nan tossed over its shoulder like a sack of potatoes.

Charlie was right on their tail and didn't slow down as the bear ran into the house of mirrors.

"No!" Mina cried.

Charlie disappeared inside after them.

Seven

Mina slowed just before entering the building. Inside, cheesy calliope music blared, but over it she could just hear Nan's angry voice telling the bear off.

There was a loud roar, and then Nan's voice cut out mid-sentence.

Mina's heart clenched. She darted around and entered the maze through the exit, hoping to cut them off. Mina slipped into the back hall and came face to face with her own reflection. She almost cried out but held in her scream. With her back to the wall, she pressed on, trying to make her way through the maze.

Wasn't this how it always was in horror movies? Hero and bad guy duke it out in a mirror maze. She could have rolled her eyes at the irony of what was happening, but she couldn't even blame the Fates, because she doubted the Fae bear had seen those movies.

A noise to her left made her freeze. It came from another mirror, behind it maybe. Mina wanted to call out for Nan or Charlie, but again, movie self-preservation told her to hold her tongue.

She made it past two more turns and didn't see or hear anything else. The floor squeaked beneath her foot, and she froze. Had she given away her position? She should have made it to the middle of the maze by now. Where had the bear gone?

A noise came from ahead, and Mina ducked behind a self-standing wave mirror and listened. She heard footsteps—light and close together. Mina moved from behind the mirror.

Charlie stood in front of her, wooden popgun hefted over his shoulder like a weapon.

"Did you find her?"

He shook his head no.

"Where did they go? I came in the exit." Mina didn't think *she* missed anything, so she continued toward the front where Charlie had come in. It would've been easy with all the twists and turns to have missed them. Maybe the bear was hiding, and she or Charlie had walked right past them.

But then Mina thought she heard scuffling, and this time it didn't sound like it was behind the mirrors. It sounded like it was under them.

She dropped to her hands and knees and pressed her ear to the floor. The sound was clearer. Something large was crawling under the floor.

"Charlie, can you go find Ever?"

He shook his head and crossed his arms.

"Please! We need help."

He didn't look happy, but he went running out the front entrance. After she was sure Charlie had gone, Mina backtracked to the spot where she'd made the floor squeak and searched for a trapdoor. She didn't want her brother to know she knew where the door was. She didn't want him anywhere near that angry Fae bear.

Mina felt along the floor until she found the edge and the metal clasp. She slowly lifted the trapdoor, expecting something large to spring out at her. When nothing terrifying immediately attacked, she opened the door and rested it back on the floor. The darkness under the house of mirrors almost caused her to chicken out.

She swung her legs over the edge and dropped down to the ground. There wasn't a lot of room below, but she immediately saw a large wheel. The fair was mobile, so the whole house was on wheels. As she let her eyes adjust, she could see a lot of light leaking in through the shabby tarp wrapped around the wheel bed.

She crawled over to the next section. Her heart sank when she noticed a large tear in the tarp where the bear had made a hasty escape. She backtracked and climbed back into the house of mirrors and called out for Charlie. When she pulled herself up out of the floor, she saw Teague—not just one Teague, many Teagues.

His reflection appeared over and over among the mirrors, each one smirking at her in unison.

Mina stood tall and tried to stare down the reflection closest to her.

"She's gone."

"No, she's not," Mina argued.

"You've lost."

"The game is only beginning."

"I'm taking each of your friends one by one, Mina. Like I promised I would. Even your Godmother friends are no match for me."

"Let Nan go!"

"Why do you demand? Don't you realize I'm not that unreasonable?"

A loud crashing noise sounded outside, and the floor rumbled below them.

"What was that?" she asked, terror filling her soul.

"Why don't we go see." He waved his hand, and the building exploded outward. Pieces of mirror shards plumed up, sparkling in the air like glitter, but none touched her because Teague placed a protective shield around them.

Mina looked out and saw people lying on the ground around her, hurt from the blast—men, women, and children. Farther up, she saw the giant troll, the same one that had been captured deep underground in the Godmothers' Guild. It was now destroying her school. Before, half-encased in the wall, his size had been impossible to tell. The troll's back had beams and pipe from the Green Mill Recycling Center melded into it, which gave him a dinosaur-like appearance.

Someone screamed, "Godzilla!"

She closed her eyes and tried to turn away as the troll's large club rose in the air and came down right over the cafeteria. The ceiling groaned as it caved in.

"Stop! There could be people inside."

"Why do you care about this place or these people, Mina? I know for a fact that you don't like school, and most—if not all—of these students have called you names. I know the resentment you have for them. I'm doing you a favor."

"It doesn't matter how bad people treat you. It's not worth hurting them."

Teague stared at her, and she didn't back down. "Interesting choice of words. Are you saying that to save your own skin?"

The glowing bubble Teague placed around them grew brighter, and Mina gasped as her feet left the ground. He hovered over the school, bringing her closer, so she could see the devastation. The troll had moved on to the gym.

The higher they flew, the more destruction she could see. The Ferris wheel had people on it, and one of the giants was spinning the wheel. People screamed inside the cars as they swung precariously.

"Make it stop!"

Constance appeared out of the crowd and ran toward the giant. She started to sing, and a few seconds later, the giant stopped shaking and spinning the Ferris wheel. His eyes got droopy, and he tottered back and forth. He let go of the wheel and fell backward, crashing into the already destroyed and abandoned dunk tank. Teague frowned at the Godmother and shrugged his shoulder. "She can't sing forever. As soon as she stops, he'll wake up again."

Other Fae from the Guild were running toward the Ferris wheel. Ken Wong stood at the operating board, trying to get the wheel to work. The operator had run away, and they couldn't get the cages open. He signaled to one of the larger Fae who looked like he was part lion. With a loud roar, he ripped the door off the hinge of the first car and helped four terrified teens out. The lion sprung on top of the empty cage and jumped onto the cart above. He pulled the door off, grabbed the first girl, and jumped down thirty feet to land on his hind paws. As soon as he deposited her next to Mr. Wong, the lion went back for the next student.

Screams came from the car, but the lion was able to get the kids in the car after that to come willingly with him as he jumped again. Another human wearing a carnival uniform came out of the crowd and shifted into a cat. He scaled the other side of the Ferris wheel and mimicked the first rescuer. She couldn't be certain, but Mina had a feeling that this Fae who had jumped in to help wasn't part of the Guild, but a good Samaritan.

"Cats always land on their feet. Well, we'll see about that." He made a motion as if to stop them, but Mina put herself in front of them.

"Please, no more."

He stopped and smiled. "Do that again. I like it when you beg."

She would have too—except that, as her gaze drifted down through their floating bubble, Mina caught sight of Charlie. He stared up at them from the ground, the only one not running away in the mass hysteria.

But her hesitation and downward glance made Teague notice her brother as well.

"Ah, the little Grimm," he said. "We really don't need two of you trying to kill me. I think one is enough." Teague signaled a red-brown griffin, and it dove toward her brother.

"No!" Mina gasped as the griffin screeched, his claws extended for the kill.

But the griffin didn't make contact. Charlie opened his mouth and screamed in anger. A loud, shrieking, piercing noise—so painful that Mina clapped her hands over her ears. The griffin was hit with a force so powerful, it knocked the beast over, and it crashed into the school.

"A siren? And he's quite powerful for one so young. No wonder he's been so quiet. That takes lots of control. I see you're shocked as well. Somebody's been keeping secrets," he taunted in a sing song voice.

"Hurts doesn't it, when those closest to you lie to you?" Teague leaned close to speak over her shoulder. "You can't trust those Godmothers."

Charlie was shaking and trembling. His little body couldn't handle the power that he'd just unleashed, and he fell to his knees on the ground and started to convulse.

"Please help him," she cried out. "Let me go to him."

Teague didn't respond. He simply stared around him, taking in the destruction. "He'll recover, Mina. He just needs time. See? He's already trying to get back up and keep fighting. You've got to admire that in one so young."

Sure enough, Charlie had made it back to his feet. He wiped white foam from his mouth with the back of his hand and turned his gaze up to them, furious. His eyes glowed with anger. Charlie turned his rage toward Teague and let forth another ear piercing shriek. The protective bubble around them cracked but didn't break.

"Too bad, I think the first attack wore him out. Now I wonder what spurred on his rage? Oh, I know. The death of his mother, perhaps?"

This time, Charlie just fell to the ground—with no convulsion. He slumped his head and appeared to be crying.

A large ogre with a bulbous nose came walking by with Ever in his hand. She kept trying to fly away, but he pinched her wings between two of his meaty fingers. When he gave a tug on them, Ever cried out in fury and pain. Mina remembered what Ever said about ogres and how they liked to eat pixie wings. He tugged again, and she screamed.

Mina cringed.

Claire strode into the middle of the fairgrounds with Grey Tail dragging Brody forcefully behind. She already looked ten years younger, and she kept touching Brody's face longingly. She had already taken a few years of his life and she was begging for more. So much was happening so fast, and Mina felt absolutely powerless.

Reid and Temple overpowered Constance. Temple put a golden gloved hand over the muse's mouth to stop her singing. The giant slowly started to wake up, and the Fae hadn't gotten all of the passengers out of the Ferris wheel.

Mina watched, helpless, as Nix ran and threw himself on Charlie just as Claire and her wolves circled him. There was little Nix could do to save him. He was fully human now. Mina turned in a circle, tears falling freely from her face as she watched her school continue to crumble beneath the onslaught of the troll.

Police were arriving, and ambulances lined the outskirts of the fairground, but they were hesitant to move in because of the giant that stomped toward their cars.

Mina had lost the war.

Utterly lost.

She wasn't a general or a fighter or a leader. She was a clumsy seventeen-year-old girl. She couldn't be responsible for all of these people dying. She didn't want to be the reason for so much tragedy.

"You said you weren't unreasonable," Mina choked out softly.

"I'm not."

"Then let's reason. What would it take for you to stop this massacre and leave my friends alone?"

Teague looked around, his hands held wide open. "You want me to stop destroying this... and the people who hurt you?"

"Yes, yes I do. And I want you to release my friends, all of them, even the Godmothers. What would it take for you to do that and to never bother them again?"

"I think you know the answer to that, Mina." Teague made their bubble fly higher and higher into the sky until they were way up in the air surrounded by clouds. "There are only two things I want. If you give them to me, I'll stop everything and let your friends live."

He stood before her, his eyes glowing with power. She tried to stand tall in front of him, but she couldn't stop the tears as they fell.

"The dagger and..." She let her voice trail off, knowing the other but unwilling to say it out loud.

"Your life." He smiled, one corner of his mouth pulling up to show his even white teeth.

Mina took a deep breath and shuddered. She held out her hand.

"Deal."

Eight

She knew the deal had to be made, but she pulled her hand back at the last second.

"Changing your mind already?" He sneered.

"No, I uh, I'd just like to add a few conditions."

He crossed his arms and snorted. "Of course you would."

"I'd like twenty-four hours before you collect on your debt."

"Two hours."

"Twelve. Take it or leave it." Mina panicked inwardly, thinking she wasn't even going to get that.

"Twelve measly hours isn't going to save you from my wrath any more than two. The ending will be the same."

Mina sighed. "I know. I just want to say my goodbyes."

"Your human emotions are so typical."

"They're not just human emotions. They're Fae as well."

"Emotions make you weak," he said, as if his own jealously and rage weren't emotions.

Apparently he only considered sentimental emotions weak. How interesting. "Twelve hours," Mina repeated and held out her hand.

Teague looked at her offered hand with a raised eyebrow. He wasn't sure what to do with it. "So Mina, twelve hours I grant you. Then I will come for you. You better have my dagger. And no funny business. He pulled her delicate hand mirror out of the air. "Remember, I'm watching your every move."

He disappeared right before her eyes—and with him, the bubble holding her thousands of feet above the ground.

Mina screamed as she fell out of the sky. Her hands clawed at the air as if, somehow, she could slow her freefall.

She couldn't inhale, she was falling so fast. Her destroyed school appeared, and what looked like ants all around it. But they weren't ants. They were people—people getting bigger.

As the ground rushed toward her face, she placed her hands in front of her, closed her eyes, and prayed. She imagined two large hands catching her and stopping her fall, saving her moments before she hit the ground. She pushed every ounce of willpower she had into her imagination.

She could hear someone else scream when they noticed her falling, or maybe she was screaming herself. Then she slammed into something warm and soft.

She grunted at the impact and looked up, but she was surrounded by darkness. Except that it wasn't completely dark. A crevice of light opened up, and Mina could see what was left of the day peering in through the crack in rock. Although it couldn't be rock. The walls shifted, opening up, and she realized she was sitting in the palm of the giant's hand.

She looked up into his eyes, and they looked straight into hers, glowing golden. When Mina turned her head, the giant turned his head too. She looked up, and the giant looked up.

Put me down. She mentally commanded the giant. Then added, *Gently,* for good measure.

The giant bent down and placed his hand on the ground. Mina scrambled out and gave herself plenty of space for safety. The giant just stood there blinking at her, awaiting orders. She wasn't sure how, but she had taken control of him. His will was hers.

Very cool, but very scary.

Teague appeared next to her. "So you think you can control my army? A giant is the weakest minded creature here. But tell me, what are you going to do with him now?"

Mina thought about using him to destroy Teague, but then she saw all of her friends still at the mercy of the rest of his army: Brody held captive by Claire, Ever pinned down in the hands of an ogre, Nix and Charlie surrounded by his griffins, and she still hadn't seen Nan. She couldn't save them all.

Go home, Giant. Mina commanded. *Go back to the Fae plane, and live a happy joyful life. Let no man, woman, beast, or Fae control you again. You are your own mind.*

He stared at her, and his eyes still glowed. He turned to walk away, probably to try and find a gate still open between the planes.

Oh, and one more thing. She mentally called out after the giant. He paused in his step and turned.

Thank you for saving me.

She wasn't sure, because she was still controlling him, but she thought she saw the barest hint of a smile cross his large face.

Teague stood before her. He looked irritated as he signaled his horde to fall back.

Nine

They weren't happy at Teague's orders, but Claire released Brody and backed away to be quickly surrounded by Grey Tail and Lone Tree. Ever yelped as the ogre dropped her on her bottom. One by one, members of his army moved away and scattered among the wreckage of the fairgrounds.

As soon as the giant disappeared, fire and rescue teams swarmed the area. Men in uniforms ran to those injured on the ground, and the GMs quickly phased and tried to hide their true selves again. Those that couldn't hide their Fae side quickly made themselves scarce.

Nix got up from the ground and helped Charlie to his feet. His red hair stood out against his pale skin. "That was too close." He reached out and ruffled Charlie's hair. "And what about you, Mr. Siren? I've got a distant cousin."

Mina ran over and hugged Charlie, fresh tears of relief pouring down her face. "Oh, Charlie."

She ran her fingers up his face. He was still warm to the touch, and his fever seemed to be out of control, but he looked fine. In fact, he glowed with power.

Ever waddled over to Mina as she rubbed her backside. "How are your wings?" Mina asked.

"Could be better. I thought they were goners for a sec there. But it's going to take more than an ogre to ground Ever Farindale." She turned and slowly flapped her deep purple and blue tinted pixie wings, wincing in pain.

Mina turned and scanned their group for Brody, but he'd disappeared. She couldn't see his blond head anywhere. She was about to turn and go look for him when Constance called her.

"Mina." The muse spoke softly.

She turned to her high school music teacher, with her short gray spiky hair and wing-tipped glasses. Her skirt and top were torn and dirty, but she didn't look injured.

"You came?" Mina said incredulously.

"We got our injured safely hidden with another inactive sect of Godmothers down in San Francisco. This one wasn't going to let us abandon you." She pointed to Nix, who blushed until his skin matched his hair and shoved his hands in his pockets.

"But how did you know where to find me?"

Constance sang a few notes and held out her wrist. A small dragon landed there and immediately began to dance around in excitement.

"Of course. Anders. How could we have forgot about him?" Mina exclaimed.

"You were meant to. He was supposed to follow you, and—when you were in trouble—come find us. There was a small group of us already on our way back to the Guild to try and salvage some of our archives when he found us. Sorry, this is all we had." She gestured to those standing behind her.

Mina couldn't help but zero in on Ferah, with her untamed red hair, standing among the GMs. She spoke wildly to the others.

Ken Wong separated himself and came over to them, whispering hurriedly to Constance. "Ferah says we have to leave. The police are asking questions, and we are a very large group standing in the open. We're sure to draw speculation."

Constance nodded her head. "She's right. We must leave. But first I need to ask you, Mina, what happened? Why did he leave?"

That was one question she wasn't ready to answer, especially not in front of her friends and brother.

She turned away. "He's toying with us, trying to intimidate me by showing he can strike any time and anywhere." She turned back to Constance. "What I want to know is what about Charlie? Did you know he's Fae?"

"Part-Fae," Constance answered. "And yes. So are you." She grabbed Mina's arm and walked closely beside her as their troop made a hasty exit, not out the front fair exit, but by the back bus-barns.

"Your mother was a powerful siren. When we learned what our future held, and how it depended on the Grimm family defeating Teague, we tried to strengthen your bloodline with Fae blood."

"How dare you meddle where you have no business meddling? These are my family's lives—not your genetic cauldron for creating weapons."

"Do you think your mother didn't love your father? Do you think we cast some sort of spell to make him fall in love with her? No, Sara and James fell in love all on their own." They squeezed through a fence behind the school, skirting the worst of the damage. "Your mother was so in love with your human father that she went to a sea witch to bind her Fae powers so she could be human. We didn't know at first that it was James Grimm that she was in love with."

"So she lied to my father?"

"Do you honestly not recognize your mother's own tale? Where a girl was so in love with a human that she was willing to give up her tail, forget her previous life, and live as a human forever so she could be with him?"

"You mean *The Little Mermaid*?" Mina scoffed. She followed Constance carefully past a sheer drop-off in the ground, actually the giant's foot print.

"What do you think a siren is, dear?" Constance smiled sadly. "A mermaid is the human term for them. Once a month, on the full moon, sirens gain their legs and walk on land, usually to cause mayhem. After all, they aren't the noblest of creatures and are tricksters. It was during your mother's moon spell when she met your father."

Mina couldn't help but think back to the stone siren that guarded the waterways under the Fates' castle. Nix had said sirens were like sea witches but worse.

"Am I going to sprout a tail?"

In the distance, the fire and rescue crews were still parked around the perimeter of the fairgrounds.

Constance laughed. "No, you and your brother won't, because that is what your mother sacrificed to become human. So it wasn't passed down to you. It does seem that Charlie picked up the siren's call, and you picked up the lure, though."

"Lure? Don't you have to sing to be able to do that? You've heard me in class. I can't sing a note."

"Lure is of the mind. It's the most powerful of curses, dear. I'm sure you've seen it firsthand. You lure others to do your bidding. You've been luring the Fae power and controlling it for years. You did it again with the giant, and you've done it with your friends."

Mina let the knowledge wash over her as they headed toward the parking area. She wasn't human, never had been. Her whole life was a lie—all because her mother was basically the little mermaid on steroids.

"And you just let it happen?"

"We didn't think it would hurt anyone if the Grimm line inherited some of her Fae powers. In fact, it would only help. Your mother was one of the strongest sirens in the sea. How else do you think you made the crystal bowl sing if you weren't already Fae, hmm? A siren doesn't have to sing to still be a siren."

"This is all too much," Mina confessed as they hustled around the block. They'd made a huge circle to get back to their cars and not be stopped by the police.

"Or is it not enough, I wonder." Constance muttered.

"Why couldn't you tell me this earlier?"

"Too much too soon. Your mother didn't want to remember her old life. And she never wanted you to know, because she was afraid you'd hate her."

"That's why all of her forgetting charms," Mina muttered as she came to the parking lot.

"But she remembered whenever you needed her to. Don't forget that, dear. Whenever she needed to remember the old ways, she could."

The GMs hurried away, and Constance needed to go with them.

"What are we going to do about that?" Mina pointed back to the destroyed school and fairgrounds. "We've left quite a lot of Fae evidence."

"We can only hide from the world for so long. It looks like our time is up. We're prepared for the human world. The only question is whether they are ready for us." She slowed down so that they fell to the back of the group. "I'm not sure why Teague backed off the way he did, but whatever you promised him, it's not worth it." Constance turned to follow her group.

Mina looked at her friends in the lot. Nix stayed close to Charlie, Ever waited by Nan's car, and they all looked to her for direction. Brody and Nan hadn't shown up.

"I thought they'd be here," Mina mumbled to herself. She felt foolish thinking somehow Brody would be waiting for them by the car. She hoped he'd only stayed behind to help, rather than gotten in danger somehow. But where was Nan? "He promised… That he'd let them all go." She kept waiting for Nan to pop out from behind a bush and say *boo*.

"Should I go back and look for them?" Nix moved Charlie closer to Ever and pointed back into the fray, at all the people who ran toward the school grounds to get pictures of what was happening.

"No!" Ever shouted and grabbed her side in pain. "We need to get far away from here as fast as possible."

Mina was torn. Ever was right—she needed to get Charlie out of here. But she couldn't abandon her friends. Finally, she understood the decision the Godmothers faced, trying to protect those who were injured or unable to protect themselves.

But she could make a different choice. Her path could be different. "Ever, stay here with Charlie," Mina commanded and then nodded to Nix.

Within moments, they were picking through the mob of bystanders trying to get to the main street.

"This is chaos!" Nix shouted over the crowd. "Hey, I see something!" He pointed to a side alley, but Mina wasn't as tall as Nix, so she couldn't see what he saw. She broke through the edge of the crowd and breathed a sigh of relief. Brody was making his way toward them, carrying someone. Long blonde hair spilled over his right arm. Mina recognized the blue shirt as belonging to her best friend.

"Nan!" Mina ran to them both.

Brody gave them an accomplished grin. "She's heavier than she looks." He sounded out of breath.

Nan's hand came up and slapped Brody upside the head. "Am not, jerk. Now put me down."

"You're wounded." Brody shifted her body so he could hold on to her better. His eyes were filled with joy as he looked down at Nan's frowning face. There was something else there too, some emotion he was trying to hold back.

"Only my pride, Brody Carmichael." Nan laughed and tried to squirm out of his grip.

Brody leaned forward and gently placed her feet on the ground, holding Nan's arm as he tried to steady her. She had a large bruise on the side of her face and a few scratches had torn through her shirt.

The minute Nan tried to move on her own, she started to fall, and she instantly turned back to Brody for support. His strong arm wrapped around her waist, and he didn't let her go.

"He saved me, Mina." Nan touched the bruise on her cheek.

"Not really," Brody confessed. "Right before those wolves attacked me, I saw some sort of beast dragging Nan into the school. I wasn't sure if she'd still be there, but—when we were freed—I needed to be sure."

"That horrible bear took me into the school, but then the building started to come down around us."

"I found her in the hallway outside the cafeteria. The bear was dead, killed in the collapse. Nan was trapped under a steel beam."

"I thought I was going to die, but once Brody found me, he wouldn't even leave to get help. He just started lifting the debris off until he could pull me out from under the beam—a regular knight in shining armor." Nan beamed at Brody.

Mina knew that look. She'd seen it plenty of times on her best friend's face. Smitten. And for some reason, Mina didn't feel a pang of jealousy. Her best friend would never intentionally try and fall for Brody. In fact, Nan tried to stay as far away from him as she could, but they were friends. It seemed like, if Mina let it, and without the Story pushing them, they might become more on their own. Without Brody being lured to fall for her.

Brody blushed at Nan's comments and met Mina's eyes, swallowing nervously. Mina just smiled and gave a slight nod in understanding.

Who was she to try and stand in the way of love, especially when it could happen between the two people

Forever

she cared about most? Besides, she'd just agreed to sacrifice her happily ever after, so theirs might be possible.

The dark cloud of her soon-coming demise loomed over her, and she couldn't help but feel sad.

Ever noticed and came over. "Do you want me to dump him in the nearest lake?"

Mina chuckled. "No, I think this is their happy ending that I've been too selfish to see. They deserve each other. I think they could be happy, if I just stepped out of the way."

"You can't really be serious." Ever groaned.

"No, I think I am," Mina admitted. "I think I've been taking away his choice and making him like me, and I've done terrible things to them on accident. I see that now. I'm not a nice person, Ever."

"That's bull. You are about the sappiest and nicest person I know. You can be a bit lame at times, but you're always nice. It's why I love hating you." Ever turned and gave her a goofy grin.

Mina wasn't so sure, she could feel that darkness from down inside her, the jealousy that would sometimes surface. She'd used it to manipulate Fae power and the Story to get what she wanted. She even let it turn her into the evil queen during one quest. It had been so easy, since she had a bit of siren deep within her.

Understanding why the Fae power came to her so easily did give her some relief. Finding out that her mother was Fae in her own right was a little disconcerting. What it meant, though, was that she really had belonged in the choosing ceremony among the others. She was Fae.

"Ever, we've got to talk. Is there anything we can do to keep Teague from hearing us?"

Ever thought for a minute while Mina's mind swirled with plans and questions.

She nodded. "Yeah. Yeah, I got it. We'll take care of it back at the house."

"There's something I have to do first," Mina said. "Before I head back to the house." She went around to the back of Brody's SUV and opened the hatch. Ever helped her get her bike out and onto the pavement. "Can you make sure Charlie gets back safe? And you may have to stop at the store for supplies, since we never made it there."

"What kind of supplies are you after?" Ever asked.

"I need to get Charlie far away from here."

Ever didn't say anything. She just nodded her head and took the money out of Mina's hand.

"What? You're not disagreeing with me?"

"No, I agree with you one hundred percent, which is why you didn't get a sarcastic reply. I'm assuming you need supplies for two people."

Mina looked hard at Ever, willing her to understand. "Yes. I'm going to ask someone to take him."

"And I can trust you not to get killed while on this errand?"

"Yeah, I think I'm safe for now. Teague won't come for me yet."

"But you think he's coming?"

"I know he is."

Ten

Mina slipped away on her bike while Ever distracted the group. Ever would make sure they all made it back to the house.

According to her watch, Mina only had eleven hours until Teague would come for her, so she needed to use the hours left to take care of business. And by business, she meant her friends—her only family.

From the school, Mina rode her bike to the nearest bus stop. She took a moment to latch the bike onto the bus's front bike rack and rode a half mile to the Country Club—where the ball had been held the night Teague attacked. Mina got her bike and rode up the sidewalk.

The gate was closed.

She parked beside the brick wall and walked around until she found a spot in the hedge she could squeeze through. Jogging up the grassy hill, she thought again how beautiful the Country Club was. It looked as lovely this evening as it had a few nights earlier.

Mina looked for the balcony she and Brody had stood on to watch the fireworks. There were a couple, but Mina found the balcony that overlooked the river. She pulled out her laser pointer and searched the bushes below it.

She wanted to kick herself for not bringing a flashlight. Even though she still had a few hours of daylight, the shadows had lengthened, and the brush under this balcony was square in the dark. Brody's class ring couldn't have rolled too far away. She hoped beyond hope that the laser would reflect off the big stone in the top of the ring. But that would be too easy, wouldn't it?

The bushes were scratching her arms up, and she was getting angry. She didn't have time for this. She wanted to do something great for her friends, and the bushes were getting in her way! Her hands tingled, and she shoved at the bush again in frustration.

The bush started to part—she jumped back. It was moving.

"What the?" The bush's branches pull themselves away from her and shifted out of her way. She shined her laser pointer into the newly cleared area.

And then she saw it. A glint reflected back at her.

The ring! Wedged under the bush. There was no way she would have found it if the bush hadn't moved.

She didn't want to spend time pondering the whys anymore. She grabbed the class ring and ran down the lawn.

The ring rested safely in her pocket as she pedaled to the bus stop. She only had to get home now. The bus would drop her off about two miles from her house, and she'd be home free.

Forever

The rain gods must hate her. She didn't know what she'd done to deserve this, but as soon as the bus dropped her off, it started to pour.

Bitter, angry, and let down, Mina pulled her red bike off the rack and started the miserable and wet ride home. The last few weeks, she'd neglected her notebook titled, "Unaccomplishments and Epic Disasters," but now she could see her next entry: *Tried to save the world. Drowned doing it.*

Her chest ached, and her legs burned as she pedaled furiously. Twice, a car drove right through a rain puddle near her. Each time, she squealed and veered toward the side of the road, dodging the car. But the second time, as she bumped into the grass and mud, she lost control of the bike for a moment. When she got back on the road, she wanted to scream. Nothing was fair! All she wanted was for her last few hours of life to at least be dry.

She came to the bottom of Kingdom Hill and got off her bike. The hill was a blast to ride down to school, but riding up it was killer on her legs. It was a half-mile incline, almost impossible to pedal. The hill was lined with forests on both sides of the road and barren of houses for the next mile. This was usually the most peaceful part of the journey.

In the rain, it was miserable. Mina walked alongside her bike and couldn't help but stare into the moss-ridden forest. Sometimes a deer or squirrel would dash into the underbrush. This time, something else caught her eye—an oddly shaped giant ash tree. It was skinny and crooked on the top with long branches. Its bark was covered with green moss, and mushrooms peppered the base.

It wouldn't have gained her attention on any other day, but she swore she saw it move. There! Its branches were shaking. Granted, it could be from the weight of the rain pelting the branches, but she didn't want to take that chance.

She picked up her pace, kept her eye on the ominous tree—its branches shuddering in her peripheral vision—and walked as fast as she could up the incline. But when she could no longer keep the tree in her eyesight, she heard it.

She'd almost been expecting it. A deep groan sounded, a cracking and snapping of branches. The cracking became more frantic—louder.

As it grew, so did her panic.

When Mina glanced back, the ash tree was gone. She ditched her bike and sprinted up the wet hill away from the noise. She gasped for breath, the sound loud in her ears.

So loud she couldn't distinguish the crashing anymore. Afraid to look back, she just ran.

The ground rumbled under her, and a deafening roar pounded her ears. She screamed seconds before a large, rough, vine-like arm scraped and wrapped around her waist and lifted her high into the air.

Feet dangling helplessly, Mina struggled against the rough bark that bit into her skin. She wriggled and pried herself out of its grasp, falling onto the muddy ground not far from the road's edge. Winded, she turned in horror to face the monstrous tree beast. It had uprooted itself and was now leaning over her.

Its roots moved along the ground in spider-like fashion, inching toward her leg. Whimpering, Mina crawled away from it. The trunk of the tree had cracked open to reveal a jagged mouth; the thick branches worked as the monster's arms. It moved toward her. The moss and leaves on the tree began to turn brown and slowly fell to the ground, dying, but she didn't have time to ponder why.

She got to her feet and ran, only to slip on the muddy terrain and fall onto her knees. A loud creak of branches was her only warning. She lifted her gaze to see one of the tree's large branches swing for her head. With a cry, Mina rolled to the side. The strike grazed her foot. She didn't think she could outmaneuver the tree monster a second time. Her only option was to get out of there.

Headlight beams blinded her in the mist. Mina rose to her feet—Brody! She tried to wave him away. Tires screeched on pavement as he braked to a stop. The tree monster roared in fury at his black SUV and took two huge menacing steps toward it.

"Oh no!" Mina cried out.

The tree swung a massive branch toward the car. Brody slammed the car into reverse as the tree pounded a branch within inches of the hood. He continued to drive away recklessly in reverse, the tires squealing as he made a hectic escape.

Mina breathed a sigh of relief that the car and driver were okay, but she couldn't help being a little disappointed that he'd left. Not to mention, she should have used the momentary distraction to run away.

She'd blown her opportunity.

"Oh, Mother Hubbard!" Mina let slip and took off. She was tired, sore, and bruised. Normally she would have pulled out the Grimoire by now. But she was on her own. Just when she thought she had outrun the tree monster, another one—a birch—appeared in front of her. The peeling white-gray bark created a face with eyes and a mouth. She was surrounded. The birch-tree monster swayed menacingly in front, while the mushroom-covered-ash-tree monster caught up and blocked her escape.

"I mean you no harm," she called out. She held up muddy palms in the air to show she was defenseless. "I didn't do anything to you. Just leave me alone!" The mushroom tree had dried out even more, and leaves kept falling to the ground. Maybe the monster couldn't survive above ground long. If that was the case, she only needed to wait.

A figure in a long black cloak appeared from the woods.

"Help!" Mina cried to the cloaked being.

But it only watched her from the tree line, neither helping nor hindering. "Please help me!" she tried again, but the figure didn't move—just continued to observe as she ran from the monsters. "Fine! A thousand curses on you!"

The figure raised its hand and pointed at her, its meaning clear. It was commanding the trees to harm her.

Mina tried to keep the monsters in sight, but the way they skittered about on their roots made it difficult. The ash tree started to shake and crack, its movements becoming stilted. The birch monster showed no signs of wilting or slowing until it stopped, and its long, gangly roots burrowed deep into the ground. Suddenly, they erupted out of the earth right in front of Mina, wrapping themselves around her legs.

She screamed and clawed at the roots, trying to pry them off. She swore she heard the monster laugh as it began to drag her into the ground. Flipping over, she dug her fingertips into the dirt, desperate to anchor herself. She glanced toward the hooded figure and noticed it had come closer as if to watch.

A low rumbling noise sounded in the distance, growing louder as it came closer. Headlight beams illuminated the tree attacking her and created a giant circular bull's-eye. The vehicle accelerated. Brody was back! He hit the curb at an intense speed, lifted into the air, and torpedoed straight into the trunk of the ash tree. *No!*

The monster shrieked as the impact severed many roots. The ones that had imprisoned her loosened, and Mina was able to wiggle free.

Brody's front wheels were halfway up the trunk of the toppled ash tree. He kept his foot on the gas, the wheels of his SUV continually spinning three feet above the ground. Was he too scared to let off it, or was he injured?

She held her breath.

He stirred and moved around inside.

She let out a sigh of relief.

Brody waved at her, trying to get her attention. His car was probably totaled, but the electric window worked...sort of. It whirred and made a loud grinding noise as it wiggled down.

"Mina, look out!" Brody shouted." His face was pale as a ghost.

Chanda Hahn

Mina turned as the ash tree toppled forward. It was
going to fall on her. She dove to the left and missed being
crushed by the thick trunk. Branches snapped, and she
imagined a rush of wind as if the tree had exhaled its last
breath.

Thump...thump...thump. Brody finally got the
driver's door opened and dropped the three feet to the
ground, his legs wobbly.

"Mina!" He crawled to where he had last seen her.

"Over here," Mina answered. She inched out from
behind the dead tree. "I'm okay."

She looked back to the tree line. The ominous
figure was gone.

"Is it dead?" Brody asked, rubbing his hand up and
down his left arm.

He refused to come any closer to either of the tree
monsters. His cheek was swollen with reddish scratches
across it from the airbags deploying. It was already starting
to bruise. One of his eyes looked swollen, and blood
trickled from a small cut on his forehead onto his white
polo.

"Brody! You're hurt!"

He was favoring his arm. She went to touch it, but
he pulled it away.

"This will be an interesting tale to tell my insurance
company." He looked his totaled car over. "Tell me I'm
not crazy." He wiped at his bruised face and winced.
"Those trees *were* attacking you...right?"

Mina scanned the scene before her. The ash tree
had fallen over dead. It had apparently been out of the
earth too long, and whatever Fae magic had kept it moving
had worn off. The birch tree was quickly drying up as they

watched. Within seconds, it was back to a regular looking tree.

Mina pointed at Brody's arm.

"I'll be fine. I just need to sit down for a second." He looked at the mangled car, the puddles of mud, and the tree corpses. "Yeah, I think I need to sit way over here."

He walked a few feet and almost collapsed as he tried to sit on the wet curb. Thankfully, it had stopped raining.

"What are you doing here?" she asked.

"I was following you. I followed you to the Country Club, and then I followed the bus. I never expected dating you to be so dangerous," he chuckled sadly.

"It's only going to get worse," Mina warned.

"I promised I'd protect you." His eyes looked glassy. "I don't go back on my promises."

"What if I released you from that promise?"

"I don't think I like where this is going." He looked down at his shoes.

"A lot has happened in the last few days, but it feels like it's been weeks."

"I know. I feel like I've aged ten years." He chuckled and grabbed her hand.

"You might have, thanks to Claire's touch," Mina admitted as she ran her hand over the back of Brody's. "She took some of your youth to sustain her."

Brody studied her, his eyes filled with sadness. He reached out with his other hand and covered hers. "Mina, what happened the night of the ball when you kept disappearing? Something changed that night, and I can't figure it out."

"I fell in love with someone else that night," she admitted... to him and to herself.

"But you were only gone from my sight for a couple of moments."

"And each of those moments felt like a lifetime on the Fae plane."

"So he's Fae? This person you fell in love with." Brody didn't seem angry. He seemed curious. Her heart swelled with relief that they could talk about this like friends.

She released a long drawn out breath, "Oh, yeah. Fae alright."

"Does he love you back?" Brody asked.

"No."

"Then he's blind."

"No, love is blind."

"Love is Grim" Brody whispered as he gently touched her face. "Why do I feel like you're saying goodbye? What are you not telling me?"

Mina reached into her pocket and pulled out his class ring. "You offered me something that, two years ago, I would have given anything for." She couldn't keep the tears of regret from creeping into her eyes or her voice. "But I can't give you what you want, because really? I lost my heart a long time ago, to a prince in a story."

"I may never get my happily-ever-after ending," she said, "but that doesn't mean you can't have yours." Mina placed the ring in his open palm. "You've given up so much for me, and I can never thank you enough. You promised to protect me, but I'm asking you to do something even greater. Protect Nan."

Brody was about to protest when Mina put her hand on his lips, stopping him. Her hand grew warm with power, and she pushed her will toward him and commanded, *Find your true love.*

Brody froze for a second, and Mina watched as her compulsion settled inside him. Why had she never noticed what she could do before? She was the one who couldn't control her own desire and kept compelling him to fall for her. And if her direction worked, she'd quickly find out if her instincts were correct.

He blinked a few times and looked at her, but there wasn't any strong emotion behind his eyes. Just trust and true friendship. Mina stood up and shivered, deeply thankful for this moment of resolution. Brody may have been able to ignore the chill of the evening, but she couldn't. The monster trees had wasted enough of her precious time.

"Let's go back."

Brody got up, and hand-in-hand, they walked the last mile to her house in silence. They took comfort from one another's touch, but it wasn't anything romantic. Mina was extra careful now to keep her feelings and desires locked up in her heart. She didn't want any stray thoughts to influence Brody.

When they finally made it up the hill and stood in front of her front door, it opened as if someone had been watching from inside.

Nan stood there. Her gaze dropped to their clasped hands, and her face fell.

Mina groaned inwardly. That wasn't what she wanted. She didn't mean to hurt her friend's feelings. How would she explain this to Nan?

She didn't have to. Brody took two steps forward, picked Nan up, even though he was injured and bruised, and kissed her.

Nan squealed in surprise but sure didn't stop him from kissing her.

Ever and Charlie happened to walk by, and Charlie stuck his finger down his throat and made barfing actions. Mina carefully squeezed past Nan and Brody as they continued to kiss. She silently closed the door and let them have privacy on the porch.

"Well, I think that was the fastest breakup and get-together in history." Ever leaned over to pull the curtain aside so she could spy.

Mina swatted her hand away. "No, he was always meant to be her prince charming. I just got in the way, and she was too good a friend to tell me her true feelings."

"So she lied to you," Ever said.

Mina thought about it, about all the jokes Nan made about not liking Brody Carmichael, even though their families were great friends. How she hadn't wanted to be the one to bring the folder to his house that fateful day when he ran over Mina's bike. Nan had liked him just as much as she did and was probably even more nervous than she was. Plus, Nan would never let herself admit to liking the same guy Mina did.

"Yeah, she lied. Not just to me, though—she lied to herself."

Ever nodded.

"Hey, you said you had a way for us to talk without being listened to?"

"Yeah. We need to get all the mirrors." She peeked back out the window again.

Nix walked in and noticed Ever looking outside. He pulled the curtain back and whistled at them.

Something loud slapped at the window, and Nix backed off.

"Leave them be," Mina commanded. "We have work to do."

Eleven

When the front door opened, and a red-faced Nan and a smiling Brody tried to sneak in, Ever pounced. She handed Brody a screwdriver.

"I need all of the bathroom mirrors taken down. You." She pointed to Nan. "Tackle the hall mirror. Nix, bring every other mirror in the house to the kitchen."

"Why?" Nan asked.

"Why must you ask why? Just trust me." Ever made a face and rolled her eyes.

Nan started unhooking the hall mirror, and Brody headed to the downstairs bathroom.

Mina went to the upstairs storage room. It had been a while since she'd entered this room. As she flipped on the light, a tremor ran up her arms. She'd been sitting on that very settee with Jared when he almost kissed her. A blush ran up her cheeks at the memory.

The large portrait of her father no longer sat on the easel, but on the floor. Now a new canvas and portrait sat in its place. The subject was a young girl, sitting in the same high back chair that was in the front living room. The girl had a slightly heart-shaped face, dark brown eyes, a hint of rosy cheeks, and long brown hair. Even though the painting stopped just past her shoulders, and only the pencil outline showed the rest, it was obvious that some magic was creating her portrait, and her fear was slowly coming to realization. Yes, that image would one day hang in this house after *she* passed.

Somehow, the house knew her time was almost up and was painting her death portrait.

Mina yelled in frustration and knocked the canvas from the easel. She picked it up and kicked right through the center of the fabric, tearing it from the staples. She stepped through it, venting her anger on it until nothing was left but a broken frame, and she was spent, sitting on the floor, staring at the mess she had made.

"Sorry, house sprite, or whoever is doing this, but I'm not ready. So no more memorial portraits until after I'm dead, got that? At least wait another eight hours." She spoke to the air, but she had a feeling that the magic house heard. "Now if you want to help me, you can show me where there are some mirrors."

Nothing happened.

"Fine, be that way." Mina began moving pictures and uncovering sheets from piles of boxes.

The curtain by the window moved. It could have been the air vents kicking on, but a sliver of moonlight fell through and pointed across the room to some boxes.

Mina checked that corner. Behind the boxes stood a large square mirror in an antique frame. She used part of the sheet to dust it off and then lifted it up carefully and carried it out. But not before saying a parting thanks.

Mina struggled under the weight of the mirror. Brody noticed and ran up the stairs to take it from her.

"Here, I got it." He gently took the mirror from her hands.

"Thanks." Mina smiled at him, surprised at how there was no awkwardness between them. Once she'd compelled him, it took only minutes to find his true love. How could Mina not feel good about that?

She walked by the front room and noticed Charlie passed out on the couch again. She stopped and brushed his hair back from his forehead. He wasn't warm anymore, just exhausted and sleeping.

Ever called her into the kitchen. Nix followed, carrying another mirror that Mina recognized from her mom's bedroom.

Ever directed the positioning of the mirrors around the kitchen, so they reflected across the island and back at each other.

"We know Teague has Mina's Godmother mirror," she said. "So he can watch her whenever he wants. But I remembered something from my gran about how to block the mirror from seeing true. We dilute her reflection by reflecting the images back at each other, within each mirror. He'll see a kaleidoscope of images, but they will be reflecting so much it will be hard for him to see or hear her." Her grin grew wide in self-appreciation.

"Like a really bad cellphone connection," Nan realized out loud.

"Exactly. Hard to make a connection if the call keeps getting dropped." Ever winked. "All plotting must be done within the safety of this mirror prism."

They sat around the kitchen island, and Mina crossed her arms and hugged herself. She took a deep steadying breath and looked over her group of friends. All of them in this together, to help her. She had to do what she could to save them, but that meant she mustn't tell them what she sacrificed to do so.

"Teague stopped his attack at the fairgrounds very suddenly. I'm not sure why. It could be that he saw the police arrive, and he wasn't ready to reveal himself yet."

"That's dumb, since hundreds of people saw his monsters attacking the school. There must be another reason," Nan spoke up as she slapped a large grayish poultice from Nix on her bruised cheek.

Nix went back to the kitchen stove to put together another poultice for Brody. She'd seen him do this before—make a mess in her kitchen, going through her cupboards mixing healing herbs.

"Teague won't stop here. He will destroy everyone unless he gets what he wants," Ever spoke firmly.

"Well, what does he want?" Nan mumbled. "Obviously it's not world peace."

"Turtle peas?" Nix asked loudly from behind his boiling pot of water. He dropped the lid, and it rattled.

"Not turtle peas—world peace," Ever snapped. "If you could keep it down a bit, maybe you could hear." She sighed dramatically and continued. "No one is safe. I believe the only reason he hasn't done more damage is that he's fixated on Mina. Maybe we can use that to our advantage."

Brody didn't look pleased at Ever's suggestion. His fists closed angrily. "No."

Ever just laughed. "You don't get it, do you? She's the best chance we have, and she'll probably have to face him in the end anyway."

"Find another way," he said.

"Okay, sheesh," Ever replied. "But you're kind of tying my hands. So our other option is that we can bring in Ferah to help us."

"Anyone except for Ferah," Mina added.

Ever made a sour face. "Yeah, well, I don't really want her on my team. I'd rather eat nails than partner up with her, but you do have a point. We've only got one shot at this, and I think I have an idea."

"What do you need us to do?" Nan jumped in. "We can help. I can—"

"No," Mina interrupted harshly. "I need you to do something else for me."

Brody's posture stiffened, and it mirrored Mina's defensive one. Would he interfere if he knew what she wanted, or would he help?

She sent Ever to gather the things she bought and asked Brody to pick up the sleeping bags from the living room. Nix was so preoccupied with banging around in the kitchen, he couldn't possibly hear Mina.

Mina pulled Nan closer while they were still within the mirrors.

"You're my best friend, right?"

"Duh, of course."

"And you love Charlie, like he was your own brother." It wasn't a question. Mina knew the answer. No one doted on Charlie more than her best friend. Nan was the only person who truly got him and his unique personality and language. She'd even punched Savannah White for calling him a name and faced out-of-school suspension.

"I'd kill anyone who touched a hair on his quirky little head," she said fiercely.

"Good, then I need you to take him."

"What do you mean?"

"Take my brother and run. Hide him from the Fae. I can't focus on what's coming next if I'm looking over my shoulder for Charlie. Is there somewhere you can go, somewhere your family owns that you can hide him?"

"Well, yeah maybe the—"

"Don't tell me. I don't want to know." Mina gripped Nan's arms. "No one can find him. No one can know, not even your parents."

"But I can't kidnap him, Mina. I'm not his legal guardian."

"Nan," Mina shot out. "Our mother's gone. He's going to end up in the system. They're going to take him. But that's the least of my worries. What if the Fae come after him? When this all dies down, you can bring him back. But remember, if something happens to me, Charlie becomes the next Grimm. He trusts you, Nan. You're the one he'd want on his side. And he'll need protection—help. He'll need you."

Nan's eyes turned glassy with tears. She left the circle of mirrors, paced the hall, rubbed her hands across her face in worry. She cried. Then she got angry. Every emotion crossed her face as she battled with what she was about to do.

Mina knew the minute Nan had made the decision to take and hide Charlie. Her posture straightened, she held her head high, and she looked Mina dead in the eye.

"No one will harm Charlie on my watch. I swear it."

"Good." Mina hugged her friend and cried.

She was asking a lot of Nan. It was illegal, and she would have to hide from her family. But Nan was used to living on her own. Her mom and stepdad were hardly ever home. When this was all over, Mina knew that he'd be taken care of, she'd see to that. If they won this battle.

"Mina. What are you going to do while I'm gone?"

"Try and survive."

There was more strategizing and planning schedules as they figured out what they were going to do about Teague. Ever had a plan that honestly might work, so Mina got Nix and Brody to agree to carry the mirrors upstairs and arrange them in her room.

Twelve

While Ever and Nix positioned the mirrors in her bedroom, Mina and Nan threw things into suitcases as quickly and quietly as they could. Charlie only woke up once, and that was when they were shuffling him out to Nan's Volkswagen beetle. When he saw Mina, he immediately closed his eyes and started crying.

He was mentally exhausted, and she felt terrible about it. She stopped in the middle of the yard and wrapped her arms around him. "Listen up, bud. Nan is going to take care of you. You're going off on an adventure together. You like adventures, don't you?"

Charlie's head bobbed yes.

"Well, she's got the best one planned, and when you get back, we will have this all figured out. Okay? Can you do this for me? Can you listen to Nan and be a good kid?"

Charlie sniffed and looked over to Nan, who sat back watching them. Hands shoved in her coat pockets, her head dipping down. Nan was crying as well.

Charlie let go of Mina and walked over to Nan, sliding his smaller hand into hers. He smiled wanly up at her and said. "I'll protect Nan."

Nan looked at their clasped hands, and the tears flowed freely.

"Ah, little buddy." She met Mina's eyes, her voice filled with promise. "You know I'd give my life for him. You know that right?"

"That's why it has to be you."

"You give the word, and we'll be back," Brody said as he packed their sleeping bags into the back of the car. She never had any doubt that once he knew what Nan was doing, he'd go with and watch over her. That was why Mina needed to get Nan to agree before she told Brody.

"You have to go quickly." Mina tried not to look at her watch in front of them.

They had spent hours packing and getting ready for this trip. She had only a few hours left. She wanted her friends far away. She didn't want Teague to stop her—or to find them if he changed his mind.

Nan opened the car door, and Mina buckled Charlie into the backseat and ran her hand over his hair. He'd need a haircut soon, and his birthday was coming up. She hoped she'd be alive to celebrate with him. She had packed his suitcase with clothes, jackets, and his favorite toys—even his *Star Wars* light saber.

"I love you, Charlie," Mina whispered as she gave him one last hug and kissed his forehead.

"Love you back," he whispered with a bear hug.

She wouldn't have let him go ever, except that he was the one who let go of her first. She wrapped the blanket from the sofa around him, and his head started to droop. Exhaustion was catching up with all of them.

"You'll explain everything to him, right?" Tears fell down Mina's cheeks as she softly closed the back door.

"I wouldn't have to if you'd let us stay to help." Nan's blue eyes were glassy but on fire with determination.

Mina shook her head. "You know this is for the best." Mina closed the passenger door, but Nan rolled the window down.

"I'll take care of them," Brody said across the roof of the car. "And I'll find a way for you to get a hold of us if you need to."

"Don't tell me. It's best if I don't know."

"Mina, it's just…" Brody trailed off.

"It's okay. I'll always love you, just not the way you deserve. But Nan will."

Those words seemed like the confirmation that Brody needed. He came around the car and pulled Mina into a hug. "Be safe."

He was going to make her cry. Mina gently pulled away, "You need to go. Get them somewhere safe."

He climbed into the driver's seat and started up. Nan leaned forward and waved as he backed her car up and drove down the driveway. Mina watched the taillights until she could no longer see them in the darkness. She knew the car would turn left, away from town and onto the highway.

She stood frozen in the middle of her driveway. Tears poured freely down her face. Her knees buckled beneath her, and she collapsed onto the gravel. It was for the best, she kept trying to tell herself.

But if it was for the best, why did it feel like she'd just ripped out another part of her soul?

The screen door slammed, and Nix stepped outside. "Mina? What's wrong?" He rushed to her side.

"He's gone," she whispered sadly.

"Who?"

"Charlie." She sniffed, wiped at her eyes, and slowly stood up to face Nix.

"How'd this happen? I promise we'll get him back." His voice grew angry, but he gathered her into a hug.

Mina took comfort from his hug but gently pulled away. "No. We won't." She watched his eyes frown in confusion. "I sent him away."

"What?"

"It's better this way. I begged Nan to take him away, and Brody went with."

"You can't do that."

"Wrong," Ever's voice cut in. "It's exactly what she should have done. She was smart." She had come out to stand on the porch and listen. "She's cutting her losses, before Teague can use them against her. She's thinking of what's ahead. And this war is no place for a young Fae boy that just lost his mother."

Nix scowled. "There could have been another way." He reached for Mina's arm, but she wrenched it free and took a step back.

"I just lost my mother," Mina hissed between clenched teeth. "I almost lost all of you. I'm not about to lose my brother. He's the only family I have left. Don't judge me. You would have done the same thing, if you were in my position."

Nix stared at her, his eyes filled with pity. "No, I wouldn't have."

"I guess that makes you better than me." She didn't really mean it, but it was easy to lash out when she was in so much pain. She stormed inside, away from Nix's pity and Ever's shock.

Mina stormed up the stairs to her room. Locking the door, she pressed her back to it and tried to hold in the sobs that threatened to tear her chest apart.

She moved toward her bed, trying to ignore the plethora of mirrors that now surrounded her room. She pulled back the covers, and something soft slid to the floor, landing with a thunk. Mina picked up the petal dress she had worn to the ball the other night and felt along the side for the hidden pocket. Her hand reached in and pulled out the dagger.

She dropped it to the floor and stared at it. She'd forgotten that she slipped it in there. It wasn't the sight of the dagger that startled her. It was the rust colored spots of Teague's dried blood on it.

She wiped it off as best as she could, placed the dagger in her bedside table, and shut the drawer. Mina crawled under the comforter and rolled over to stare across the room and into the mirror that faced her bed.

He was winning. The Story was winning, and she was losing the will to fight. She heard knocking on her bedroom door but ignored it. She needed to mourn, to sink into her feelings and feel the pain, the betrayal, and the anger. Anger at her mother, anger at herself. When she had thought through every scenario, it always came down to what was best for her brother.

113

She was down to two hours when a crazy idea came to her. She climbed out of bed and got dressed. This time, she was going over-prepared. She changed into jeans, boots, a white t-shirt, and her olive green jacket. In her backpack, she loaded food, water, and a flashlight. She looked at her nightstand, debating on whether to bring the dagger. She needed a weapon, but having one on her might make her life forfeit sooner than she had planned. When she was as packed as she could be, she grabbed the seam ripper from the top of her dresser.

There was more to using the seam ripper than just opening up a gate between the planes. With enough willpower, maybe she could direct where it opened a gate. How else could she explain her fall from the tower to land in Wilhelm Grimm's hospital room? Or how Queen Maeve was able to zone in on her and show up wherever Mina was with the seam ripper.

Now, it was Mina's turn to do some popping-in-uninvited of her own.

She held the silver lipstick-sized tube and clicked the small gem. *The Fates. Take me to the Fates.*

The seam ripper glowed, and she drew a large oval, creating a gate between her world and the Fae one outside of the mirror-circle. The portal glowed, and she tried to look through to the other side.

Worry and doubt wedged themselves in the bottom of her stomach, but Mina pushed those feelings aside. She needed help, and she wasn't going to sit back and let her friends do all the work.

Taking a deep breath, Mina closed her eyes and stepped through the gate.

Thirteen

It was night, and Mina was not surrounded by the normal sweet aroma of the Fae plane, but by an odorous sulfur-like smell that burned her nose and made her gag.

"Ugh." Mina covered her nose with her shirt. Had she ended up in the wrong place? Was she even on the Fae plane? She would have doubted it, but she looked up at the night sky and saw continually moving stars above. The Fae plane could be as fantastic as stories made it out to be, but it was also as deadly—with sea witches, giants, trolls, ogres and more. She couldn't let her guard down for one second.

She pulled her small flashlight out of her backpack and began walking. Mina didn't get far before she slipped and sunk into mud. She struggled to regain her footing on the path, but then the very next step, she was knee deep in the mud again.

She flashed the light around in an arc to see that she was surrounded by swamp and curly green grass. Maybe it hadn't worked? Maybe trying to direct the seam ripper had failed. She wasn't anywhere near the Fates' palace. She was in the middle of a stinking swamp.

The hair on the back of her neck stood on end. The odd chirping and grunting noises of the swamp creatures suddenly stopped. All was silent, except the slushing and sucking noises she made as she tried to free herself from the mud and get onto the path. Once in the grass, she froze and crouched low, listening in fear as she tried to silence her frantic breathing.

After a minute of silence, Mina stood up and carefully continued her trek through the swamp grass. A squelch and popping sound followed each of her steps, but something warned her to move, to run. Mina tried, but suddenly slid waist-deep into water. She tried to wade through it, but she was too late.

Lights exploded around her, blinding her. She was unable to blink or even cover her eyes from the onslaught of the bright light. But that was their way of keeping her from seeing them.

She could hear voices, see shadows move beyond the light, but she couldn't identify her captors.

"So you have returned, have you?" A woman's voice echoed with authority through the swamp. "Do you see the mess you have caused, child?"

Mina couldn't see her, but she recognized the voice of Queen Maeve. The balls of light dimmed, and she could see the queen standing in front of her. Her dark brown dress lacked the finer adornments and was a sharp contrast to the shimmering silver colors she preferred. Her hair was plaited in a long simple braid down her back. King Lucian came up next to her in similar clothes in earth tones.

Mina suspected it was to help camouflage them in the swamps. She wasn't sure, but she had a feeling that they weren't here by choice. They were hiding.

116

The hold on Mina's body lessened, and without the support of the power holding her in place, she slipped and fell into the muddy water, barely catching herself before her head went under. She stood up to face the Fates and tried to keep her body from shaking with the cold.

"I came to ask for help."

Queen Maeve barked a derisive laugh. "Help! I blame you for this." She waved her hand to the swamp around her. "This is our home now, thanks to you. All you had to do was stay on the human plane, never let him cross back over. But now we're doomed." Her regal face crumpled, and Lucian slipped his arms around his wife.

"Now, now, darling. Everything will be alright," he whispered softly to her.

"What happened?" Mina asked. "Why are you in the swamp?"

"Because of our son," Lucian answered. "He's too powerful. Even our armies. He controls them all now, the giants, griffins, ogres, trolls. We dare not go up against him and what's left of our royal guard alone. This is all that is still loyal to us."

The Fae light around her dimmed. Beyond the Fates, about twenty or so soldiers from the palace stood in the nearby reeds. Their uniforms and armor were covered with mud and starting to rust. They looked tired and worn out. Not fit to storm the palace and fight Teague. Among them, she recognized Captain Plaith. But their numbers were dismal.

"What do we do now?" Mina asked.

"We?" Queen Maeve scoffed. "You've done enough."

"Now, Maeve," Lucian chastised.

She gave him a seething look. "I wouldn't trust that human any more than I'd trust a sea witch."

"Well, she can't be all human. You saw how the bowl reacted to her in the test. She's strong, and... ahem... our son has a fondness for the girl. She could be our only hope."

"You once came to me for help," Mina reminded the Fates. "When the Grimoire ended up in the hands of a renegade Reaper, you sent me after it to protect a part of your son."

"That Reaper would have destroyed him—or worse, reunited him with himself."

"But I saved him, at least a part of him."

"You were the one who turned him into the beast that he is now! He wasn't like this until that night in the tower. That night that you poisoned our son against us."

"You don't know what happened, do you?"King Lucian turned to her, looking extremely interested. "What exactly happened?"

"He was stabbed with the dagger of Erjad, and he was dying, but I healed him... Only I didn't know that a piece of the dagger was still inside. It changed him and turned him into..." She trailed off, not needing to say any more about their son.

"And how did this dagger end up in our son? You were the one who was with him." King Lucian's eyes glowed, and Mina felt pressure around her throat. She grasped at the power that began to strangle her. *So that's where Teague got his temper.*

Her mouth opened and closed as she tried to breathe. She looked at the king's glowing eyes, and she wasn't afraid. She closed her own eyes and imagined his power snapping back on the king like a rubber band. She felt the power break.

King Lucian cried out in pain. He gasped, looking at her in awe. "How did you do that?" A small smile formed at the corner of his lips. "You used my own power against me."

Mina ignored the king, rubbing at her throat. She stared directly at Queen Maeve and said two words. "The Godmothers."

Queen Maeve sighed and rubbed her forehead. "I wondered. They've always had it out for the ruling family. But they used to be mere pests, with the occasional assassination attempt. They believe we are evil dictators."

Mina raised an eyebrow and scoffed. "Do you blame them? Look what's come to pass. They acted based on a prophecy that foretold all of this. Do you know what it's like to watch your loved ones being hunted—toyed with—only to fall victim to mindless quests? In fact, they *weren't* quests. They were traps. You *never* intended to break the curse over my family."

"Of course not. Teague was set on destroying your family, no matter what we did. We could neither stop him nor close the gates between the planes—not when our son was on the human plane.

Tears of frustration filled Mina's eyes. "Well, you should have. He would have been happy—at least a part of him would have. I would have seen to that. And then Teague wouldn't have killed my family."

"Perhaps there is truth in what you say. But it's too late for that now," Queen Maeve admitted sadly.

"What about splitting him again?" Mina asked, her voice filled with desperation.

119

"We never wanted him split. Just his powers bound."

"The first who attempted and failed now sleeps in stone at the bottom of the lake." King Lucian's voice carried an edge of anger, and Mina couldn't help but wonder if he referred to the siren.

"The second Fae split him into two. Although she didn't fail, she didn't do what we asked. That sprite was not who she said she was, and we banished her to the human plane," Queen Maeve said.

"Oh," Mina said sadly.

"Even if we were able to split him again, there's no guarantee that Teague's personality would divide down the same path. You could end up with two different personas of the current Teague," the queen said sadly. "And as dangerous and unpredictable as he is, I'm not sure that's worth the risk."

"Plus he would never let us get that close to him again," King Lucian said. "We barely escaped with our lives at our last encounter. You on the other hand..." His voice trailed off as he studied her thoughtfully.

"How?" Mina asked. "You're the ruling Fates. How did one boy overpower the both of you?"

Queen Maeve looked pained at the question. She brought her finger up to her lips and made a shushing noise. "Follow us."

She beckoned Mina to follow her through the reeds. A few feet away, the grass parted before the Fates, mud slurping out of the way, reeds bending backward to clear a path so they could move to an area outside of the swamp. They walked to a grove of willow trees.

King Lucian pulled the low hanging branches apart and let his wife enter the shelter of one, and then Mina. As Mina passed through, she could hear the faint sound of crying.

Apparently, in the Fae plane, the willows really did weep. Mina had never seen a weeping willow so large or beautiful. Its long, hanging branches appeared more white than green as they formed a swaying rooftop.

Within the protection of the boughs, King Lucian waved his hand, and gold magic wove up and around the tree, encasing them within a cage of power.

"No!" Mina rushed to the side, but King Lucian stopped her.

"Don't touch the ward. You will be instantly killed."

Those words didn't make her feel any safer. She pulled away from the king and stood awkwardly in the center of the cage.

"It's only a sound barrier to keep prying ears from hearing," Queen Maeve waved her hand, and silver willow branches slowly dropped from above to form a small swing for the queen to sit in. She smoothed out her skirts and watched her husband expectantly.

King Lucian rubbed his beard and nodded. He prepared to sit on air, when a large purple mushroom formed beneath him, creating the perfect stool.

Mina felt a little bit perturbed that no one offered her a seat, but why should they? They were the Fates. They created their own seats. Using anger more than common sense, Mina focused on a small blue flower. Envisioning what she had in mind, she felt the prickle of power come to her and pushed it toward the flower.

She couldn't hold back the smirk when the flower grew and morphed—not into just a larger version of itself. Three of the petals grew exponentially larger, one creating the back and two others forming armrests. Mina didn't just create for herself a chair to sit on in front of the Fates. She went so far as to challenge them by fashioning herself a flower throne. She was about to sit on her throne when she noticed how covered in mud she was.

Well, that wouldn't do. She pushed the power and made the mud disappear from her clothes. Then, crossing her legs, she settled back in the throne and waited.

King Lucian laughed. "Well done. Well done, girl. I see you have not only power, but sass. I like that. I like that very much."

Queen Maeve just shook her head at her husband's verbal adoration.

"You were about to say?" Mina prompted them with a nod of her head. Her smile did not dim in the light of the king's laughter.

"What we are about to tell you cannot leave this tree." Queen Maeve warned, her voice threatening.

Mina would have none of it. She leaned forward on her throne, her voice matching the queen's with its own threat. "One of your Death Reapers took my mother. I make no such promises. I'm here for revenge. I'm not worried about wounding your pride."

This time it was Maeve's turn to look shocked but pleased. "Very well. But you must know this is very sensitive information we are going to share."

"Then why share it with me?" Mina asked. "Especially if you blame me for what happened to your son."

Queen Maeve stilled her eyes, slowly closing them with barely hidden anger. "Even though I may not trust you, and despite what the Godmothers believe, we do care for our people. And you, child, can save not only your world but ours as well."

"How exactly can I do that?"

King Lucian crossed his arms and spoke slowly. "We are chosen as the Fates, because we are the most powerful Fae. We marry into powerful lineages to protect our line."

"That's why you have the tests," Mina answered.

"Exactly," the king said. "But if one far stronger than us comes to power, they can wrest that title from us. Our son was strong, the Fae magic almost too much for him to handle. He feared he would lose control of the power. We had hoped that by finding his match, it would help balance him, and one day the pair would become the Fates. But in his fury, he has taken that from us all on his own. He is now the lone Fate, and with that title he holds control of the army."

"How did he gain control of the army?"

"Similar to the sweetsuckle bees," Queen Maeve answered, referring to a Fae bee. "Just as the queen bee controls the swarms of soldiers, the Fate controls our armies."

"We need to turn our enemy into our greatest weapon," King Lucian said.

"Stop it." Mina stood and stared down at the king and queen. "I am not a pawn."

Her anger was so evident, and her power flowed forth so violently, that the mushroom under the king withered back into the ground, and he fell into the grass.

123

The queen's swing dropped her on the ground and retreated back into the canopy above. "I am a Grimm."

King Lucian recovered first. He stood up, dusting the dirt from the back of his trousers. "*That* is the power we need if you are to succeed where we have failed."

Queen Maeve gave him a hauntingly sad look.

"Succeed by doing what exactly?" Mina snapped.

King Lucian didn't look thrilled himself, but he swallowed and looked deep into Mina's eyes. "By killing our son."

Fourteen

There was never any doubt in Mina's mind that it would come down to death—hers or Teague's. But for the command to come from his own parents! Their willingness to betray their own flesh and blood so they could once again rule as the Fates turned her blood cold. No wonder Teague was so conflicted. His own parents had just put a bounty out on his head.

At first Mina started to empathize with the Fates, but she didn't expect them to betray their own son.

"I can see the accusation in your eyes," Queen Maeve said firmly. She came and stood before Mina. Her chin held high as she looked down her nose at her. "You don't understand how we, his own parents, can wish that upon our son. But you don't know what havoc he has wreaked in our world. Thousands have died. Thousands more will as well."

"He's your son!"

"That beast!" Maeve's hand shook as she pointed outward toward the swamp. "Is not my son."

"Deep inside, he is still the same young man, under an evil spell. I came here seeking help. Hoping you would stop him from destroying my world."

"How can we," Queen Maeve whispered, a tear slowly sliding down her dainty white cheek, "when we couldn't stop him from destroying ours?"

Mina's heart was breaking for Teague. She remembered how she felt when her mom abandoned her, but that was only until she realized that *her* family would do whatever it took to rescue her. By making the greatest sacrifice of all. Her life.

Maybe if the Fates had been willing to risk themselves, they might have been able to help him. Didn't they understand that he was scared of ruling? Of losing control? He became the very thing he feared. He'd never wanted this to happen. But instead of searching for another solution, Teague's parents gave up and were resorting to murder.

She would have to stop him without their help, because she certainly wasn't going to help them regain power to a throne that rested on the blood of their son. Even Teague was able to dethrone his parents without killing them.

How horrible it must be to have such heartless parents. She was so furious, she had problems reining in her anger.

She stormed to the wall of willow branches and waited while King Lucian unwove the ward to release her. When it was down, and she could no longer see the glowing spider web of power, she turned and said her farewell to the Royals before her.

"So while my world crumbles, you hide in your swamp kingdom...scared of your own son. No wonder it was easy for him to steal control from you two. You're cowards."

Mina walked out of the boughs and into the swamp. She heard the roar of King Lucian's angry retort, but she didn't dare look back. She pulled out her seam ripper, created a gate, and stepped back to her world.

The gate slowly closed, and she didn't even care if something followed her through. She didn't think the king and queen would send anyone after her. Not when their whole plan started and ended with her doing all the work. The weight of her current plan fell on her shoulders like a ton of bricks as soon as came through the gate.

Her back-up plan had failed, and the task laid before her made her nervous, agitated, and resigned. She hoped she was strong enough for what was to come, prayed that she was brave enough to both save her brother and end the curse on both their worlds. Maybe she'd be alive in the end to tell the story to her kids one day.

Mina put her seam ripper in her pocket, looked around her bedroom, and wondered how much time she had left. Had time passed at all while she'd been on the Fae plane, or—like Brody said—had it been mere moments? She made her way to the kitchen.

Ever sat at the breakfast table eating toast with peanut butter and marshmallows on it. She raised one dark eyebrow and offered Mina a piece. "Want some? It's great for curing the blues, and we have some time to kill."

"Ugh, no," Mina rubbed her face and sat on the stool, burying her face in her arms.

"Coffee?" Ever held up a mug with the words. *Coffee is my happily ever after.* "It's just black. Nothing weird in it. I promise."

"No, I can't handle that stuff unless there's tons of cream and sugar."

"I'm on it." Ever slid from her chair and went to fill an empty mug. She poured in a splash of cream. Then she waved her finger in the air, and a pink and white striped tube appeared next to her. The paper tube opened, poured into the cup, and the spoon stirred on its own.

"What is that?" Mina asked, her piqued curiosity overriding her burden for a moment.

"Sugar," Ever answered, handing her the cup. The spoon swirled twice more in the mug and came to a slow stop.

"What kind of sugar?"

"Only the best ever." Ever smiled and clinked her cup against Mina's. She took a swig and rolled her eyes in pleasure.

Mina stared at the empty wrapper on the counter. A Pixy Stix. Of course Ever would find a use for her addiction to the Fae named candy.

Not wanting to offend her, Mina took a sip and tried to keep her face as neutral as possible. Huh. It wasn't half bad.

Mina glanced around the kitchen and then to the hall, looking for Nix.

"He's not here," Ever answered. "He left after you went upstairs."

"Yeah."

"You know, you treated him like garbage."

"I know." Mina grumbled, feeling worse.

Forever

"I get why you did it. It's easier to push them away so they don't get hurt. Like you did with Nan, Brody, and Charlie. You sent the ones you love the most away. And you started to treat Nix bad, hoping he'll abandon you too. You're trying to protect him."

Mina didn't answer. She didn't have to. The truth was written across her face.

Ever just continued to talk. "And since you barely tolerate me, you won't send me away, because I'm not important to you."

Mina's head snapped up. "That's not true at all."

"Relax, Gimp. I know I'm your favorite." She smiled wryly and took another bite of her peanut butter marshmallow toast. "Plus, you need me," she said around her mouthful of food.

Mina sat there staring at Ever. Finally, she reached for that offered piece of toast and took a bite. Something crackled in her throat. Mina coughed into her napkin, and shot Ever an awful look. "Pop rocks?"

Ever opened her mouth, so Mina could hear the popping noise. "It's the best."

"You're worse than Charlie." Mina coughed again as a stray piece of popping candy lodged in her throat.

"Naw, he's just got the great Fae taste in food. Always has."

"Why is that?" Mina asked, wiping her mouth.

"Because Charlie and you are a part of our world as much as yours—and magic is your legacy. You can feel how it flows naturally to you. You just need the confidence to control it."

"That's what scares me. I can feel it hovering, especially whenever I've been scared or angry—the

129

weakness of all sirens. Everything Nix wanted to avoid. Neither of those emotions are great influences on my power."

"Sirens are some of the strongest Fae around. If you start practicing, maybe you'll be a match for Teague."

There's not enough time.

"I'll never be a match for him."

Ever tossed her toast back onto the plate and shoved away from the table. "How can you say that about yourself?"

Mina winced. Did Ever not remember that he could be watching them? Teague was always watching. Of course, it was possible that was the *reason* Ever was being so adamant and loud in her confession. She was trying to taunt him.

"Do you still not realize your potential?" Ever went on. "You passed the Fates' tests! You, who are a half-breed, not even born on our plane, have more Fae power at your fingertips than some of the strongest Fae families."

"Why is that?" Mina asked, frustrated with her own ignorance.

"Beats me, but I wouldn't be looking a gift dog in the mouth."

"Horse. You mean gift horse?"

"Dog... horse. Whatever. Your kind talks funny." Ever picked up her backpack from the floor by the door and put her arm through the black straps. So, promise to not leave the house until I get back."

"I won't leave the house," Mina promised.

A sly look passed between them.

Ever sighed and shook her head. "I hate leaving you this soon, especially after yesterday."

"Go," Mina answered. "It's more important that you find help."

Ever gave her a long look, a silent communication. "We'll beat him Mina. For what he did to your family."

Mina only nodded. If she spoke, Ever would be able to read the doubt and fear in her voice. She needed to act scared, not wired up.

As soon as Ever left, Mina locked the door after her. She sat at the kitchen table and watched the clock's second hand tick. Then, she went back up to her room, laid across the covers of her bed and waited for the end.

Fifteen

"Mina..." The voice drawled out her name, the whisper echoing throughout the room.

Mina sat up in bed and stared around her empty bedroom, the hair on the back of her arms lifting with the flow of power that radiated throughout the room. The air was so full of magnified Fae power, she could almost choke on it.

It was the mirrors. Not only were they distorting the looking glass to keep Teague from spying on her, they also seemed to be bouncing his power back on itself and magnifying it.

"Why do you try and hide from me, Mina... Mina... Mina?" Teague's voice was unmistakable, as was his tone of displeasure. He was using power to amplify his voice, causing it to scatter and repeat through multiple mirrors.

"I'm not hiding. I'm right here." She threw off the cover and stood next to her bed. His image faded in and out as he tried to see her. The mirror-protection was working. He couldn't focus on her.

"Ah, I see what you've done. But you can't stay in the circle forever. Have you gone back on our deal?"

"Of course not. But I want a guarantee you won't go after my friends," Mina yelled.

"Give me the dagger, and I'll leave your friends alone. No other bargains will be made. I could send a Reaper after your brother right now to help you understand the necessity of following through."

Her body started to tremble. How could she win against him? Despite what Ever said, here, now, in this moment, she doubted her strength. If she risked the fight and lost, she'd only guarantee the death of everyone she loved. A tear slid down her cheek. "Okay, you win. Take the dagger, but leave my friends and family alone."

"Step away from the circle," he demanded.

Mina stepped away from the protection of her circle. A glow of light appeared under the hallway door. The knob turned, and the door opened. Teague.

He came in and studied the display of mirrors. "Very impressive for a human."

As he moved toward her, she backed up. The back of her knees bumped against her bed.

He chuckled at her fear and reached out for her face. She turned away, but he gently plucked a strand of hair off her cheek and tucked it behind her ear. "Where is it? Do not make me ask again." His voice was softer than she expected.

Her eyes flicked to her nightstand and back to him.

Teague pulled open the small drawer filled with her hair brush, numerous hair bands, and pens. His hand lingered over her blue notebook of Unaccomplishments and Epic Disasters. He pulled it out, flipped open a few pages, and skimmed them.

"You really are bad luck, aren't you? Some would say cursed." He tossed the notebook onto her bed. "Of course, that could be in part because of me."

Teague reached back in and dug around until he pulled out the dagger. He stared overly long at the small missing tip. His free hand touched the spot over his heart where the tip lay. An expression of contemplation flickered across his face, and she saw a chance.

"Teague," Mina whispered his name. "That dagger is evil. It's changed you. If you'd let me help you, we could remove the rest, and you'd be back to normal."

"And why would I want that?" His eyes went dark, and he turned on her. "I've never felt so alive... so powerful... so in control of my own destiny."

"Fine. So does this mean it's over?" she asked. "That you'll leave me and my family alone?"

He turned to her, his face lighting up in an evil grin. "I'll spare your friends, but I'm not done with you." Within seconds, he was pressed up against her, his hand cupped around her face, his thumb just brushing the corner of her lip.

Mina's breath caught as he leaned forward to kiss her. She pinched her eyes shut, scared to fight, scared to breathe as his lips barely brushed hers.

"My only wish," he whispered, "is for you to share my fate."

Her eyes shot open. The dagger glinted as his arm lifted to plunge it into her.

"No!" Mina screamed and reeled backward falling onto her bed.

Her fall made her even more vulnerable. He smiled.

The door burst open, and Ever exploded into the room flying straight for the dagger in his hand. She grabbed his wrist mid-lunge and yanked backward.

"Now, Mina!" Ever shouted, as she struggled with Teague to pull him closer to their target.

Mina pulled all of the power through the mirrors into the room. The mirrors glowed, lights flickered, and the paintings on the wall shook.

Teague blasted Ever against the wall, leaving a spidery crack up the plaster. She looked a bit dazed, but the pixie shook it off and flew toward him again, grabbing the hand with the dagger. Teague seized her in a net of power, frozen, her hand still wrapped around his wrist.

Mina didn't have much time. The mirrors were charged, but Ever was too close to Teague to go through with their plan.

Ever's eyes flicked to Mina. "Do it!"

The joint attack surprised Teague. He spun his attention on Mina. She aimed the concentrated power from the mirrors at the knife and Teague. Power shot into him, making him glow, turning a bright white.

He screamed in frustration and countered her power with his own. Teague was stronger. He released his hold on Ever.

Screaming, she fell to the floor with a thud.

Teague began to laugh.

That worried Mina.

"Don't quit, Mina. Keep going," Ever shouted. "This *has* to work!" She got back up and flew behind Teague. Grabbing him around the waist, Ever lifted him into the air. He roared as the pixie pulled him toward the center of the circle of mirrors.

"Come on, Mina," the pixie yelled over the glowing ball of light that now almost engulfed her.

"Move. I can't do it," Mina hesitated, desperate to keep from hurting her friend.

"It's my job to protect *you*, Gimp. Forget about me. Think of your family!"

Teague slashed Ever across the arm with the poisoned dagger. She yelped and let go to grab her arm.

Mina had no choice. With all her might, she focused the magnified Fae power and, with a metaphysical push, shoved it straight into the center of Teague's chest.

He released his own burst of power as he started to fade in and out.

"This is for my mother!" Mina screamed.

Her arms and hands tingled as she sent another burst of power into Teague, pressing him toward the glowing circle. He held up his hands and began to separate into rays of light but fought being pushed into the circle.

"Aaahhh!" Ever jumped into the air and charged Teague, knocking them into the bright light. Teague split into seven forms of himself, and Ever and several Teagues were dragged into the mirrors.

The power backlashed, sending Mina spinning through the air to land on her bed. The house shook, and she heard the unmistakable sound of glass breaking.

"No!" Mina ran to the edge of the circle and looked within. Three of the mirrors were cracked and dark. Ever banged at the other side of the intact bathroom mirror.

When the power flowed out of the room, and it was safe for Mina to enter the circle, she ran to Ever's mirror and pressed her hands to it. Ever met her gaze and slammed her fist into the mirror.

At first, Mina thought the pixie was trying to get out, but then she saw a shadowy figure pull himself up off the bathroom floor behind her. Ever wasn't trying to get out, she was trying to break the mirror and trap herself inside, with a version of Teague.

It had worked. Ever's secret plan to try and once again divide Teague's power and trap him within the mirrors worked. And Mina was the only person strong enough to do it.

Ever had said it was like a prism. Fae were in essence magic, and magic had seven colors—like a spectrum. She had thought of—not just splitting him in two—but using a prism and mirrors to split him seven ways. Each one would weaken a part of him. Then Mina and Ever would simply have to destroy the mirror and trap him inside. He'd never be able to cross over and hurt one of them again.

Except that Ever was trapped in one of the mirrors with him.

Thankfully, she wasn't split. She hadn't been in the center with the prism long enough. But she was injured and with a shadow form of Teague. Which one would he be? Would he be evil? Good? Something else?

Beads of sweat appeared across Ever's forehead, and her eyes started to look glazed.

"Oh no no no no!" The effects of the poisoned dagger were causing Ever to fade fast. Mina pressed herself to the mirror and called out. "What do I do?"

Ever bent down out of sight and stood back up, her right hand hidden out of sight. Ever smiled sadly and mouthed the words. "It's too late for me. Break the other mirrors."

She raised her hand and held up the towel bar she'd pulled off the wall.

Teague came into focus, running toward the mirror, just as Ever smashed the bar into it.

It shattered.

What had Ever done? Did she not think Mina could save her?

Mina stared at the broken mirror before wracking her brain for answers, but she didn't have any. Ever sacrificed herself for the plan by destroying the mirror from the other side.

Then her bedroom door burst open with a flash of light as someone blasted her in the chest. Pain surged through her body as she flew through the far mirror.

Sixteen

Mina landed on something cold and hard. The glow of the portal she had been hurled through closed up, leaving her in pitch black. What mirror was she in? It wasn't the bathroom, hall, or kitchen. The darkness surrounding her made her shiver. Was it the house trying to help her again? Where had Nix even found this mirror?

She sat up and groaned in pain, her foot scraping across what sounded like stone. Mina felt around her and along the freezing cold floor. There. A wall. Better to have that to her back than be wide open to who knew what. As she shifted, she heard something slide across stone. Someone or something was in the darkness with her.

"Who's there?" she called out softly.

No one answered, but she heard a slight cough. Terrified of being attacked in the dark, she scrambled along the wall until she felt a somewhat familiar shelf. She sighed in relief when she felt a paint can, toolbox, and next to it a flashlight. Nix had found a mirror in the basement. Clicking it on, she swung the beam in an arc while she kept her senses on high alert.

The light illuminated a leg in dark jeans. She followed the leg up to a body in a red shirt and hesitated just before reaching the face. Did she send up a silent prayer? She wasn't sure. Gathering her courage, she shined the beam on the person's face, and his hand came up to block the light.

"Ow!" The voice grumbled. "Give a guy a break."

"Sorry." Mina moved the beam away but brought it back close enough that she could see his face clearly. Her heart was already thudding loudly in her ears, and the flashlight shook in her hands.

It looked like him, but he had his face turned away from the light as if he was purposely avoiding looking at her. She had to know.

"Is it really you?"

"Go away." His voice was low, almost growling at her.

"Not until you tell me who you are."

The man lunged at her, his voice rising in animalistic pitch. "Go away!"

Chains attached to the floor below him brought him up short. His body convulsed, and he stopped struggling against his bonds. He slowly turned his back on her, chains rustling. Now she had a full view of his back.

But she knew.

"Jared. It *is* you!" Mina moved to just outside the reach of his chains and tried to sit on the floor.

"It's me, Mina."

He hadn't changed. His dark hair was longer, unkempt from lack of care. His face looked thinner, but it was still just as handsome beneath the layers of grime. She hadn't seen his eyes, but she didn't really want to know their color.

She told herself it wouldn't matter. This was Jared.

He turned and gave her a long searching look. She waited for recognition to flare in his eyes, for the smile to reach his lips.

He just sneered. "Mina. What a pathetic name—for a pathetic girl."

"I'm not pathetic. You are. You're the one lying here in filth and dirt."

His head rolled to the side, as if holding it up took too much effort. This time he did smile cruelly as he shook the silver manacles in front of him and shook the chains at her. "I, at least, have a reason, for it. You do not belong here. You need to leave," he warned.

"I'm not leaving without you," Mina promised, moving forward slowly, unthreateningly. She motioned to his manacles, and he held them up for her to inspect.

Her heart dropped when she saw how bloody and mangled his wrists were under the metal. No padding protected his skin from the iron, which was terribly painful to Fae. On someone not as strong, it might have killed them or driven them mad. Of course, she wasn't sure how much time had passed on this mirror plane. How long had he been here? Was he still safe?

She closed her eyes, and her hand glowed over the lock. A loud click followed, and the first manacle fell from his wrist.

Jared groaned in pain as some of his skin came off with the manacle, but he held out his left hand as she did the same to the second lock. This time, he clenched his teeth as she held the manacle still and carefully pulled it off, mindful of his wounds.

His breathing had quickened from the pain. She bit her lip and studied the raw and bloody wrists. He needed more than just bandages—he needed a hospital. She ran to the basement door and pulled on the handle, only to find a solid brick wall. They were trapped in the mirror. A reflection of the Grimm family basement. A brick room with no windows, and the only way out blocked by a brick wall. It was the perfect cell. Designed to withhold Teague. Of course there wouldn't be an easy way out.

"Okay, this might hurt." She spoke soothingly as she placed her hands above his wrists and concentrated on healing his hands. She watched her work with surprised satisfaction—his wrists glowed, and the skin started to heal. When she was done, she frowned. Terrible scars remained on his wrists.

"I don't understand. I thought it would heal."

Jared rubbed his wrists. "Nothing can fully heal iron wounds. I'd been bound for a long time. I'm lucky to be alive." He turned his back on her once again as he sat on the cold stone floor.

"What are you doing?"

She'd freed him. He should be jumping for joy, thanking her, kissing her even. Instead, he sat back down.

He leaned his head back against the wall and closed his eyes like he was asleep. "I'm sitting," he answered dryly. "It's a bit cold, but I'm used to the cold."

"No, why aren't you trying to escape? I freed you. You should be thankful."

He opened his eyes to slits. "Do you see a another door besides the one you tried? And thanks. You want me to say thanks. You came in here to my home—"

"Prison," she interrupted.

"Prison," he repeated. "With no clue what you've done or who you're messing with."

"I know exactly what I've done. I've come to save you." Mina ground her teeth.

"I don't need saving."

"You don't mean to stay here." She gestured to the small room.

"This is where I belong." He closed his eyes and leaned his head back.

Mina came to sit by him and touched his arm. "No, you don't, Jared."

He pulled his arm away from her. "I'm not Jared."

She tried to not let his words hurt her. She steeled her resolve and her voice. "Teague can't imprison you any longer. I've trapped him in seven mirrors. Four of those are destroyed already. All I need to do is destroy the others, and we'll win. Teague will be destroyed and…" She couldn't finish.

"I'll be destroyed as well," he finished for her. "It's why I have to stay here."

"Well, I'm not leaving without you."

"Fine by me. Enjoy your stay, although I have to say, the meals are few and far between, the beds are non-existent, and the company is horrible." He flashed his teeth at her, then pulled his knees up and rested his head on his forearms.

"Jared…"

He groaned. "Girl, I swear. Stop calling me that cursed name. I am not this… this person."

"Mina."

"Whatever," he rolled his shoulders and ignored her.

How could she convince him she was here to help? "Okay, well I meant it. I'm not leaving unless you come with me. I'll use the seam ripper. We have to try to escape. You can't give up hope."

"Not going to happen." He yawned and proceeded to stretch out on the cold floor, his back to her.

Mina sat down and pulled her knees up to her chin for warmth. She could wait him out. She was almost certain of it. She knew Jared could be stubborn, but she was going to have to show him that she was serious.

Mina rocked back and forth trying to get her body to warm up. As Jared slept, she held back the desire to go over and kick him in the stomach for being so stupid. Instead, she settled for walking as far as she dared in the dark, while trying to keep an eye on him.

The longer they stayed in the basement, the more it seemed like the darkness was creeping up on them. The shelves and boxes slowly disappeared, and they were surrounded by it. A darkness that continued forever. Finally, perhaps hours later, she came back and sat on the cold floor as close as she dared to Jared without waking him up. Soon, the chill set in, and drowsiness overtook her.

She couldn't hold her head up anymore. Mina let herself slide to the ground, and she heard the sound of chattering. Was that her teeth? It didn't matter, because staying awake was a fight she didn't mind losing.

Forever

Sometime during her sleep, she dreamed someone grumbled and cursed about her freezing to death. Something heavy and warm draped over her, and she wrapped herself up in the safety of it.

After all, what harm could come from sleep?

Chanda Hahn

Seventeen

Mina opened her eyes and blinked in confusion at her surroundings. Where was she?
It took a few seconds before she comprehended.

She was in the mirror. But she was no longer freezing. She was in fact quite warm, or at least her back was. She tried to move away, but a weight across her waist pulled her back against the warmth.

She froze. A soft brush of warm air caressed her neck, and she couldn't help but notice the masculine arm around her stomach, holding her possessively. Mina turned over and looked into the deep gray eyes of Jared. He had moved over and spooned her to keep her warm. Now, those mesmerizing eyes were looking at her with what? Regret?

She couldn't read them.

He leaned forward and whispered into her ear. "You are the most insufferable girl when you're freezing. Whining and shivering. I could hear your teeth clattering. I had to keep you warm, just so I could get some sleep."

She smiled softly at him. "Liar."

His gray eyes darkened, and she thought she saw a hint of blue. She needed to remember—he might not really be the Jared that she knew.

"Who am I?" she asked, unwilling to pull herself out of his embrace.

"A dream." He tugged her closer. "An annoying dream that has come to plague me. Although you haven't disappeared yet. But you will. You always disappear."

So that was what was bothering him.

"I won't leave if you won't," she whispered back.

Just the softest of smiles worked at the corner of his mouth.

"There's only one way to prove you're not a dream." His hand came up and brushed against the side of her cheek. "And that's to do this." He leaned forward and pressed his lips to hers.

She didn't move, lost in the feel of his mouth brushing against hers in a gentle caress. He pulled back suddenly, his eyes filled with confusion. "Wait…how?"

Mina didn't hesitate. She wrapped her hand around his head and pulled him back into the kiss.

He didn't hold back this time. He deepened the kiss. His lips claimed hers, and she let her hands roam freely in his hair, afraid that she really would wake up, and he'd be gone.

It was a kiss of longing, a kiss of desperation, a kiss of remembering.

Their lips remembered their one shared kiss long ago.

This time when he let her go, there were tears in his eyes. "No. Fates No, tell me you're not here. You can't be here."

147

"I am. I came for you."

He closed his eyes in pain and pulled away from her to sit up on the floor. His demeanor changed, and he stiffened. Immediately, she felt the absence of his warmth.

"If you're here, then you know."

"Know?" She sat up and reached to comfort him, but he pulled away.

"Know I'm a fake. A fraud…a…a copy." It was obvious that the admission pained him. "I'm the reason you're cursed, the reason for the things that happened to you—and your family. I told you in the beginning not to trust me."

"You are the only one I trust."

He turned to her, his gray eyes filled with tears. "But you can't. I'm not Jared. It's just a name I stole from a memory, because I didn't want to remember all of the horrible things I did. I'm *him*." He said the word with disdain. "And he hates you… but at the same time, parts of me can't stay away from you."

"I know. But it doesn't change the way I feel about you."

"It should."

"I still can't be trusted. You need to finish what you started and destroy the mirrors."

"No. Not unless you come with me. I can save you. I can free you."

"Mina, just you knowing who I really am is enough for me. I can die happy."

"Now wait a minute. Who said anything about anyone dying here?"

"I can't leave here," he said simply. "I wasn't joking when I said that I'm imprisoned here. I always have been and always will be the prince."

"I don't believe that."

"Last time I was dangerous enough to be split in two." He came and took her hand. "I know how you feel about me, how I feel about you. But when I became whole again, I took those memories of Jared and locked them up, deep inside, banished them to the in-between. That is all that's left of me. The Jared you knew is just a memory."

"No, you're more than just a memory to me."

He shook his head. "No, Mina. If you can't let go of the memory of Jared, then there's no hope of ever saving me. The real me. I'm still poisoned and filled with hate. And I don't understand what happened between us."

"I don't believe you."

"It doesn't matter if you believe me or not. Look at me," he demanded. She closed her eyes and turned away.

He came forward and grabbed her shoulders. "Mina. Look at me."

She could feel the sobs coming on, and she clenched her jaw to try and hold back the overpowering feelings. But she looked into his deep gray eyes, at his strong defined jaw. She had a feeling she wouldn't like what was coming next.

"I told you, Royals can shift. Because we're the strongest Fae."

"No, stop." She squeezed her eyes shut again.

He touched her cheek softly, and her breath caught. She refused to open her eyes. But then his grip on her changed, and his lips once again pressed on hers. This time, she couldn't help opening her eyes.

She gasped and pulled away.

"I've tried to deny it, even held onto this form in memory. But you have to see the truth." His eyes were still gray, but Jared's appearance had changed. His hair was darker, his face a bit more angular. He was Teague.

She tried to comprehend the person in front of her. Even his voice had changed. "What about your eyes?" Mina asked. "Why are your eyes still gray then?"

"Well, because a copy of a copy is never as clear as the original. Blue eyes have always been and always will be the true Teague's one tell."

"Can you see me?" Jared asked "Through this?" He gestured to his face. Even though the face was different, his expression was the same.

Could she?

"Look!" He pointed to the darkness surrounding them. As she watched, hairline cracks splintered her world. "Someone is breaking the mirror. If you don't leave, you'll die."

The cracks fanned out, becoming bigger. Mina held onto him. If they were going to die, she wanted to die with him—together.

He pressed his forehead to hers. "I love you, Mina," he said breathlessly.

"I love you too." Mina cried. Her heart was breaking at the thought of gaining him and losing him so quickly.

He looked at her, full of grief. "Please," he begged as the walls around them started to crumble and fall. "Say my name."

"Jared." She grasped onto him desperately, scared of being separated.

"No, no more lies. Please. *My* name."

Mina looked up into his pain filled eyes and knew what he was asking. Fae were tricksters, full of lies. They couldn't be trusted, but here he was baring his heart and soul, wanting a piece of him to be recognized.

In that moment, their last, as the mirror finally shattered around them, trapping them together, she knew the truth. "I love you, Teague."

Eighteen

M ina flailed and fell out of bed onto the floor with a painful thud. She stared at the morning light pouring into her room. Her alarm clock showed a quarter past seven. Fifteen minutes.

She sat on the floor, her hands covering her mouth in horror at what she had just experienced. It had felt so real—even following their plan down to a T.

Ever had been stabbed and then destroyed, and Mina had tried to save somebody she thought was Jared and ended up dying as well.

But how? Someone else must have come in after her and smashed the mirror.

Was it a dream? A warning of something to come? Looking up in alarm, she saw that the mirrors were still intact. Mina and Ever hadn't trapped him in the mirrors yet. In fact, Teague hadn't even arrived.

There was still time. Not a whole lot, but enough that maybe, just maybe, she could save one more person before she died. This had to be more than a dream. It was a premonition. There was still another enemy to watch out for.

She grabbed the wooden bat from behind her bed post. She couldn't risk losing Ever too. If she could just swing the bat and break the mirror, that timeline would be over. She hefted the bat, grunted and swung—but she pulled up short, changed direction, and hit the floor.

Screaming in frustration, Mina pounded the floor until her anger was spent. She tossed the bat on the floor and wiped her wrist across her brow, staring at the mirrors. This plan was supposed to save her life, but it would cost Ever's. She didn't want to sacrifice herself to save everyone, but she knew she had to. Destroying their mirrors trap was the only way to protect Ever.

Mina gripped the baseball bat again and swung. One by one, she destroyed each of the mirrors. Shards of glass littered the floor. She stepped toward the next, glass popping beneath her feet. She broke every single mirror.

Except her mother's.

"Why mom?" Mina asked. She could just make out her own outline, blurred through her tears, and for a moment, convince herself she was talking to her mother.

"Why did you hide so much from us? Why couldn't you have told us and given us the best chance to survive?"

Mina could imagine her mother's voice answering, telling her she had the best chance ever—*now*—of saving not only herself, but her people, the Fae.

Angry tears slid down her cheeks. As Mina looked back up at the mirror, she knew what she had to do.

She grabbed her Unaccomplishments and Epic Disasters notebook and flipped it open.

"You are a new Grimoire. You are not made from Teague's life but mine. No longer will you hold tales of my unaccomplishments and epic disasters. You will hold my greatest triumphs and happily-ever-afters." She closed her eyes and felt her hands grow warm as power spread through her fingertips.

The notebook lifted off of the bed and spun in the air, before gently landing open on the bed. No longer a spiral notebook, the new Grimoire was a leather-bound journal with gold letters. She placed it on her bedside table, and on top of it the seam ripper. She hoped Ever would find it and know that she was passing the quests off to her. Ever would find the others and help protect her brother. Besides, she was better at being a Grimm and fighting Fae than Mina had ever been. She only wished she had thought of creating more Grimoires sooner, but they were made of journals. Hours of heart had gone into each book, and she had a suspicion that's why they held the power they did.

Ever was hiding in a room down the hall waiting to ambush Teague. To make sure she didn't repeat the dream, Mina needed to get away from the house. She grabbed a cross over bag from her messy floor and shoved in the dagger.

As she took off running down the stairs, she heard the closet door open. Ever called out in surprise, "What's all the noise? Where are you going? What about the plan?"

Forget the plan. Her current plan was to get as far away from her friends as she could before Teague came for her. She ran through the kitchen and out the back door across the grass.

She looked at the watch on her hand as she ran. She only had two minutes before her twelve hours were up. Mina didn't want to die, and she realized what must have run through her mother's mind as she faced Death to protect her children: Love for others can make even the scaredest of souls become brave in the face of danger.

Ever hung her head out a second-floor window. "Don't do it, Mina!"

She began a countdown in her head. When she only had a few seconds left, she stopped running and held her hand over the stitch in her side. She had almost reached the tree line.

"Mina." His voice echoed through the air, taunting her.

"I'm here," she answered.

"So am I," he said from right behind her.

He was just as she pictured in her dream, wearing the same exact clothes, even the same exact expression of triumph. "I've come for what's mine."

"It's in my bag."

"Give it to me." He stepped forward and held out his hand.

Mina carefully opened up the crossover bag and reached inside, her fingers brushing the dagger. "Remember what you promised. You'd leave my friends and family alone if I gave you the dagger and my life."

She sucked in her breath and squeezed the blade until she felt the sharp sting as it sliced her skin. A burning sensation followed, but she held in the gasp and tried to mask the pain. She wanted to be the one in control, and this was the fastest way to seal the deal and protect her friends.

"Yes, I get the dagger and your life. In exchange, they go free. I promise. Now give me the dagger." His eyes searched hers and looked at her bag in worry. He noticed how long she was drawing out handing him the weapon.

Mina lost her equilibrium and had problems focusing. A cold shock went through her body as she pulled the cursed dagger out of the bag and held it out to Teague. There was no mistaking the long bleeding cut along her hand from the poisoned dagger.

"Mina, what have you done?" She thought she saw a hint of worry flash across his face, but she must have imagined it.

He wanted her life, but he hadn't specified how.

"Here," she whispered, her lips trembling as she fell to her knees. "I give you both the dagger and my life"—breathing became hard as she fought to make her lungs work—"freely." Then the poison froze her limbs. The only thing she could feel as she hit the ground was the coldness of the wet grass against her cheek.

Then her world went dark.

Nineteen

Pain seized Mina, and she woke up gasping. Teague, face grim, leaned over her. Her stomach knotted, and she curled up in a ball to try and protect herself.

"Make it stop," she cried out.

Teague cursed in anger.

"Kill me," she begged. Never in her life or death— if that's what this was—had she ever thought she'd beg Teague to kill her. But she meant it. "Just kill me and get it over with."

"Not yet." She swore his eyes turned gray for a minute. She watched his hands glow brightly when he brought them near her arm. "I have to burn the poison out of your bloodstream."

Another searing pain laced up her hand, and she blacked out.

When she came to again, she had to fight to open her eyes, crusted shut from dried tears. She lay in a pile of straw in a dank, dark room. Mina's first thought was "dungeon," and her second thought was that she wasn't dead. Iron bracelets adorned each of her wrists with small etched writing that looked Fae. Her skin burned and itched in slight irritation. She tried to use power to get them off, but it only hurt her wrists and turned them bright red. She quickly abandoned that idea. It seemed—though the bands were light—there was enough iron in the cuffs to limit her power. She studied the burns on her wrists and noticed that her palm had been well bandaged.

Peeling back the white cloth, she saw that the cut had already healed. But the scar was still there, jagged and pink.

How long had she been here? She pulled off the bandage and let it fall to the straw. There wasn't much room in her cell, just enough space to stand and walk five paces from one side to the other. A Fae light floated in the middle of the area, giving her light to see by, but little else was in the room. There wasn't even a door.

How strange. "I'm either still dreaming… or dead."

"No, you're not dead, though you should be," Teague's voice rang out around her. A hole opened in the brick wall, and he stepped through it. He wore his royal robes again with the silver-leaf emblem on the collar. Which probably meant they were at the Fae palace, and she was in his dungeon "You thought to rob me of my prize, dear Mina. We can't have that. I said I wanted your life, and I shall have it, but only I will decide when your short lifespan will be over. Do you understand?" He grasped her chin and made her look up at him.

She searched his eyes for a hint of gray. "And when will that be?"

"Soon, if you don't stop asking annoying questions." He thrust her chin downward and forced her gaze away.

"Fine," she snapped, instantly regretting it.

Every inch of her wanted to fight and defy him, but if surviving was a possibility—if holding back her anger could help—she had to rein that in. She'd told Nan she was going to survive.

Teague wouldn't admit it, because he preferred looking cruel and in control. But he saved her life, gave her a second chance. She wasn't sure why he'd done it, but she hoped it was because part of him was still good.

She had seen it in her vision. Good still existed in him. She just needed to find it.

"How's your hand?" He turned away from her, clasped his hands behind his back, and pretended to talk to the wall.

"It's fine."

"And how do you fare?" Again without turning around.

"Fine as well."

"Is that the only word in your vocabulary?" He spun, the irritation across his face obvious.

Which just set her off. "I don't know. I'm sure there's a lot of really interesting vocabulary words I'd like to call you right now, but somehow this dungeon doesn't seem like the ideal time and place to let loose those choice words."

Teague started to laugh, and he didn't stop. "There! That's the fire and the wit I remember."

"Oh, I'm sure you didn't extend my life just so you could have intellectual battles. But then again, I'm sure you get plenty of stimulating conversations with the ogres each day."

"You have no idea why I did what I did!"

"No, I don't," she yelled back. "So explain."

159

"I plan on making you suffer like I suffered."

"I don't understa…"

Teague had vanished.

He came again hours later for more of the same. Taunting and teasing—they battled with wits and words. It became a frustrating habit, actually. Each time, Teague riled her until they were yelling at each other, and then he'd disappear, leaving her miserable.

She'd stared at the Fae light that floated above her cell and realized she could make it dim or glow brighter with just a thought. She had spent her hours trying to make the wall open up like Teague had and escape. But it must be warded against her, because the only thing she could actually control in her whole cell was the Fae light.

After another few hours, she grew hungry. Her stomach growled, but she wasn't going to beg for food from Teague. She was too proud for that.

The light above her disappeared into the wall and left her in darkness.

"Hey wait!" Mina called out in shock. But then she stopped herself. She could handle being in the dark. She wasn't scared.

Minutes later, the Fae light reappeared, floating just above her as if it had never left. The bricks in the wall folded out to reveal a slot, and a tray of food appeared. As soon as Mina took the tray, the bricks moved back and formed a solid wall again.

The meal was simple—bread, a sweet grain mixture similar to oatmeal, and warm cider. For prison food, it wasn't half-bad. Mina finished the food and then put the tray by the wall and stretched out on the straw. She fell asleep only to wake up with a familiar sensation. There wasn't a toilet in her cell.

"This is so embarrassing." Mina wanted to cry as she looked around for options.

Again, the Fae light bobbed and floated through the wall. When it returned, the bricks shifted to reveal a door.

This was the first time a door had appeared. Mina wasn't sure what to make of it, but she had a feeling the light had responded to her current need. She tried the brass pull handle, and it opened to reveal a simple water closet to relieve herself, along with necessities like soap and water. Mina took way longer than she needed and used the soap and water to scrub her face, hands, and as much of her body as she could reach. She didn't have a comb, so she did the best she could, running her hands through her long brown hair to pull out the snarls.

When she came out, the closet disappeared.

That became her daily routine. Mina would sleep on the straw and then spend hours talking to herself, pondering aloud what had happened to her friends and family. Was Teague leaving the human plane alone? When he didn't come to torment her, that was its own special torture—she assumed he was destroying her plane as she sat there helpless.

Her plane? There was a good part of her that wanted to go and explore the Fae world and learn about her mother's family. She had learned all she wanted to know about the Grimm line, but she desperately wanted to know about her mother's parents. Were they still out there? Did she have cousins, aunts, uncles?

Only twice did she give in to her sadness and cry over the loss of her mother and brother. She missed them terribly, and after days, even wished for Ever's company. When she thought she'd been in the dungeon over a week, she almost began to miss Teague and his temper.

Mina amused herself by creating a game of sorts with the straw. She would bend a piece around and around creating a ball, which she would hold between her finger and thumb on her left hand and then flick with her right at a brick on the far wall. She even scratched a round target onto the brick.

She flicked the ball at the target.

Teague appeared and caught the ball midair.

"You know that almost hit me." He looked at the crumpled straw in his hand.

"Oh no, you were almost impaled by a piece of straw and died," Mina said. "Too bad."

"It wouldn't have killed me." Teague frowned and discarded the homemade ball.

"Oh, bad sportsmanship, minus two points." She picked up another straw ball and took aim at the target. She flicked it, and it hit low on the target.

Teague stood off to the side, watching her as she played her game. She didn't ask him to join in, even though she kinda thought he wanted to. He seemed really interested in just watching her. He even made a chair materialize, so he could sit comfortably. He didn't speak.

After an hour, he disappeared again.

He appeared again the next afternoon when she was scratching another target on the wall. She turned around, and he was next to her with his own pile of straw balls—his were green. He picked one up and flicked it at her. It bounced off her forehead, and she flinched.

"Two points." Teague grinned and reached for another ball.

"I'm not the target." Mina pointed at the second one, higher up the wall. "That is."

"Could have fooled me. I'm winning, two to zero," he crowed.

"My game, my rules." She kneeled in front of her stack. She'd had a feeling he would appear today just as she was setting up the game. "Zero-zero."

"Fine," he grumbled. But she could see the challenge light up his eyes.

She didn't want to admit it, but she was excited at the prospect of beating him.

"And no cheating," Mina remembered to add at the last minute.

Teague's shoulders wilted a little at the reminder.

They took turns aiming and flicking their balls at the targets, and since she had never played the game two-player, they had to argue the change in rules extensively and loudly. Teague frequently demanded that he was right, but Mina reminded him she made up the game, so choosing the rules was her prerogative.

"You want to decide the rules, make up your own game."

His eyes flashed a darker blue.

"Maybe tomorrow will be the day I take your life," he warned before he disappeared.

He didn't come back the next day, and Mina didn't feel like picking up her straw game again. She even broke up all the balls she'd made into smaller pieces of unusable straw.

Sleeping on the straw was getting tiresome. It was itchy, uncomfortable, and it gave her a rash, but she'd never tell Teague that. At least the straw kept her inches away from freezing to death. Still, it poked and prodded and kept getting under her clothes.

Frustrated, she finally decided if she froze to death, she froze to death. She wasn't going to ask Teague for help. She moved to sleep on the stone. At first, she was fine and fell asleep easily without the poking and prodding of the straw, but sometime during the night, her teeth started to chatter. The Fae light dimmed and relit, but she didn't stir.

She vaguely remembered the sound of bricks scraping against each other. Someone lifted her and carried her up stairs. She didn't open her eyes to see the warm person who carried her. Instead, she might have snuggled against his shoulder.

She heard a curse and received a nuzzle in return. He placed her on something soft and laid a blanket over her. Bricks scraped again.

When she awoke, she studied her new prison. It still lacked a door and window, but it had a bed—a real four-poster bed with a sapphire blue coverlet. There was even a pillow. Mina squealed in delight and hugged the satin pillow. The bed was so wonderful that she couldn't hold back the tears. She looked around the cell and noticed more. There was a small, square table with two chairs and a chess board, another end table with a bowl of water and a glass, and even a few books.

It was so glorious after her weeks in the dungeon, she felt like a princess in a palace. This time, when she needed to use the water closet, the wall opened to reveal a very large bathtub, full with warm soapy water.

Mina happily spent the next few hours soaking in the tub, scrubbing her skin raw. She soaked her wrists under the water, and the iron cuffs clanked against the tub. She tried to rub her skin beneath the enchanted bracelets, and it felt soothing.

The whole *thing* was soothing. Mina even went so far as to drain the water and refill it with bubbles and soap, so she could soak a second time. She dunked her head under the water and held her breath, imagining what it was like to be a siren. It was hard to imagine something other than the cartoon-mermaid version, but she knew better than to imagine that. She tried to picture her mother as a young mergirl with a tail—desperately in love.

What had it been like for her mother to give up her tail to be with her father? No matter how she imagined it, it didn't seem real. She couldn't envision her mom as anything other than the normal, overly petrified mother who worked as a house cleaner. That didn't suggest powerful siren, and yet she had seen Charlie scream. His call was so powerful, it cracked the magic ward around her. How come she hadn't gotten that gift?

Suddenly, two hands reached into the water, grabbed her shoulders, and pulled her up through the bubbles.

Mina gasped in shock as bubbles ran down her face. She sputtered and splashed in the water when she realized Teague was in the same room as her. Mina quickly checked the bubbles, glad to see the tub was still full of them. They were high enough there was no way he could see anything.

Teague stood there, furious, his shirt and pants soaking wet and covered with bubbles.

"What are you doing in here?" Mina yelled at him. "Get out!"

"Not until I'm sure you're not drowning yourself in the bathtub!" He flicked the bubbles off of his arms and tried to roll up his wet sleeves. Water dripped from him and puddled all around him on the stone floor. A moment later, his face paled and then turned bright red. He spun his back to her.

"Of course I'm not drowning myself! I was only under for a few seconds."

"Few seconds! A few seconds. More like a few minutes."

"That's impossible," Mina answered.

"No, it's not!" he pointed up at the Fae light that bobbed up and down. "You had been under for five minutes. "I'm not sure if a Siren can even stay under that long. The Fae light wouldn't have alerted me if it didn't believe you were in danger."

It was certainly clear she'd upset him. She wanted to get out, but she couldn't with him in the room. "Can you hand me a towel?"

Teague's shoulders hunched as he tried to look to the side to find a towel for her, but he realized how undignified it was. In a fit of temper, he blasted through the wall and left her in her warm tub of bubbles alone.

The Fae light bobbed up and down, visibly distressed.

"You've been spying on me?" Mina accused it in an annoyed tone, even though she had assumed it was. The light bobbed sadly in affirmation. "Shame on you."

The light softly dimmed.

Mina couldn't hold a grudge against her silent light protector, so she quickly added, "It's fine, just... is there no one else for you to go to for help but him?"

The light dimmed again, and she assumed that meant no.

"What about guards? Are there guards?"

The Fae light brightened in an affirmative.

"So can you go to them?"

The light dimmed. No.

She tried to not show her frustration as she dried off and went back into the room with the large towel around her. The Fae light danced for joy by her bed. Mina was pleased to see clothes—clean clothes. Teague hadn't provided a red dress this time, like he had during the betrothal process, and she was thankful he remembered.

Twenty

M ina was getting used to long days of solitude. She didn't know day from night anymore, because she just slept whenever she was tired, and the Fae light would dim.

So maybe she hadn't been in the prison that long, maybe it was just days instead of weeks. She couldn't really judge it by her meals, because when she ate Fae food it was quite filling.

She started to talk her little Fae light, since it seemed to understand her, or at least blink and flicker in response to her questions. And it seemed to anticipate her mood and needs pretty quickly.

One time she actually mumbled out loud, "I'm actually starting to miss his company." The light began to head for the wall, and Mina stopped it. "Don't you dare tell him. Remember he's the one who wants to make me suffer and punish me. Don't let my soft side fool you."

The light bobbed and flickered up toward the ceiling. She thought it seemed awfully dim and wondered if maybe she had hurt its feelings. *Look at me, worried about a magic light's feelings!* The imprisonment must be getting to her more than she thought. Teague was watching out for her. All she had to do was wait and he'd come...eventually. Hopefully before she starved to death. Still, it was hard to not get depressed and worry about how many days or nights she'd live before he'd put an end to it.

It was also hard not to worry about Charlie.

The time for eating had long passed, and the wall opened up with another tray of food. Mina ignored the tray and curled up in her bed and waited until the food disappeared. A few hours later, another tray appeared with even more appealing food. The smell of roasted chicken, spices, and fruit tempted her to move from her bed, but she didn't give in. The tray moved from the wall to the small table in her room with invisible hands.

Mina just closed her eyes and pretended it wasn't there. An hour later, the food was gone. Her stomach grumbled with hunger, but it was easy to forget about it with sleep. Sleep and hunger were interchangeable in her book.

The sound of the bricks moving told her there would be another attempt to coax her to eat. And then the smell of her favorite food wafted to her nose—homemade dumplings and chocolate cake. Back home, Mina would never tire of eating them, but this time? They didn't make her hungry. They only made her miss her Godmother more. Tears filled her eyes.

"Please stop it. I'm not hungry." Mina spoke out loud to the room. "Make it go away." This time it didn't take hours. It took seconds for the tray of food to disappear with the scraping sound.

"Thank you," she whispered softly to no one.

Her Fae light dimmed.

"Are you dying?" His irritated voice spoke in the darkness.

"No." Mina rolled her eyes, but she wouldn't turn to look at him. She didn't know where in the room he was anyway.

"Are you sick, then?"

"In a way."

The Fae light illuminated the room, and she could see Teague standing next to her bed looking down at her. He wore pants, brown leather boots, and a green long-sleeved tunic.

"Well, get better," he demanded, as if that command alone could solve her problems.

"I'm homesick."

"Oh." Her answer seemed to startle him. "Of course you are. You're in my prison. You're here to be miserable." He sounded like he was trying to convince himself.

"And I am." Mina rolled over on her other side, so she didn't have to look at his face. "Why would you tell me to get better? Isn't this exactly what you wanted?"

"Yes?" He answered as if he doubted his answer. The bed dipped as he sat next to her. She heard his long drawn out sigh. "I think so," he said.

Silence followed. The bed shifted again, and she turned her head to see that he had made himself comfortable. His boots were crossed at the ankles, his right arm cushioned his head, and his left lay across his stomach. He stared up at the ceiling.

"What are you doing?"

"I'm relaxing."

"In my bed?"

"No my bed. The bed is mine. That rug is mine, the chair is mine. It's all mine." He turned to look at her, and she saw a glint in his eye. "You're mine."

"Only because of this." She held up her wrists to show him the iron cuffs. By now she'd grown accustomed to them and could ignore them, but she hated what they represented.

"So you're saying if I removed them, you'd leave?"

"No, because I promised I wouldn't. To save my friends. I'll stay here with you forever, or until you chose to end my life."

"But you're unhappy."

"I'm lonely, and I miss my brother."

"Why do you miss him?"

She closed her eyes and counted backward from twenty as she tried not to snap at him. "Because he's family, and I love him. Haven't you ever missed someone so much it hurts?"

He didn't answer her right away. "Yes, and as you'd say, it drove me crazy." He turned on his side and leaned his head on his elbow studying her. "Why do you think I'm not happy?"

"You can never be happy, because your heart has been poisoned by the dagger." Mina turned back, unwilling to look at him while he relaxed in her bed. It may be his cell and his prison, but he was invading her sanctuary, her bed, and she didn't like it.

"No, there were moments when I was," he spoke softly. "When I dethroned my parents and banished them to the swamplands for what they had done to me—that made me happy. When I finally found you after a hundred years, and I began to spin your life into tales, like I had done to your ancestors—that made me happy. When I wreaked havoc on your school—that made me happy."

"That's because you're a monster." She didn't care if she angered him and brought out the beast.

"You're right," Teague answered his voice going low. "It seems that I'm happiest when I'm tormenting the Grimms. Now that I have you, I'm bored. Thank you for reminding me that there's still another Grimm left to torment. I'll say hello to your brother for you." He sat up abruptly and left.

"No wait!" Mina cried out in desperation, but it was too late. She was left alone in her cell to ponder what horrible fate would befall her younger brother and her friends.

She paced constantly now and worried her thumbnail as she watched for signs of Teague's return. She was desperate to hear whether he'd found Charlie and the others and—if he had—what he was doing to them. Mina had even begged the Fae light to bring Teague to her, but he never came.

She had cried enough tears to last a lifetime, and she couldn't cry anymore. She spent hours trying to summon Fae power to her to open the wall, but nothing happened. She screamed at the wall and wished she had her brother's gift. She pounded, and dug her fingers into the mortar, trying to pull out the brick, but only ended up with bruised and scraped hands. Before she had tried to play the obedient servant, to live a quiet and solitary life, and to avoid angering Teague, but those days were gone.

"There's your fire." Teague said appearing beside her.

She turned, fist raised and tried to hit him for being away so long, but he caught her wrist mid-strike. Mina fell into Teague and buried her face in his chest, fresh tears surprising her. Maybe because they came from a well of relief rather than worry. She clung to his jacket.

The shift from attacking to clinging took Teague aback. He didn't know how to fight her.

"Please tell me he's still alive. Please just tell me he's okay. Even if he's not, lie to me and tell me he is," she gasped out between sobs as she held onto his shirt.

His grip on her wrist loosened, and he let go of it, gently placing his hands on her shoulders. He didn't push her away, but paused a few moments. Then Teague very slowly wrapped his arms around her and touched his chin to her head.

"He's alive," he answered.

Mina gasped in relief. "Thank you, thank you, thank you," she repeated into his chest. She could smell the scent of his clothes, the faint smell of the soap he used. As she looked up along his jaw, her heart raced. It had been so long since she had human contact, she didn't realize she craved it.

It was so easy to pretend he wasn't evil, but she knew so very much of him was. Even as her ear pressed to his chest, she could hear the heartbeat pounding softly, quickening in excitement. Her hand was pressed ever so softly over his chest, right over where she knew the scar was, and she wondered just briefly if she could use her power to lure the poisoned tip out.

But that could destroy him if she wasn't careful. Maybe what she could focus on was slowly pulling the poison from him. But clearly, she couldn't do that from within this warded prison. She needed to be free. She needed to earn his trust, but he'd see through her if she lied. So she couldn't lie to him, ever.

She let her fingers brush against his chest and thought about her feelings for him—for Teague—back during the choosing ceremony. They were conflicted, but when given the choice at the time, she did choose to stay with him. And right after she had chosen him, someone else had come in and ruined things, poisoned his heart against her. Why should she not fight for what they could have had? Shouldn't love conquer all?

Mina lifted her gaze to Teague, only to see he was already staring down at her, his eyes half-closed, his face a mask. She ached to know what he was feeling. Was it in any way similar to her feelings? He swallowed, and she did the same. He leaned forward, his head bent low, so she closed her eyes and lifted her mouth.

"What are you plotting?" he whispered into her ear. It wasn't said in anger, but in a teasing tone.

"I'm plotting my own demise," she teased, keeping her eyes closed. "Because I know that falling for you will be the death of me."

She heard a swift intake of breath, as his hands dropped from her shoulders.

And then she was left standing alone.

Twenty-One

The next morning when she woke up, Teague was sitting there watching her. "Would you like to come with me?" There was a twinkle in his eye, and he looked like an eager child.

"Where to?" she asked hesitantly.

"Does it matter if you get out of the cell for a while?"

"I guess it doesn't," she said, moving toward the exit. "Yes. I'd like to get out awhile—anywhere."

He blocked the door with his body so she almost ran into him. "Not so fast. I can't let you out without a warning."

"A warning?"

"Promise me you're not going to run away. Not now. Not ever," he said softly.

She hesitated at his tone. It wasn't a command. Teague wasn't demanding it of her. He was asking her, needing her reassurance.

"I promise." She had to press him, find out how much he was softening toward her. She lifted up her iron cuffs.

"No, I can't." He looked disappointed in himself.

"It's okay." She shrugged it off and looked back to Teague. "Let's go."

"Aren't you the eager one?" He offered a rueful smile. "Well, come along." He held his hand out in front of him.

For the first time in weeks, Mina left her prison. Outside her cell, the floor moved beneath them like an escalator as it carried them up and then left along a passage. The bricks continued to move out of their way, opening up for them and closing behind them after Teague passed through. Finally, they were deposited in the main hall. She turned to watch as Teague stepped through the wall after her, and their passage disappeared.

The palace looked nothing like she remembered it. Gone were the elaborate tapestries, statues, and sparkling marble columns. Instead there were fragments of burned cloth, scorched walls and columns, and headless statues. Cobwebs and layers of dust had laid claim to the place. She was looking at the destruction Teague caused the day he was reunited with Jared. That day, the Fates lost the war. He had banished them to the swamp. No hand, human or Fae, had restored the palace to its glory.

He led her up the winding stairs to the second floor and out onto a balcony that overlooked the lake. She glanced across the water, imagining the invisible veil that sat midway. One of the griffins flew low over the water. But something was wrong with the picture.

The surrounding lands—now as brown and ugly as the swamp where the Fates hid—used to be green and flowing with life.

"It's dying," Mina stated.

"I know," Teague snapped.

"Can you stop it?"

He turned to her, his mouth an angry line. His nostrils flared, and she could see that he was barely keeping it under control. "I'm...I'm not sure I want to."

"This was your plan all along, to destroy everything you loved?"

He looked pained, and his hand kept going to his chest and scratching. "I'm not... I don't... I..." He hissed between his teeth and pulled away. Turning to give her his back, he leaned over the balcony and caught his breath.

"Teague, what's wrong? Are you hurt?"

"No," he growled. A few seconds later, he straightened and turned to look back at her. She felt uncomfortable under his gaze.

"Teague." Mina walked over to him. "Does this hurt?" She touched his chest.

He turned away and mumbled. "It's been hurting more and more lately. It's enough to drive someone mad. But I ignore it. The pain makes me weak."

"No, ignoring your feelings is weakness. Listening to your heart is a sign of strength."

"That being said from a girl."

"I may be a girl, but I can kick your butt...in a game anyway."

He snorted. "I know how uncoordinated you are."

She shrugged. "Okay, I'll cheat. That's the Fae way, isn't it?"

He grimaced. "Yeah, it *is* our motto."

Mina reached for his hand. He immediately stiffened.

"Why am I here, Teague? What do you want with me?"

"I don't know anymore," he said simply, and he walked off, leaving her alone on the balcony. She waited a few minutes, gazing out across the dying land, but he didn't return.

This was a test. It had to be. She wanted to believe he really didn't know, that he was changing. But part of her feared he was waiting somewhere to see if she'd run away, so he'd have an excuse to kill her on the spot. The poison in his heart wasn't his fault, but it certainly made him dangerous to try to predict.

She retraced her steps through the empty palace. Where was everyone? There were no servants, no guards, barely any signs of life. And what little there were seemed to be dying. The large double doors of the main hall taunted her, tempting her to try and escape. But she was invested. She needed to follow through for so many reasons. Her pulse raced, wishing it were as easy as walking away, but it couldn't be.

Besides, she didn't have the seam ripper. And if she did leave, Teague would have every excuse to destroy her brother and friends.

This was the test. He wanted her to break her word, so he could destroy everything important to her.

She clenched her fists and headed in the opposite direction. She would not be the one to break her promise. Teague was a trickster, a cheat, and a liar—the most dangerous one alive.

After a few turns, her little Fae light surprised her in the hall—at least she thought it was her Fae light.

"Can you take me back to my room please?" she asked.

The light bobbed in response and floated about happily. Mina followed with cautious steps down a wing with double doors on the end. The light stopped in front of a door on the left, not quite at the end.

"This can't be the door to my room. There was no door. We traveled through the walls and ended up…" She turned and tried to follow the direction of the walls with her eyes. She shrugged and opened the door.

It was her room—as far as she could tell. But this time, when she entered, she made sure to wedge a book in the doorway to keep it from closing and locking her inside. She didn't want to upset Teague, but she also didn't want to be locked in again.

She waited hours. He never returned to either lock her door or close it.

The next morning, she changed clothes and ate the food delivered to her. Then she decided to explore the palace. There had to be someone left. She found her way to the sitting rooms, where she had waited during the choosing ceremony. The wing full of rooms the girls had stayed in, the library, and the palace kitchen—all of them empty.

The kitchen was depressing. Everything had been abandoned, left as it was when the servants ran away or disappeared. Old bread on the table was hard and dry, dirty pots and plates left in the sink. No fire had been made in ages, which meant no food had been prepared recently here either. So whoever was preparing her meals wasn't doing it from the kitchens. She did find buckets, mops, soap, and the water pump. She could do more than just mope around the palace.

She spent a few hours working in the kitchen, cleaning out the fireplace, finding the woodshed, and restocking the logs in the grate. She found some kindling and searched for a way to start the fire but was at a loss. She couldn't find any matches. Then she noticed an odd red Fae light hanging just outside the window.

Mina opened the window, and it came in and moved toward her stack of logs, brightening. She jumped as a spark of light shot out, and her kindling lit. A few seconds later, she heard the crackle of wood and could feel the glow of the fire. Mina blew on the flame and fed it more kindling until a steady fire burned.

She smiled at the Fae light. "Thank you."

Mina heated water over the fire and brought it carefully to the sink and added soap shavings from a jar on the shelf. She washed dishes for what seemed like hours. More Fae lights joined her, watching her move about the kitchen as she tried her best to put things away. If she moved a pot to the wrong spot, a light would move over and direct her to the right place.

Soon, she began to talk to the lights like she did her personal light, the one that watched over her in her room. And she realized they were all different. Some were larger than the others. Some had a hint of a different color. Some moved slowly. Others zipped about the kitchen.

She laughed as a few of the lights seemed to get in a tizzy over who got to guide her. One of them began to pull on her shirt, and Mina followed as it led her to a wooden chair. She sat down and watched as two of the larger Fae lights attempted to move a large broom between them. Two more joined in and, all together, they were able to sweep the floor.

Entertained, Mina clapped in encouragement to them, and they shone brighter. But something suddenly startled them, and they scattered, hiding.

Teague stood behind her, surprised.

"What did you do?"

"Cleaned." Why did she feel unsure now of all she and her Fae friends had accomplished?

"Why?"

"It needed to be done and..." She paused in thought before answering. "And because it made me happy."

He gave her the most disgusted look, and she had to cover her mouth to hide her smile. It really did make her happy. She had found a purpose, something to occupy her thoughts from worry.

"Like mother like daughter," he said as he gazed around the kitchen, his face unreadable.

He said that as if it were an insult, not a compliment, and his careless words stabbed at her barely healed heart. She tried to not let him know how much those words hurt her.

"I guess," she answered stiffly.

"You did this by yourself?"

"I had help from the lights."

He turned to her in surprise. "Really? Interesting. Where are they now?"

"I'm not sure." She glanced around the kitchen and couldn't find a single one.

Teague gave her an odd stare and abruptly left. It took a few minutes before she could get her heart rate under control. She thought she was in trouble.

She made herself get back to cleaning and, after a few minutes, the Fae lights came out of hiding. They helped her tackle the hallway. They swept, mopped, and washed the high arched windows. Before she knew it, it was evening, and she was famished. When she returned to her room, warm food waited. She devoured it all and slept soundly, her door never closing.

The next morning when she went to the kitchen for soap and water, even more Fae lights greeted her.

"Are you here to help?"

They bobbed and blinked excitedly.

"Well, then we need to take down the remnants of the old tapestries, and we need to replace or repair the paintings. I hate to get rid of them, but they need to be fixed. Can you handle that?"

Before she had even finished, a third of the lights dashed out the open window. Another group—the ones she figured she worked with yesterday—worked together to carry large pots to the pump.

Mina went out to the main hall with a bucket and started gathering large pieces of the broken column. She didn't know how they were actually going to clean up the pillar. She definitely wasn't strong enough to move it. The double door behind her banged wide open, and she smelled it before she dared turn to look. A large fur-covered beast stood peering over her shoulder.

Twenty-Two

M ina swallowed a scream and scrambled backward, tripping over the rubble she was trying to clear. The white-haired beast stared at her, its gruesome teeth lifting into a half-smile, making her knees shake. He was huge— easily over twelve feet tall—with white and gray tufted fur covering his whole body. His nose was apelike, and his teeth were large and flat. Her first thought was *Yeti*.

His furred hand reached for her, and she rolled out of the way, scraping her stomach across the sharp pieces of marble and stone. When she stopped moving, she had time to notice it wasn't attacking. It was actually hefting the large broken column onto its shoulders and turning to walk back out the doors. A few minutes later, he returned and picked up another piece of the colonnade and dragged it out.

"Careful," Mina called out, utterly relieved. "We don't want to scratch the floors."

A long rumbling sound echoed from the thing. She wasn't sure, but it could've been laughter. She worked side by side with the furred beast for a good part of the afternoon. He took down the broken tapestries and paintings and put them on the floor, and he cleared the rooms of the large debris, stone, and destroyed doors.

The Fae lights returned and worked on cleaning the scorch marks from the walls and clearing cobwebs.

The beast carefully opened up another door and entered the throne room. Mina followed at a distance. This room was the worst. Both of the Royal thrones were destroyed, burned to a crisp. The curtains were in a pile on the floor, and the portrait of the Fates had been blown up. All that was left was the frame.

They got to work cleaning up the throne room, and it felt weird. She wanted the palace to be put back together, but she didn't know why. Maybe the Fae part of her soul wanted order restored. More Fae lights came in to help, and the yeti cleared out the destroyed chairs. Within a few hours, even the pillars were fixed.

"Well, now that it's cleaned, what do we do? We can't leave it empty." Mina said to the Fae lights as she looked around the Great Hall.

A small Fae light spun in circles to get her attention, signaling her to follow it. It led her up the stairs and down an empty hall to a large storage room. The beast followed her, always a few yards back.

The Fae light zipped into the locking mechanism, and the lock grew brighter from within. A loud click followed, and the door swung outward to reveal darkness.

The Fae light pulled on a curtain, and a few seconds later, the room was bathed in light. Mina gasped. It was like walking into a museum. There were tapestries, paintings, and statues all carefully stored on swinging racks or marble shelves.

She took her time walking among the paintings and studying each and every one, while the yeti waited in the hallway. Quite a few paintings depicted the Fates at various celebrations or events.

Mina paused when she came to one in particular. Teague was obviously happy, excited about something. The joy, deep in his eyes, made her wish desperately that she knew how to make him look that way again.

The painting showed his betrothal ceremony.

She remembered that day. The artist had captured the moment perfectly. Teague stood in front of the twelve girls who would take part in the choosing ceremony. Most of the girls' faces were hidden, since the painting portrayed them looking up at Teague, but Mina could easily recognize Ever's long black hair, Annalora's gold-blonde locks and her deep amber dress. She smiled when she recognized Dinah's beautiful tanned skin and dark green hair. But there was one girl who wasn't looking at the prince, one girl whose head was slightly turned toward the painter, and he had captured her worried expression as she looked for an escape route. She wore an elegant white dress of moon crystals and feathers. The painter had centered her in the painting, the only one of the twelve whose face was visible.

And it was also obvious that the prince was looking straight at her. Even now, Mina's stomach filled with butterflies at seeing his reaction to her.

"This one. I want this one in the throne room." Mina pointed to the painting.

The Fae lights carefully entered and took the painting out.

Mina paused and moved to the next painting— another of the ceremony, although she couldn't remember when it took place. Teague stood in the middle, with the final four girls on either side of him. Most of the girls were smiling and trying to appear as regal as they could. Only Mina, next to Annalora, looked as if she wanted to be somewhere else. And once again, Teague was staring at her over Annalora's head. It was obvious that the artist had figured out, before everyone else did, the story being played out. He could see the feelings Teague had for her.

The next portrait made her step back. Teague's Royal engagement portrait. He stood tall and proud, his face lacking the joy so obvious in the earlier paintings as he held the hand of his future bride. It wasn't Mina.

Teague held Ever's hand.

She stopped, unable to look at any more. She wanted to run out of there and hide from all of her mistakes. How could that painting be true? The artist had captured so many moments of the choosing, but this seemed out of place. Ever hadn't made it to the tower. Mina had.

Maybe she wasn't supposed to make it.

Mina was confused and taken aback, and then she was filled with guilt again.

She pushed back her feelings and moved on to the next painting—another engagement portrait. But this one featured Teague and Annalora. Curiosity pushed her to keep moving the frames, and she wasn't surprised when she noticed a third depicting Dinah and Teague. Three engagement portraits painted for three possible outcomes.

Longing to see her own portrait with Teague, she searched the whole room top to bottom. It wasn't there. Puzzled and a bit annoyed, she moved on with her original task and picked some tapestries. She chose fantastically colored pieces featuring the woods, mountains, and valleys—the life of the Fae world.

Then Mina came to a section that housed the thrones, and the yeti joined her. She studied the various matching sets of ornate chairs and saw some inlaid with gold, others with diamonds and gems. But none of them fit Teague. Then she spotted a dark ebony chair with a deep blue cushion. She could make out fine engraved detail in the wood. It was masculine but not flashy.

"What do you think of this chair for him?" There was no need to say who she meant. Both she and the yeti knew it was for Teague.

He paused, tilting his head in thought. Then he grunted. He moved forward and picked up a set, one in each hand.

"No, just one throne."

He turned and gave her a steely look before giving her his back and shuffling out the door with both chairs. She winced when the wood door slammed against the outer wall as he exited.

After she had picked everything she thought Teague would like, she left and locked the room. By the time she entered the throne room, it was finished. The yeti and the Fae lights had hung the new curtains, tapestries, and painting. She stopped mid-step when she saw the chairs she had picked out for Teague sitting on the dais.

One was occupied by a ghost from past.

"Playing house, I see." Annalora smiled cruelly. Her braided hair hung over her shoulder. The olive green of her dress made her look sickly—or maybe her gnome heritage was simply showing through.

"What are you doing here?" Mina asked, defensive.

"I should ask you the same thing. You shouldn't be here."

"I'm not exactly here willingly. But why are *you* here, Annalora?"

"I'm coming to pay my respects to my prince and offer my services," she answered snidely.

"What services would he need from you?" Mina scoffed.

Annalora's face turned ugly and red. "Teague's banished the king and queen. I've talked to them, and they have no intention of attacking him and retaking the throne. They are waiting for another solution. So I've come up with my own."

"Which is?" Mina asked sarcastically, knowing the Fates were waiting on her to solve their dilemma.

"Our world is dying. A queen should know what that means." Her eyes narrowed. "I do."

"This is not my home. So I don't exactly keep up to date on Fae World 101." Mina said, pretending to not care.

Annalora sneered. "All good things come to those who are patient. And I am very patient. You don't belong here, Mina. You never did. If you hadn't've shown up, none of this would have happened." Annalora gestured to the palace.

"You're the one who killed Dinah and tried to kill Ever and me." Mina stepped forward.

Annalora stiffened but continued. "Well, I blame you for stealing the throne from me."

"That's all you ever cared about. The throne. You never cared about the prince, just his title and position.

"That's how it should be." Annalora's voice rose in anger. "The job comes first. You don't need love to rule. I know that. Teague knows that. All of the Fates before married for power, not love. Her voice calmed, and she took a deep breath. "But I also thank you for returning my throne to me. Giving me a second chance." She rubbed her hands along the dark ebony wood.

Mina wanted to march up there and yank her out of the chair by her hair. "The throne will never be yours."

"Teague will have to choose someone eventually," Annalora answered slyly. "Why not me? Besides, you're the one who betrayed him and made him this way. Not that I'm complaining. I kind of like him ruthless. And I can see by the iron cuffs that you've not redeemed yourself. You're nothing more than a slave."

The whole time they argued, the Fae lights had darted in and out of the room, clearly alarmed by Annalora's sudden appearance.

Mina felt the build-up of power and sensed Teague's approach moments before the Fae lights disappeared. Teague marched down the room and stood in front of Annalora, who quickly jumped up and out of the throne.

"My King." She spoke softly and curtsied.

Teague's eyebrow rose in question, and he turned to give Mina a look as if to ask why she didn't show him the same respect.

"Annalora, what a surprise to see you here." Teague kept his voice neutral.

"It shouldn't be, considering the signs. I knew when the river dried up that you would need to choose. I'm only sorry I didn't come sooner." She stood and gently placed her hand on her chest, trying to show how saddened she really was.

Mina's mind was flooded with questions, but she didn't want to interrupt.

"So you've come expecting what exactly?"

"Nothing more than a second chance."

"That's an interesting proposition."

"One only a fool would turn down in this predicament," Annalora answered. "And you and I know that neither of us are fools."

"No. That we are not," Teague answered respectfully. "I didn't think ruling would drain me this fast."

"It's because you've brought your armies across the planes and back again. That takes a lot of power, and the balance is off. But if you accept me, we will be unstoppable. I'll help you destroy the human plane."

Mina tried to hide her shock. If taking his whole army across the planes and coming back weakened him and drained him, that must be why he'd kept them away from the palace. He couldn't risk being further drained, and he would never risk losing control.

If there was even the slightest chance that he would take Annalora up on that offer, then Mina needed to get back and warn the others. Maybe she *could* escape and get away if she caught him at a weak moment.

"You give me much to think about Annalora." Teague stepped up onto the dais and turned to sit on the throne with Annalora standing near the other chair.

Mina couldn't handle the rush of emotions she felt at seeing them next to each other, when she'd done all this work to make Teague smile, so she spun and left the room. Once again, Annalora wasn't going to stop until she ruined everything. Mina had no choice but to stop her.

Twenty-Three

When Mina entered the hall, the yeti and the Fae lights waited just outside the doors as if they'd been there the whole time.

"Thank you for all of your hard work. I couldn't have done it without you. I'm tired, and I think we should all take a break for a while."

She wasn't sure, but she thought they looked a little sad at their dismissal. Mina looked down the hall at the tall double doors that led outside and found herself moving toward them. She pushed open the right hand door, stepped into the sun, and let its rays shine on her. The warmth felt wonderful, but a shadow fell across her face, and she looked up to see a griffin glide overhead to land in a large tower above.

It was the one reminder that she needed to keep her on track.

She looked down and realized she had walked within feet of the bridge that led across the lake and to freedom. She stared at the bridge and then down at her enchanted cuffs. If she crossed, her promise would be broken. She quickly moved back away from the bridge and turned to walk beneath a covered alcove which led around the side of the palace but still overlooked the lake.

Mina leaned on the stone banister and looked out across the water. In the distance, she could make out the waterfall she and Nix had come down. Both the falls and the lake had receded in size. She could tell from the water lines along the rocks.

"That can't be a good sign." Mina's skin tingled, and she turned to see Teague watching her.

"I'm surprised you didn't try to run away."

"You would have gone after my brother if I did."

"You're absolutely correct."

"It wouldn't have mattered. I won't run away."

"You did before," he said softly, reminding her of the time she tried to run away during the choosing ceremony.

"I was scared. I wasn't supposed to be here, in this world in the past. I was on a mission to save my family, and the shoes didn't give me a choice on when I went back."

"But you didn't save them. You failed."

"No, I did. I saved them. But you took them away from me one by one. And I won't fail the only family I have left."

"Why is family so important to you?"

"Why isn't it to you? I know that your parents cared about you in their own demented way. When I lost the Grimoire, your mother demanded that I do everything in my power to save you."

"You lie. They tried to destroy me."

"Yes, but they didn't intend to. They were terrified, and what they did was wrong. But how is what you're doing now to me any different?"

"You did even worse. You betrayed me, played me for a fool." He leveled his gaze at the water, refusing to make eye contact.

"I was willing to give up everything for you. I chose you."

"No, you chose *Jared*," he snapped.

"He's you! I wish I'd never said his name. It was— he was—always just a part of you that I love. You are one and the same, Teague. I've gotten past his name, can you?"

"You tried to kill me."

"Actually, despite everything you've done to me over the years, I tried to save you." Mina reached out to touch the area above his heart. "I'm still trying, and maybe one day you'll realize that."

Teague's eyes were cloudy, and she wasn't sure if it was because of his anger or the setting sun. Either way, Mina was emotionally exhausted. She hadn't seen Annalora leave, which meant she was still somewhere within earshot.

Mina waited, and when he didn't say anything else, she assumed it mean she was free to go. She moved away, and he called her name.

She stopped and took in his profile, his dark hair, and deep blue eyes. "Yes?"

"If you ever try to run away…" He pointed across the bridge and waved his hand. One of the Reapers appeared in the middle of the bridge. "You won't get far."

Every time she thought she might be gaining ground and earning his trust and understanding, he would resort to his insecurities and threaten her. She so longed for him to see that she wouldn't lie to him. She only wanted him to be happy and her family and friends to be safe. If that meant staying, then she didn't want to escape.

His warning sent chills down her spine but irritated her just as much. She held her head high and leveled her gaze at Teague. "I won't."

She wasn't sure, but she thought he looked relieved by her promise. This time, he let her go without stopping her, and she went back into the palace. Annalora stood on the top step.

"You're still here? I thought you got scared of little old me and ran away."

"I'm not scared of you."

"You should be," Annalora answered.

"Is that a threat?"

"It doesn't have to be if you just leave."

"Not happening."

"Then I'll just have to get rid of you."

"Good luck with that." Mina tossed the words over her shoulder and headed back to her room.

This time when she got to her cell, she closed the door and pushed a table in front of it. She could put up a big front with Annalora, but she really was scared the girl would try and murder her in her sleep.

The next day, Mina worked in the library. This room had been relatively untouched from the trauma of the war. Only dust showed that no one had disturbed it for years. Mina found solace in the quietness, knowing Annalora would never be caught dead in here. Today more Fae lights swirled and danced around the room, carrying feathers. Mina laughed as they dusted the top shelves and it rained down on her. Though it did make her sneeze.

The sound entertained the Fae lights, so more and more of them brushed the dust toward her. In a bout of silliness, Mina threw her hands up in the air and danced as she tried to avoid the falling dust motes. Until she bumped into a shelf and knocked over a few precariously stacked books.

"One day you're cleaning the kitchen and redecorating my throne room, and the next you're destroying my library. What did books and Stories ever do to you?" Teague teased.

Mina threw him a disgusted look.

"Oh wait, never mind," Teague caught himself in his own joke and started laughing hard.

Mina couldn't help but crack a smile. But she laughed even harder when the Fae lights accidentally swept a pile of accumulated dust off the shelves and right onto his head.

Teague reached up to brush it off and looked at his dirty hands. "What the...?" He glared up at the lights, who scattered and hid within the bookshelves.

"Don't get mad. They've been trying so hard to help."

"They'd be a better help if they just obeyed my order."

An abandoned dusting feather rocked softly down. Mina tried to catch it, but it landed on her head. Teague reached up and gently pulled the feather off. The feather—

larger than any she had seen in her world—was dark black with a bright gold tip.

"Hmm, a griffin feather." He held it out to her, and she twirled it in a ray of sunshine and watched as the gold moved subtly with the light.

"It means the Fae lights been up in the aerie."

"The aerie?"

"The griffins' nesting grounds are the mountain behind the castle. It's dangerous for anyone to be up there because of the newly hatched kitlings."

"Kitlings, as in babies? Can I see them?" she asked excitedly.

Teague looked at her as if she had grown two heads. "No, the mother would kill anyone who trespassed. I wouldn't dare take on an angry griffin for no reason."

"Oh." She tried to keep her disappointment at bay. After a few awkwardly silent moments passed, Mina decided to pick up the books she'd knocked over and put them where they belong. Teague moved over to a chair, sat down, and picked up a book. He began reading.

The system of books had no order, nothing like the Dewey decimal system of her library. She really had no idea where to put the book on the creation of the Fates. She turned and tried to find a spot on the shelf she'd dislodged the book from, but the section housed a genealogy of the Fae families. She had to wonder at the books that were left out if Teague had been searching for answers to heal the Fae world.

"Nope, not there," Teague said without looking as he flipped a page in his book.

She gave him an irritated look and moved over to the next shelf. This shelf was filled with books on the

Great Siren War. She wanted to hold onto a few and tuck them away to read up on her heritage, but she didn't want Teague to see her take them. Since obviously he had been researching *her* lineage. She reached up to put it away.

"Not there either."

She turned and caught the barest smile quickly disappear under his stoic façade.

Finally, she came to a shelf which looked like it was full of love sonnets. Frustrated, she quickly shoved the book there and turned, hands on her hips, to wait for his smug look, but the chair was empty. He was already next to her, pulling the book back down off the shelf. He gave her a wry smile that would have melted her heart if she wasn't sure another snide comment was coming.

"Menlo." He shook the book in the air. "Belongs next to Menlay." He switched hands and gently reached over her shoulder to shelve the book, bringing him within inches of her. Mina quickly handed him the next, hoping it belonged on the other side of the room.

He briefly glanced at the book and smiled again as he leaned closer and reached just above her head to put the book away. When he came back down on the balls of his feet, he was so close, she could hardly take a breath. Her head bumped into the wood shelf. She heard a wobble and looked up just as a decorative vase fell from above.

Teague grabbed her shoulders and pulled her into him as he jerked a few steps back. The vase crashed to the ground, barely missing her. Mina was flush against his body, her head resting against his chest, and she froze, unable to move. She could hear frantic beating, and it took her a second to realize she was hearing Teague's heart. She glanced up at him, and he stared at her wide-eyed, his expression utterly confused.

As if he couldn't comprehend his own racing heart.

"Thanks," she whispered, unwilling to be the one to pull away.

"You're welcome." His arms held on too.

"I'll clean that up," Mina said softly.

"Leave it," he demanded and moved his head lower.

"Prince Teague, are you in here?" Annalora called in an overly sweet voice.

She thought Teague cursed softly in Fae under his breath, but he pushed her away and took large steps toward the door to cut off Annalora.

Mina retreated behind the tall stacks of books as Annalora came to him and smiled brightly.

"Annalora, you're looking for me?"

"Yes, I wanted to talk to you some more about what I had said earlier. Have you had a chance to think it over?"

"I have. I'm not sure what you're proposing will solve my exact problem."

"Of course it will. It's a fact that the land will be healed when you choose your queen. Everyone knows that. The fate of our world has always been connected to the Fates. I can see the toll it's taking on you, and I'm willing to share your burden. Together we can heal the land, and you will live."

"I'm searching for other alternatives."

"You're dying. I know it because the land is dying. You're not strong enough to sustain the land by yourself and control the armies. Others will come and try to overthrow you if you don't bind yourself to another."

"How dare you say that I am weak!" Teague's eyes blazed, and the books on the shelves behind him started to shake and move in their place. "Do you not know who I am?"

"I know who you are." She pushed on his chest right in the spot where the tip of the dagger lay, and he gasped in pain. The shelves stopped moving. "I also know that the tip is moving closer to your heart. It's weakening you at the same time you're drawing strength from it. I can help you. You can draw your strength from me. I will rule by your side."

He rubbed his chest and glared at her. "You do yourself no favors speaking to me with such disrespect. I will think on it more—if I find myself desperate."

"You do that. Because you're more desperate than you're willing to admit. I don't know how much time you even have left." She strode back out the library doors.

As soon as they shut, Teague spun and blasted through a whole shelf of books, scattering the pages into the air.

Mina cried out as another shelf started to topple toward her. She barely dodged it. "Teague," Mina called. "Teague, it's okay. You'll figure something out."

He just raged on in pain and fury. The dark side of Teague came out as his fear erupted, and he took it out on his precious library.

Mina knew better than to stay nearby, so she took off running for the door, flinging it open just as a large table crashed into the wall next to her. She ran down the hall and into the main foyer and stopped by one of the columns. Fresh tears streamed down her face as she realized that freedom may come faster than she realized. All she had to do was wait for Teague to die.

Twenty-Four

Mina left the library and Teague's destructive anger behind. She was so torn. What was the right thing to do? She ran blindly, not even caring where she was headed, as her feet pounded on, doubts and questions that filled her mind.

Until she collided into a wall of flesh.

"Oomph." Mina groaned as strong hands grabbed her forearms, and she looked up into the tanned and bearded face of a shirtless stranger.

"Come, we will get you out of here." The man gripped her arm and tugged her after him.

"No, wait! I can't leave!"

Her abductor ignored her and pulled her down the hall and out the front door. She struggled against the older man. His brown beard was tinged in gray, his eyes a dark hazel, filled with worry. On his arms, she could see the fine white spidery lines of scars that had long since healed over. A long necklace of seashells was the only adornment on his upper body.

"Stop! I can't cross the bridge. The Reaper will kill me."

"Who said anything about crossing the bridge?" He pulled up short and pushed her to the railing. Was he going to throw her over? He quickly flung his legs over and yanked her with him as he jumped into the water.

Mina didn't have time to scream as the cold water rushed over her face. She tried to kick and swim for the surface, but the kidnapper dragged her under with powerful strength. Her chest ached, but she held her breath as he pulled her through the lake.

She opened her eyes enough to see a flash of silver scales move near her face. This couldn't be. The person dragging her to her death was a merman?

Feeling the intense pressure and burn build again, she clawed at the hand that held her forearm. The man turned around, surprised at her distress. He immediately pulled her up to the surface.

When her head broke the water, sweet succulent air rushed into her lungs. But instead of taking the moment to savor her breath, she turned on the merman. "Are you trying to kill me?"

"No, quite the opposite. I'm here to rescue you." He looked taken aback by her outburst, but he didn't stop with his plan. He just flipped her over, put his arm around her neck, and continued to swim at impossible speed across the lake. When he came to the waterfall, he slowed just before the rocks.

"Trust your instincts." He gestured with his finger toward the water. "We're going down."

"What? No, I can't." She kicked out against his body.

He grunted when she made contact but only tightened his grip. "You can, and you will. Now on the count of three. One, two"—he propelled himself up and out of the water using his tail—"three."

He dove back under the water, dragging her beside him deep, deep below the surface.

The battering, rushing water pounded against her back, and her hair whipped around as they swam through the rough currents. She decided it would be suicide to fight him and switched her efforts to trying to swim with him.

The deeper they swam, the darker it grew until Mina saw the underwater cave he was heading toward. Panic seized her, but his strong grip on her wrist tugged her toward the cave.

Her previous fears of being underwater and fighting the sea witch rushed to the surface of her mind. She'd never liked swimming. Or maybe she did, and it was her mother who didn't like the water. She distinctly remembered a beach trip with her parents when she was a child. Her mother wouldn't go near the water. It was her father who had taught her how to swim and to not be afraid of the ocean. She'd felt safe with him.

Once her dad passed away, her mom never took them to the ocean again. The memory of what she'd given up must have been too painful for her.

Her trip down memory lane helped ease her fears as they swam through the dark underwater tunnel. Some creature or plant brushed past her leg, making her want to scream out and release her breath. Too much like that dream that had plagued her before she'd gone back in time. The darkness began to lighten, and Mina couldn't hold it any longer. She rushed to swim upward, but the man turned, saw her distress, and pressed his mouth to hers the same way Nix had done. Fresh oxygen flowed into her taxed lungs.

Loud thoughts pushed past her fears, and she heard him speak as clear as fresh air into her head. *If you relax, your body will do what comes natural and slow down your heart. You will be able to stay under much longer.*

Yeah right, Mina thought back. *You kidnapped me! And this was exactly how I was dragged underwater to my death by the sea witch. How is this not panic-worthy?*

He flinched at her onslaught of thought. *A sea witch. Nasty creatures, but you are much stronger than them. We're almost through.* His eyes squinted underwater, and she could see his teeth in a strangely reassuring smile, before he turned to swim further. *We will have to catch the underwater current to make it out of here. Let it pull you. Don't fight it.*

She tried to let her thoughts soothe her again and swim in sync with the mysterious man. It was hard to see, but she felt the water pull at her as they turned into the current. Once in, the water rushed and pushed at them. She tried to clear her mind and just focus on counting as they moved through the water.

The light grew brighter, and the water began to feel warmer against her skin. They broke the surface, and she gulped in fresh air. They were in a large cove. Rivulets of salt water streamed down her face, burning her eyes, but once they slowed, she was able to focus on the large three-masted ship in front of them. The closer they came, the more detail she was able to make out on the vessel, from its brightly colored sails to the hand-carved mermaid on the ship's bow.

He pulled her over to the boat, and a rope ladder dropped over the side for them to climb up. The man pushed her in front of him on the ladder, and his arms kept her from trying to jump back into the water. As if she could even think of going back in. Her limbs and body and the shock of what had just happened were too much for her system. She was positive that if she fell in, she would just sink to the ocean floor.

When she got to the top, strong hands grabbed her under the arms and helped her onto the deck. Exhausted, Mina slumped against the railing.

"Welcome to the fastest siren ship on the seas. *Serenity.*" The man swept his arms outward, gesturing to the beautiful Fae ship. Her eyes followed the arc of his arms and took in the vast array of wild and sea-loving Fae who all stood, staring at her.

"Oy, Ternan, that was fast. We weren't expecting you back for another few hours at least."

Ternan, the bearded man who saved her, grinned and shook his head, spraying the water over the others near him. "I expected that as well, but I came upon her in grim circumstances. The prince was on a vile rampage, intent on destroying the palace. It proved just the distraction I needed to sneak in and pull her out. Not to mention there was a serious lack of guards."

"Well, it was a good thing you got to her when you did." A woman with green highlights in her long brown hair stepped out of the crowd of onlookers. Her face was tanned with a hint of freckles across the bridge of her nose. She wore a vest showing off strong, tan arms with light, tattoo-like patterns, criss-crossing her skin. Her pants were a dark green with decorative netting wrapped around like a skirt. She looked mysterious and very much a siren of the sea. "Mina, darling, are you okay?"

"Who are you?" Mina asked, studying the faces of the gathered Fae. Many looked like they were one with the sea, hints of netting or shells embroidered into their shirts and clothing. Most of them—even the males—had long hair that was braided or left hanging down their backs, and intricate patterns lightly danced across their skin.

The woman who addressed her seemed slightly taken aback by her question. "Well, I know we've never met, but after your mother's death, we felt it was our duty to take care of you… and your brother as soon as we find him."

"That still doesn't answer my question," Mina said, her bottom lip shivering from cold.

"Why, I'm Winona, Ternan's wife. Your grandmother."

Twenty-Five

The vividly colored sails of the ship rose as the siren crew prepared to depart. Mina found a barrel to sit on as she watched her grandparents for the first time, trying to take in this information. Her mother had said to find them, but—she'd never imagined this. A good part of her wanted to reject them for not being a part of her life before now. The other part could see the family resemblance, and it made her want to run and hug them.

But they were strangers, and they'd abandoned her family.

Ternan came and leaned against the railing, crossing his arms. He scratched his beard and tried to make small talk. "You look like her... your mother."

"And my father," she shot back.

He looked pained at her answer. "Aye, that you do. You need to realize that it was her choice to leave her mother and me and cut all ties. She felt it was safer that way—for you, for us."

Mina got up off of the barrel and stared across the water as they sailed away from the small cove. "It would

207

have been better if it stayed that way. You don't know what you've done."

"We saved you from that lunatic prince," Ternan answered, his voice gruff. He pointed back the way they had come.

"I made a bargain. I'd stay with him, and Charlie would be safe. Since you interfered, you've doomed him and my friends."

Ternan was about to say something when a wooden hatch slammed open and interrupted him.

"Mina?" Ever shot up from below deck. When she saw her, Ever threw her arms around her. "You're okay?"

"What are you doing here?" Mina asked.

"I'm saving you, you Gimp. No wait, I can't call you that anymore." She cast a worried glance toward Mina's grandfather. "At least not out loud." Ever was dressed in siren garb, black pants, white netted tank top over a blue-purple tank.

Mina grabbed Ever by her arm and pulled her starboard and away from the prying eyes of the sirens, who never seemed to stop watching her. "No, what are you doing here, on the Fae plane?"

"Well, you're the one who abandoned our plan and just surrendered herself to the enemy. We had a perfectly good trap all worked out."

"I had a vision—a premonition. Our trap would have backfired, and you would've ended up trapped inside one of the mirrors with the nastiest part of Teague's personality and gotten stabbed by the poisoned knife. I watched you sacrifice yourself to trap the two of you in the mirror forever. And I couldn't go through with it." Tears of frustration burned at the corner of Mina's eyes. "I've lost too many friends and family to this curse. I couldn't lose you."

Ever stood in front of Mina and placed her hands on her shoulders. "There's something special about you, Mina." All teasing was gone from her tone. "I don't know, but when I look at you, I see more than the girl in front of me. I see a dangerous Grimm, a powerful siren, and a leader. Our futures are intertwined, and I know protecting you means protecting everyone I love—Fae and human alike. Giving my life to protect you is not that big of a sacrifice. I've found a purpose, and that purpose…besides annoying you…is to protect you."

"But not if it means your death."

Ever's face crinkled in anger. "I'm a pixie. No one ever expects much from us. They see our race as troublemakers, but I'm more than they think. I'm more than the label Fae put on me, and I will prove it."

"I understand wanting to be more than a label," Mina answered, "but you have to promise me that you'll be careful."

Ever nodded her head. "I'll try my best. Now about this dream of yours. Is this a new super power or something?"

"Or something."

"And the plan didn't work."

Mina shook her head. "I wish it had. And there's more. After I watched you die, someone came in and blasted me into the mirror as well."

"Who?"

"I don't know. I never saw them. But I knew I couldn't take the chance of all that happening."

"So you just surrendered yourself to Teague?"

"Yes, and I'd do it again if it meant protecting everyone. That's the sacrifice I made." She paused and looked over at Ever's clothes. "But how did you end up here?"

"Well, you left me with the seam ripper, so the first thing I had to do was come over. But then, instead of storming the castle like I wanted to, I needed help. So I went looking for your family."

Ever leaned her elbows on the railing and nodded at a cute siren boy with sun-bleached blond hair past his shoulders. "I didn't know that sirens were this good-looking. It took a few weeks of searching since they spend most of their life sailing and exploring underwater caves. They're pretty much the gypsies of the sea, and it's kind of better for all Fae that they are. They're too powerful in large groups."

"How'd you find them?"

"She didn't. I did." Nix swung down with a rope from the crow's nest."

"Nix, you're here on the Fae plane, and you're okay?"

He looked relieved. "Yeah, I wasn't sure if I could cross back over since part of me died on this plane. The Godmothers weren't sure I'd survive the crossing either, but you were worth the risk. Turns out I'm fine because I'm fully human now. You didn't abandon me, and I won't abandon you."

"Nix insisted on coming with, especially when I told him I was going to search for your family."

"Yeah, I know enough about them since nixies and sirens are both water races, though the two don't particularly get along. They don't trust us when we turn sea witch, which I understand. But I'm not a nixie anymore, so don't worry. I have no power, no gifts. So far they've been putting up with me."

"Oh, I've heard them talk of throwing you overboard a few times," Ever chided.

Nix didn't miss a beat. "That's because of my good looks. The men feel threatened."

Ever rolled her eyes. "That's not what I hear. I hear you cheat at games."

Nix looked aghast at the accusation. "I only cheat to win."

"Is there another reason for cheating?" Mina chuckled.

His mouth gaped opened, and his finger froze midair as he began a rebuttal but thought better of it. "Um, nope there isn't."

"So how'd you find them?"

Nix recovered and became serious. "It's always wise to know where your enemy is, so you can avoid them at all costs. Growing up, we always heard the water sprites and sirens inhabited Dead Man's Cove, so Ever and I had to make it there and wait for one to come up from the underground caverns or for a ship to pass by. Well, we got impatient and built a boat."

"A raft," Ever corrected.

"It was a fine ship."

"It was barely staying afloat. It was nothing more than logs tied together with vines."

"It had a mast," he said.

"With no sail."

"Stop dismissing our vessel. She was the finest one I've ever captained," Nix pouted.

"She fell apart when we got near the cove and the rocks."

Nix's cheeks went beet red, and he scratched his head. "Yeah, well that was my plan all along."

"Oh, that's not what you told me. We were going to go out to the cove, sail near the rocks, and wait for one of them to try and lure us to our death." Ever placed her hands on her hips.

"But it didn't happen, did it?"

"No, our boat fell apart, and we began to sink. The sirens saved us."

"Yeah, who'd have thought the myths were wrong?" He offered a sheepish shrug. "Sometimes sirens are the good guys too."

Ever turned her back on Nix. "Well, anyway. We found them, and it took some convincing that we were legit and knew the daughter of Sarafina. It turns out your family is one of the oldest and strongest family lines, and... well..." She paused, and her head dropped. "If you had really lived on the Fae plane all those years ago, you probably *would* have been sent to the choosing ceremony for the prince."

"But I wasn't even born then."

"It doesn't seem to matter. You always find a way of surprising everyone. But it seemed that Ternan and Winona knew right away who we were. They had been keeping an eye on you for some time. They didn't even ask questions but sailed straight here to save you. I gotta admit. Your family rocks."

Mina looked over at the water and watched in amazement as something large and white shot out of the water and dove back beneath the waves. It looked like a creature that was half-fish and half… unicorn.

Ever coughed to get her attention, and Mina apologized. "They're strangers," Mina added.

"They don't have to be. You were worried you didn't have anyone to take care of Charlie. I'd say your family is a great place to start," Ever coaxed.

"I'm his family." Sure, her mom had told her to find them, but they were making things worse. Not better.

"They're his family as well, Mina. Don't you think Charlie would like to meet his grandparents?"

"We don't need them, if you could help me go back," Mina whispered urgently.

"To the human plane? No problem."

"No back to the palace."

"Mina, have you gone mad?"

"I promised him I wouldn't run away."

Ever scoffed at her. "Well, that's a dumb promise. Of course you'd run away. Who'd want to stay with him as crazy and evil as he's become? I bet he treated you horrible while you were there."

"Uh no, it actually wasn't that bad. For the most part, he was reasonable and okay company. Or he was until Annalora showed up."

"What does that ugly gnome-head want?"

"She seems to think he'll choose her as his next queen."

"Well, that would explain her sudden appearance."

"How so?"

"Because he does——"

One of the sirens came and beckoned for Mina to join him.

Ever stayed where she was, but Mina followed the young man down a few steps and into the captain's quarters. Ternan stood at the window, looking forlorn. Winona was sitting in a chair, her hands folded in her lap. Mina stood in front of her siren grandparents and waited for one of them to speak first.

It was Winona who stood up and approached her. "There's something we should tell you."

"We're not really related. I knew it," she said, a defense mechanism.

Winona frowned. "No, you're the spitting image of our daughter. There's no doubt that you're kin. But with Sarafina's death, we've been left without an heir."

"You mean you don't have anyone else? Why would you let my mother go to the human plane then?"

Ternan was the one to answer. "We had two daughters. Sarafina was the youngest and always followed her heart. Our oldest displeased the Fates and was turned to stone. She now rests in the bottom of the lake beside the palace."

Mina's heart pounded, and she felt sick. That was her *aunt?* She'd been so close to joining her in death.

"I've seen her," Mina whispered under her breath. "I've heard her call to me."

Winona's head dropped in despair, while Ternan's voice rose in anger. "We have no love for the Fates and their cruel ways."

"I need to go back. You don't understand. I can't stay with you."

"Nonsense. You're family. You will be accepted here among us," Winona spoke up.

"No, I made a deal—willingly. I said I'd stay with the prince, and he promised to leave my friends alone. If I left, they'd be hurt or killed." She decided not to mention that she was worried for the prince himself.

"Well, then we must get to your friends first," Ternan announced.

"Yes. And your brother," Winona agreed. "With Sarafina gone, we are no longer barred from interacting with her children. Let's bring them home."

Mina felt a moment of relief that she wasn't alone in her quest to protect her brother, but the Fae plane wasn't any safer than the human plane. She'd have to find him, trust the sirens, and find a way to keep them all safe from Teague.

They called Ever into the room and spoke quickly about what they were going to do and how they were going to find Charlie.

"The seam ripper is only strong enough to open a gate for a few people. We'd never be able to take everyone with us," Ever said.

"We will have to use one of the natural gates then," Ternan stated.

"It won't do us any good unless we know where Charlie is." Ever looked to Mina for an answer.

"I don't know. The whole point was that I wouldn't know where they've taken him."

"She can find him," Winona said firmly to Ever. "Mina has the closest connection to him of any of us."

"I don't know how." Mina felt the mounting pressure being placed on her and began to doubt.

"In your dreams. The pixie told me of your dreams, that you see things," Winona encouraged.

"No, mostly nightmares. But then sometimes it feels real," Mina answered, a slight panic rising within her.

"Can you honestly tell me you've never dreamed something, a conversation that never came true?"

The premonition of Ever's death. And more than that. Mina thought back to her many restless nights and the pieces of her dreams that came true. Of being pulled underwater by Teague, though he was pulling her underground. Or the conversations she had with him. Her heart raced, and breathing became a challenge.

It was true. She was seeing bits of the future. "But how can I do it on purpose?"

"Just think about him while you fall asleep. Your subconscience will seek him out," Winona said.

Mina felt all of the eyes on her and swallowed. "I'll try, but I think I'm too wound up to sleep."

Winona smiled. "I have a tea for that. I'll brew you a cup and let you sleep. Take your time. The dream will come."

"But what if I'm too late?"

"Then we will have to fight Teague to steal him back," Ternan answered.

"You're not afraid of him?" Mina asked.

"No. In fact, it will be our pleasure to inflict a little payback on the Royals for what King Lucian did to our daughter." He grinned evilly.

Mina felt a moment of indecisiveness arise at her grandfather's eagerness for war. Was she really in the right place to find help for Charlie? She couldn't go back to Teague now, so she prayed that she was doing the right thing.

Twenty-Six

Sleep didn't come easily. Mina had lain down on a small padded bench in the captain's quarters with a pillow and blanket. She tried to focus her mind on her brother, but too many questions, thoughts, and fears plagued her—not to mention, she was in the middle of the ocean on a Fae ship, surrounded by her mother's family. Instead of relief, a flood of angry thoughts rushed at her. Her mother shouldn't have kept them from her. She lied.

Mina punched the pillow and tried to get comfortable again, but the gentle sway of the waves didn't help. They only reminded her she wasn't on land. She stared at the warm cup of tea on a small table to her right. Her first instinct was to avoid the sea blue liquid with its unique aroma. She'd never in her life seen blue tea, and she didn't know what it would do to her—or if it was even safe. And she had only just met her mother's parents. They might be lying about the effects of the tea.

But what other choice did she have?

Mina picked up the blue tea to give it a cursory sniff and picked up motes of fruit and honey. Tipping the cup, she drank the first few sips slowly before she gained enough courage to finish it off. She laid back down on the pillow and tried to concentrate on Charlie.

But her mind couldn't stay away from Teague.

He was furious. She could see his stiff angry posture as he stormed about the castle, searching for her. Her heart ached to see that she was causing him so much pain and anger.

"You promised me!" he yelled into the empty room. He stormed through the halls and burst through the doors to his own room. He went to a table and snatched up a small silver hand mirror and spoke her name. In the dream, she could see the mirror shimmer as it changed from his reflection to an image of her.

Confusion marred his face as he met her eyes. "You ran away to be with the sirens." His voice wavered. "I told you what would happen if you broke our deal," he said, his voice suddenly like steel. "You'll have to come back to me if you want your brother." His hands held the mirror so tightly his knuckles turned white. He slammed the mirror back down onto the table then turned and yelled out the door.

"Summon the Reapers and my army. She has broken my trust for the last time." Mina could see shadows move to do his bidding. She wanted to scream at him that whatever he was seeing was a lie, that she hadn't abandoned him, hadn't left him.

Her dream shifted. It was night, and she was running for her life. She could hear the low growl of the omen on her tail. She was running down an unfamiliar street. She tripped in the darkness and landed on the pavement. Her hands and knees were scraped, and she looked desperately around in the darkness for the omen, pulling out a small hand mirror to glance over her shoulder. There it was, mere feet from her, with its eyes pale as death and his snarling mouth.

It lunged, and she dropped the mirror.

She cried out in her sleep and woke up covered in sweat. Winona sat in a chair off to the side of the room, watching over her.

Mina covered her mouth with her hands and tried to keep from crying out, but she was wracked with silent sobs. Winona rushed forward and kneeled beside the couch. "What is it? What did you see?"

"My death," she whispered. Her body went cold. "I don't make it in time to save them."

She was quiet afterward, solemn. Nothing Nix or Ever did could bring her out of the spiral of depression her mind had sunk to. She hadn't dreamed of her brother. She couldn't find his location, and there was nothing she could do for another twenty-four hours or until it was safe for her to take the tea again. Mina was so overwhelmed that she knew there was no way she'd fall asleep naturally. Not when she didn't know how many days she had left to live.

She sat on a crate of supplies and stared across the sea at the setting sun.

The image of the omen's eyes bothered her so much, she finally gathered the courage to ask Winona about it. She went to stand near her grandmother. "What is an omen exactly? Is it a Reaper or something else?"

"An omen is the form the Death Reaper takes before he strikes and takes your soul. They are a different breed of Reapers, unlike the ones that guard the Fates. Because they are already dead."

"So can it be killed?" Mina asked.

"No. Only the dead can challenge Death to become the next omen. Then they must spend their half-life collecting souls."

"How horrible." Mina shuddered.

"It is," Winona agreed.

"Who'd want to become a Death Reaper?"

"Someone desperate enough to want a second chance at life, even if it's only a half-life."

"Then is there a way to stop it?" she asked.

"There's lore of a bone whistle that can control the Reaper, but I think that's all it is—a tale. Because nothing can stop Death when he strikes."

"It's how I lost Mom," Mina whispered. "The omen stole her soul."

"I know, but I also know that she loved you and would have traded her life for yours in a heartbeat, love. Don't ever mistake her sacrifice for weakness."

Mina stared at her hands and saw the half-moon fingernail indents she had left on her palms. She made herself relax and looked up as Winona moved to Ternan's side.

While they'd talked about the omen, Ternan had his siren crew unfurl every sail—crimson, copper, aquamarine. They were trying to beat the sunset and make it to specific coordinates. Ternan and his first mate were hunched over a sea map calculating distance and wind speed.

Nix asked Winona if she thought they'd make it.

"Of course, dear boy. This is the fastest siren ship ever built. The sirens were the first to discover the sea gate to the human plane, although the humans were the first to discover its sister—the Bermuda Triangle. This one is closest to us, and we've risked many of our lives keeping the Fae from using it to cross the planes."

"Luring them to their death, you mean," Nix said.

Winona's chin lifted in challenge, but she laughed good-naturedly. "Aye. The only ones that come sailing here for the gate are up to no good. They're the low down, dirtiest scum that walks the Fae world. So yes, we call them to their doom, and no one has cared or stopped us. In fact, we do the world a favor."

"And that's how my mother met my father." Mina spoke up.

"Somehow the young man sailed through the gate into our world while he was chasing the Loch Ness beast across the planes."

"You mean the Loch Ness Monster is real?" Mina asked in disbelief.

"Well, they're certainly not all from your Loch Ness, but the beasts like deep lakes on both planes," Winona said. "James followed it through the gate, and, when he did, it attacked and capsized his vessel. It was our youngest daughter, your mother, who saved him. We told her to let him drown since he wasn't one of us, but she couldn't. She cried for days when we made a raft and sent him back through the gate to his own plane. There was nothing we could do to help her. She was young and in love, and she begged us to let her go after him."

"And you let her?" Mina asked. Then she saw Ternan's face of disgust. "...right?"

"Of course not. We'd never tell her to expose her Fae side to a human. But when we forbade it, she went to a sea witch for help and had her powers bound. That wasn't enough for her though. She wanted to forget all about us and went to a guild of rogue Fae for help."

"I believe they call themselves the Godmothers," Winona corrected.

Ternan growled out, "Whatever, but they helped her. Before they altered her memories, she contacted us and told us never to try to reach her again. It wasn't until years later that we realized she'd fallen for a Grimm. It kind of changed some things since he already knew about the Fae, but it hurt that she wanted nothing to do with us. Wanted to be human, to raise human children."

"So we watched you, in our dreams," Winona said, "and waited, hoping one day, you would need us. And that day is today." Winona came over and put her arm around Mina in a side hug.

Winona's eyes locked on the iron cuffs around Mina's wrists. "How dare he?" Winona gripped the band harder, fuming. "How dare someone shackle the power of a siren!" Her hair crackled with static electricity as her anger rose to the surface.

Mina watched in awe.

Winona held out her hand and power raced to her, her hair whipping about from the abundance of energy. "No one lays a hand on my granddaughter."

Winona touched the cuffs, and Mina felt the current of power blast through them, turning them black. Whatever magic had blocked her was killed. Her bonds clicked open and fell to the deck with a thud.

Mina hadn't known what she was missing, but when the Fae power came rushing back to her, it was as strong and as sharp as regaining the ability to see after being blind. She needed to grab a hold of Winona's arm to steady herself. Her wrists weren't rubbed raw like Jared's, she could only assume that it didn't hurt her as much because she was only half Fae.

Winona smirked and raised her eyebrow. "Now that is just a taste of our power. Shall I teach you the rest?"

Mina's mouth was dry, and she had to swallow a few times before her verbal yes spilled out. "Teach me anything and everything I need, so I can save my friends."

"Very good," Ternan grunted, watching the exchange. "There's the siren spirit. But you'll have to delay your lessons until we are through the gate. Any outlash of power can collapse it around us, trapping us between the planes forever." He gestured to the setting sun.

Mina ran to the front of the ship to watch the miracle that was about to happen.

She saw nothing on the horizon except for two giant stone monoliths that rose out of the sea. Heads popped out of the water to watch them.

Mina couldn't help but be drawn in by the beautiful aquatic features of the sirens. The fleeting sun reflected off their tails and scales as they swam alongside the ship.

A few came up and called out, a loud piercing shriek, but it didn't damage the boat. If it had been anything like her brother's gift, it could very well tear them to pieces. These calls were more of a warning to the boat. The closer they came, the more violent the attacks became.

Until Ternan strode to the bow holding a giant gold trident. He raised it, and the sirens in the water jumped high into the air and flicked their tails in a salute before diving deep below the waves. This continued the last mile. When they reached the twin monoliths, the sirens that guarded the gate left them as the ship continued toward it.

"Almost," Winona called out. "Starboard," she yelled to the young siren with dreadlocks who currently stood at the helm. "We can't breach the gate too early, or we'll miss our chance completely. We won't have time to turn around. We've got one chance tonight. We can't afford to have to wait till tomorrow."

Ever came and stood nervously next to Mina. "I've only ever passed through one of the smaller gates between our worlds or used the seam ripper. I've heard of the Sister Rocks and the rumor it was a gate, but I've never imagined actually seeing it or passing through."

"Why are we not using the seam ripper to open a gate between the planes? It's too small?"

"Do you see how many sirens are on this ship? The seam ripper would only let two or three max through before it closed, and it's too dangerous to open in the same spot over and over. You're bringing an army through, so you need one of the natural gates. Just like Teague would have used."

Nix looked at the setting sun and the gate and voiced his concern, "We're not going to make it!"

"Yes, we are!" Ternan bellowed. He ran toward the stern of the ship. He held his hands up in the air, and

Winona did the same. Soon every siren on the boat raised their hands in unison, facing the sea behind them.

The ship stilled on the water, and they dropped down suddenly. Mina looked over her shoulder, and a giant wave surged up behind them. A wave that would surely break their boat apart.

"Hold on!" Ternan shouted. He controlled the wave, causing it to break and rush under the ship. It lifted the boat and propelled them toward the Sister Rocks.

Ever and Mina screamed. Nix pushed them against the middle mast and wrapped a rope around their waists, securing them to the large wooden post. Water rushed over the side, and the wave dropped again. People screamed—most in excitement—as they were airborne for a few seconds before slamming back into the water. The sun just touched the horizon.

The gate opened, a spiral of bright colors.

But they were off course, charging straight toward the right monolith.

"Turn! Port, port!" Winona hollered to the first mate on the helm. He spun the wheel, trying to keep the ship from crashing.

Everyone held their breath.

The boat cleared the monolith and sailed toward the open gate.

Another wave came up from behind and spilled over the railings, making the ship rock and reel. Nix lost his grip on the rope. Mina and Ever grabbed his hands as the ship tilted to the side, buffeted by another wave across the deck.

The wave partially swallowed them for a heartbeat, and when it passed, they looked around.

Nix was gone.

Ever fought against the ropes that tied her to the mast and screamed in despair. "Nix!" she howled as they left the Fae plane behind them.

Twenty-Seven

When they passed through the gate, a relative silence followed.

Ever's loud wail of sorrow cut through the wind like a sword. "No, no, no!"

Mina's fingers worked tirelessly at the knot, but she couldn't get the rope undone. One of the sirens rushed over to untie them. The rope fell to the deck with a thud, and Ever ran to the railing and looked over.

"You stupid nixie!" Her fist pounded the railing. "You always think of others first. For once, why couldn't you be selfish and save yourself?" She collapsed to her knees, bawling.

Mina gently wrapped her hands around Ever's shoulders, surprised when she turned, and buried her head in Mina's shoulder.

"Oh Nix, I'm so sorry for all the names I called you," Ever confessed. "For putting salt in the Pixy Stix when you kept stealing them. For telling you cartoons were real."

"What do you mean—they're not real?" Nix shouted from the other side of the ship.

They turned to see Nix's head as he peeked over the side rail. He hauled himself up, swung his legs over, and hopped onto the deck. Then he used his hands to flick the water out of his hair.

Ever ran across the deck and threw herself into his arms. "Don't you ever do anything that stupid and dangerous again, do you hear me?"

Nix blushed at Ever's show of affection. "O-oh. O-okay. I don't think I'll b-be dragged through a gate off the side of a siren ship again."

"Good, you big lug." Ever reached up to circle her arms around his neck and kissed him on the lips.

Nix was only momentarily taken aback before he returned the kiss with fervor.

"Well, I've got to hand it to them. They *are* a cute couple." Winona smiled sweetly.

"They deserve each other, and I mean that in the best way possible." Mina grinned. The joy she felt was slowly replaced by shock as she realized where they'd come out of the portal. Of all the places for them to appear in the human plane. "You've got to be kidding me! We just passed under the Golden Gate Bridge?"

"I've always thought that was such a horrid name. It's not even gold," Winona said dryly.

Behind them, the iron and steel bridge looked almost black against the rising sun. She was still nowhere near home, but what could she expect from a natural Fae gate?

"We'll attract too much attention in this ship. And, um, you'll all probably attract attention too." Mina blurted out as she looked at her kin. Their crazy hair styles, unique tattoos, and the pearlescent scales that lay just beneath the skin, reflecting the light, would definitely make them stand out.

Winona whistled loudly and made a series of high pitched notes. Four male sirens scrambled up the masts. Mina watched as their hands glowed, and they began to weave a glamour over their ship. It instantly changed in appearance to mimic a smaller-masted vessel they'd just passed. The siren figurehead disappeared. The rough Fae wood morphed into a painted blue with white stripes. Even the colorful sails became stark white. Honestly, the ship lost much of its beauty.

The young siren with the dreadlocks came up to her wearing boat shoes, a polo, and white shorts. The crew suddenly looked like they were competing in a regatta. Mina tried to stifle her laugh.

"What?" Dreadlocks asked. "Is this not right?"

"No, it's fine. It's just not what I was expecting," she answered.

He held out his hand. "I'm Kino."

Mina shook Kino's hand. "Nice to meet you. I'm Mina."

"Oh, you don't have to introduce yourself. We all know who you are. Your grandparents weren't the only ones waiting a long time for you."

"What?"

"Ternan and Winona are not just any sirens. They pretty much rule the sea, which means one day? All of this will be yours. On both planes."

"Uh, no thank you. The last few encounters I've had with the ocean or water have not ended well."

Kino grinned. "That's because you thought you were human. Now that you know you're part-siren, it will call to you like a lover. One day, you'll answer."

"Nope, I'll let it go to voicemail." She held up her hand to her ear. "Please leave a message after the beep."

Kino laughed. "Well, I guess that's one way to avoid responsibility."

"This isn't my responsibility. It never was. I already have too much on my plate with a cursed prince hunting me down. I'm not ready for more."

Kino bent over, gripping his stomach in laughter. "Oh, if you weren't already taken, I'd try to win your hand."

"What do you mean?" She freaked. How could he come to the conclusion that she was taken?

"It's written on your face. You're in love with someone. And I hope he loves you in return, because princess, if he don't, Kino's going to show him what happens when you mess with family."

"Uh…"

Ternan stepped up as they reached the pier. The sirens, all completely camouflaged, began to secure their ship to the posts. Her grandfather wore a deep blue jacket and captain's hat. Of course his costume wasn't complete without the old wooden pipe he was shoving—was that seaweed?—into. He might as well have stepped out of an ad for a seafood restaurant.

But she wasn't going to be the one to correct the king of the sea. Thankfully Winona's attire was more toned down. She wore white shorts, a blue tank top, and boat shoes, and her hair was all brown and tamed into a simple braid.

Forever

"What now?" Mina asked.

"You to tell us where to find your brother," Winona answered. "We can wait for another dream, or you can try your Fae intuition."

"I don't know how trustworthy that is," Mina answered.

When they were docked and the gangplank secured, Kino escorted Mina, Ever, and Nix off the ship, and they set off on a quest for a payphone.

"They're going to be harder to find than I thought," Ever grumbled. "Now, I'm kicking myself for having broken my phone. Sorry, Mina."

"Don't be, now you get a taste of what my life is like."

They had to walk among the shops of the pier. Kino tried to play it cool, but he was just as excited as Nix was at the musical stairs, the street performers, and the mirror maze.

Mina cringed at the mirror-maze memories that flooded her—and this maze was even larger. "Okay, does anyone have any spare change?" she asked.

Ever looked sheepish, and Kino looked confused.

Nix was the one who produced quarters out of his pants pocket. Of course nixies were hoarders, so it was no surprise that he also pulled out a bunch of rocks and bottle caps.

Mina inserted two quarters into the payphone and dialed Nan's cell. It went right to voicemail. Feeling rushed, she tried to spout off all of the directions she could. She'd been rehearsing them in her mind on the way over.

"Nan, it's me. He's coming after you, but it will be okay. I've got friends, and they're here to help. They can

231

protect Charlie. We just have to find you. I need you to meet me at the place we ran away to when we were fourteen. I'll be there twice a day waiting for you at your lucky time and—"

Beep.

Her voice message was cut off.

"What kind of message was that?" Kino asked. "That didn't sound very clear."

"It's perfectly clear when your best friend is a movie buff. She once convinced me to run away and find an old fortune teller machine, so it could magically transform us into adults."

"What magic is this?" Kina sounded skeptical.

"It's the magic of Twentieth Century Fox and *Big*, a movie from the 1980s."

The only thing she could do was wait, and it was going to be the hardest wait she'd ever had to endure. Kino begged to stay and wander the pier, but Mina didn't want to be anywhere near a local landmark in case Teague was watching her through her mirror.

Nix was just as bad as Kino, watching all of the people along the pier in fascination.

But then Kino saw the aquarium. "Did you see what they've done? They're holding that octopus captive. We must rescue him and free all of the sea creatures. How do your kind live like this, enslaving the sea's most beautiful and smartest of creatures?" He ranted and seemed sort of unstable the whole walk back to the ship.

Mina let Ever try and explain to the siren how an aquarium works.

"Money? This is all about profit? It's even worse than I thought," Kino grumbled.

"Oh, brother." Ever shook her head and strictly forbid him from going to the aquarium or even mentioning to anyone else what he'd seen. "We are here to lay low until we can find Charlie. We are not here to cause a scene. Do you got that?" She jabbed her finger into Kino's chest.

He didn't look happy, but he shrugged. When they got back to the boat, he immediately disappeared below decks and ignored them.

"Well, it didn't take long for you to make enemies," Nix commented. "I thought I'd be the one to get on the bad side of the sirens."

"He couldn't see the big picture," Ever said. "He has to remember this isn't his world, and the rules are different here. If he wants to stay, he needs to shape up or ship out."

"Oh, I see what you did there!" Nix started to laugh, and Ever just glared at him until he fell into silence. But that didn't last either. His shoulders continued to shake, and a loud snort slipped through.

Mina walked to the captain's chambers and knocked politely on the door.

"Come in," her grandfather called.

She carefully pushed open the wood door and entered.

Ternan bent over a map he had picked up from a visitor center, marking it with little green colored pebbles.

Winona carefully settled something she was holding into a trunk and picked up a little cloth-covered bundle. "Any luck?"

"No, I left a message. Hopefully she'll get it and meet me here." She walked over and sat on a small stool near Winona.

"Does your friend know this area?"

"Yes, she'd come out here during the summer for drama camps. Once in the middle of her parents' divorce, Nan decided to run away and come here. She bought a bus ticket, and I came with her—only to convince her to come back—but I was grounded for a month."

"You should have been grounded longer. Your mother was soft."

Mina nodded her head in affirmation. "Probably, but I gave her a heads up what I was doing, that I wasn't letting Nan go by herself. And if we weren't back in twelve hours, she was going to come and get me."

"Smart. I take it you both made it back."

"Yeah, we missed the first bus back, so we had to take a later one, which is why I was grounded for the month."

"How did you convince your friend to come back?"

"Nothing I said would change her mind, until I told her Charlie wouldn't be the same without her in his life. He always was her weak spot."

Winona smiled sadly and fidgeted with the item she had pulled from the trunk.

"When your mother chose your father over her heritage, she gave up everything that reminded her of us. I've kept it all, if you're interested in learning a bit more about your mother."

Mina peeked at the opened trunk and the indiscernible items inside. "I would like that."

Winona smiled, the corners of her lips quivering slightly. "I think she'd like that too." She handed Mina the bundle she had in her hands.

Forever

The cloth held something hard, and Mina slowly unwrapped it to find a lovely gold seashell on a small chain. "It's beautiful."

"It's yours," Winona offered. "Anything you want out of your mother's trunk is yours."

"I don't know what to say."

"Then don't say anything." Winona stood up and moved away from the trunk, giving Mina space to peruse her mother's items. It was mostly clothes of blues and greens decorated with shells, some books, a delicate white netted top. There were a few other trinkets, but then Mina found a piece of parchment tucked inside a book cover.

She pulled it out and saw her father's likeness carefully drawn in coal. He'd been very young at the time—before he grew out his mustache—possibly in his early twenties. Studying her mother's love for her father, forbidden but blooming all the same, felt like an invasion of privacy. Mina carefully tucked the picture back into the book and placed it in the bottom of the trunk.

"Tell me about her, before, when she was a siren," she said.

"Oh, she was a handful—stubborn and one of the strongest in her gifts. I can see that her bloodline passed on to each of you. So it's not just your father's curse you were born with, but your mother's gifts as well."

"But why would she hide it—from my father, from me?"

"Your father, James, hated the Fae, because they killed his brother. When your mother saved his life, he didn't know she was a siren. But they fell in love so deeply, he willingly shared his secret, his curse. When Sara learned how much he hated the Fae, she chose to keep her identity

235

a secret. But Ternan told you all of that already—about her deal with the sprite and all."

"Wait. A sprite, you say?"

"Yes. One of the most powerful nixies of all. She was once employed at the castle as one of the Queen's own handmaidens, before she was banished."

"I bet you I know what she was banished for," Mina breathed out excitedly. Her heart was racing. She'd once asked the Godmothers, and no one knew where this sprite had disappeared to. "You don't happen to know where I can find her, do you?"

Ternan's expression soured. "Now why would you want to stir up trouble with her?"

"Because I think she can help me."

"Nay, she can't help anyone but herself. She's a conniving, deceitful—"

"Ternan," Winona gently warned. "You cannot let what happened with our daughter cloud your judgment."

"Wait...what bargain did they make? I thought Ternan said my mom got help from a *sea witch*."

Winona closed her eyes and whispered softly to herself. When she opened her eyes, there were tears in the corners. "Ternan spoke the truth when he called her a sea witch earlier. Sprites are entities of water like us, and they go by many names—depending on their choices. Water sprites, nixies—or the deplorable one—sea witch."

"It's true, they can't be trusted," Winona said.

"And now *both* of our daughters are dead," Ternan growled angrily.

"I'll soon be dead, if I don't find another way to stop what's about to happen," Mina said.

"We could protect you. We could help you," her grandmother said.

She shook her head. "I need to find this sprite, this sea witch. Please, if you know anything… Help me."

Both of her grandparents looked pained at the prospect. Winona spoke up first. "She's here on the human plane. This is where she was banished after the Fates were unhappy with the deal they had made."

"Where?"

"We do not know. We know only the name which she goes by here."

"Which is?"

"Taz Clara."

"That's it? That's all you can tell me?"

"That's all anyone knows. Truly, if you don't find her, that may be for the better."

Mina felt frustrated. No plan she came up with worked. She couldn't find Charlie, and now—when the possibility of finding the one who'd split Teague rallied her spirits—she had only a name. Taz Clara.

She left Ternan and Winona's room and made her way below deck to the sleeping quarters. It was pretty empty except for a few sirens who looked to be taking an afternoon nap. Ever and Nix were chatting while they swung in their hammocks.

Nix nodded at Mina. "Those two are unoccupied." Next to him, there were two hammocks folded up, waiting to be stretched out and hung on far hooks for an occupant.

Mina grabbed the heavy cloth and hooked the ring on a post, then unwound it till she found the other ring. It took a few tries to get the hammock opened enough to where she could sit in it and lay back without falling out.

From her position in the hammock, she could see Ever and Nix as they whispered softly to each other.

"Hey, Nix," Mina called. "Did you ever know a sea witch by the name of Taz Clara?"

Nix shivered and looked away. "No. And thank goodness. I've never even run into her, since I never left the Fae plane growing up. I've heard stories about her, though. She's one of the most powerful and dangerous sea witches out there. You've heard the phrase, be careful what you wish for? Well, that phrase came into existence because of her."

"Please don't tell me you're actually thinking of looking for her." Ever grimaced.

Mina stayed quiet and decided not to answer. It seemed like Nix wasn't the person to ask to help with her personal quest.

"I was just wondering," Mina added when he wouldn't stop staring at her. After his pointed stare finally dropped away, Mina relaxed in her bed. She had quite a few hours before she'd head to the pier to see if Nan had gotten her message.

If she hadn't made it, Mina would have to wait until morning. She'd rather do that on the ship than to traipse about San Francisco, though. She didn't want any nasty surprises from Teague or his fun friends, as in Claire or Temple.

Unlike last night, the soft swaying of the ship on the water and the heat were actually making Mina sleepy right then. Maybe the stress was wearing her down, but she had the time, so she decided to close her eyes for just a few minutes.

Twenty-Eight

They were in a car. Mina couldn't see much in her dream, but she could see that Brody was driving, and it was daylight. Nan set down her cell phone and looked over at Brody.

"You wouldn't believe who that was."

"Mina?" he asked hopefully.

Nan started to tear up and nodded. "Yes! After weeks of nothing, we finally hear from her."

"Does she want us to come back? Is it safe to bring Charlie home?" Brody glanced at Nan and then refocused on the road.

Nan peeked into the back seat where Charlie was fast asleep in what looked like a bed of comics. Mina could just make out a white bag with golden arches.

"No Brody, it's not safe. It's was a warning. He's coming for us."

"Well, what do we do? She must have given us some instructions other than that."

Nan bit her lip and pulled out a map out of the glove compartment. "She studied it for a second. We need to get off of this exit here and take this interstate south. If we hurry, we can get there by tomorrow night."

"Are you sure about this, Nan?" he reached out to cup her cheek. "You trust this message? It could be a trap." The look he gave her was one of affection, and Mina only felt the slightest bit hurt.

Nan covered Brody's hand against her face and threaded her fingers through his, bringing it down to her lap. "Positive. That was Mina. She even spoke in code. Not very good code, but there were enough clues that only she would have known. We're going to San Francisco."

"That's hours away!"

"Then we better start driving."

Brody adjusted the rearview mirror. "You're sure we're no longer safe?"

"Not on our own anymore. We need Mina."

"Then we'll go." Gravel crunched under his tires as he pulled the car over. He waited for traffic to pass and then did a U-turn.

Nan gazed fondly at sleeping Charlie. "Did you hear that, bud?" she whispered. "We're going to find your sister."

Mina woke up to the swaying of the boat. Ever and Nix had left, and she was the only one sleeping. She carefully crawled out of the hammock and placed her feet on the floor. If she could believe her dreams, then Nan had gotten her message, and they were on their way. But how long before they made it here? It would help if she had a clue whether the dream was of the future or the past. She rubbed her temples to try to make sense of it.

Her stomach growled, and she realized it had been a while since she had eaten real food. She went above deck and saw that most of the sirens were diving off the ship into the water. Kino appeared to be hosting a contest.

Ever sat as judge, calling out scores for each of the participants. Kino went to the side rail and did a forward somersault.

"Nine!" Ever yelled.

Nix was up next. He crawled onto the railing, turned to face her, and blew her a kiss. He jumped and executed a backward tuck, his head just missing the railing.

Ever jumped up and cheered when he appeared above the water. "Ten, ten, ten!"

"Maybe I need to flirt with the judge more." Kino laughed and flicked water at Nix.

A shadow passed over Mina.

"You've seen him, your brother, in your dreams," Winona said from a few steps above her, her arm wrapped around Ternan's waist. "I can tell. You seemed more relaxed."

"Yes, they're coming. I don't know when, but they're coming."

Ternan answered, "Which means they may lead trouble right to us."

"Well, what would you have me do?"

"Nothing," Ternan said. "We wouldn't have it any other way. We can handle trouble, but I think you need to start figuring out your gifts with your grandmother now, while I show these guppies how it's done." He grinned, pulled off his blue jacket, tossed the hat to the ground, and jumped up on the railing.

All of the jostling and cheering and calls stopped, everyone's eyes on the King of the Sirens. Ternan raised his hands above his head, the scars even lighter than the siren tattoos on his tanned arms in the sunlight.

Mina let out a sound of surprise as the ship shifted on the water and rose high into the air, creating an even greater distance to the water.

Ternan rose to his tiptoes, bent his knees, and jumped into the air, doing a reverse three-and-a-half somersault with a half twist.

"Show off," Winona chuckled and nudged Mina in the arm. "Do you want to have a try?"

Mina shook her head violently. "No, I've had enough of the water."

Her grandmother frowned. "It seems you've been dark water bitten."

"What?"

"It means you have a fear of deep water."

"Well, you're probably right. The last few times I've had to swim underwater have been traumatizing."

"Maybe one day you'll get over your fear."

"Maybe."

"So tell me what you've been experiencing or what you can do so far."

"I'm not sure exactly what I'm able to do. Most of the things I've ever done have been on accident or tied to extreme heightened emotion. I caused a car accident, shifted or changed items, created the Grimoire, and took control of the mind of a giant. Charlie, who never spoke until Mom died, all of a sudden can open his mouth and cause mass destruction. My gifts seem to be a mess."

"Well, the two of you have very different gifts—but important ones. Charlie's gift is very rare—it's known as the call. When angry or afraid, a siren who has this gift can open his mouth and destroy whole ships with the vibration of his vocal chords alone. We usually try not to have more than one calling siren in a group at any one time. For instance, Kino is the only siren on this ship that has the power to call. Any more than that, and if tempers flared, we'd be adrift at sea. Now, mind you, we are creatures of the sea, but we enjoy riding in a grand Fae vessel."

"That makes sense." Mina chuckled. Just because she had legs and could do it, didn't mean she would walk across the United States on foot.

"You, my dear, have what's known as the lure. It's one of the most dangerous and volatile gifts."

Goosebumps ran up her arms. "How so?"

"Most sirens have a smidge of the lure. They're able to sing and control non-sirens or trick their minds, but not like you can. You actually summon the Fae magic to do your bidding, and you use its allure on others. Your gift is tied to your emotions, so if it's not properly reined in, you'll find yourself affecting the world around you just by your own thoughts and desires. You're even more powerful if you're around water or rain. The magic listens, and things happen."

"Yes," Mina answered. "My jealousy caused my friend to die in car accident."

"It can push your deepest desires into being."

Heartbroken, Mina wondered again if that's what she had done with Brody. Had she been so infatuated with him that she pushed him into falling in love with her? Yes, she could blame Teague for the first time, because he was intent on making her follow the Story quests to a T.

But what about the other times, when Brody'd lose his memories but then be drawn to her? Was she making him obsess about her?

"I suddenly don't feel very good." Mina had to go find somewhere to sit, which happened to be the deck steps.

"Oh Mina, it's okay. We've all done things that we regret, but it may be what has kept you alive. If Teague is so filled with hate toward you, maybe your gift is also what kept him infatuated with you. Thank the stars that you sympathize with him a little, because he seems to be reluctant to harm you."

"But what if I've been doing this since the beginning? What if I made Teague fall in love with me, like I did Brody? What if I doomed myself?"

"Don't be so hard on yourself. I don't think you've given your own charming self enough credit." She tapped Mina's wrists. "You were shackled and your powers bound while in the palace. If you felt any kindness or compassion toward him in those circumstances, then you can believe what you felt was real."

A rush of relief ran through her. There were moments.

Yes. Moments when she felt a tug at her heart and could see the softening of Teague's eyes. And she hadn't imagined the time when he almost kissed her. So, despite her own misgivings, a real connection did exist between them. More connection than Winona realized.

"So what do I do now?"

"Well, I think you know what you're capable of, so it's just practicing to see if you can get it under control and make it work when you're not angry, threatened, or scared."

"Okay, give me something."

"You said you've changed your appearance before. Change it again. Most Fae are capable of a simple glamour. Let's see yours."

Mina tried to relax and clear her mind. She could do this—she had to.

She concentrated on her pants, ones from her mother's trunk. She didn't really want to change or alter them—she liked them the way they were, but she needed to practice on something. Picturing them as a deep blue instead, she felt Fae power rush to her. Her fingers tingled, and the hair on the back of her arms rose. When she opened her eyes, her pants were blue. She grinned in triumph at Winona.

"Good. But clothes are one thing. Can you change your hair, your face?"

"Why would I want to?"

"What if you had to go into hiding, and your life depended on it?"

"Point taken."

Winona took a small seashell out of her pocket and waved her hand over it, turning it into a seashell-shaped compact mirror. She opened the mirrored shell and handed it to Mina. "Now try your hair."

How many times had Mina stared in the mirror at her plain brown hair and boring eyes and wished for something different? But now, given the chance, she wasn't sure she wanted to change.

"How about blonde?" Mina tried to imagine Nan's blonde locks on her head. The power came again willingly, rushing to her and almost overwhelming her, but it disappeared just as fast as it came.

Mina held the mirror up to her face and frowned. It was the same face, the same color of hair. "What did I do wrong?"

"Nothing I can tell," Winona answered. "Try again, just so I can be sure."

"Okay." Once again Mina pictured in her mind what she wanted and tried to imagine the color change. This time, she imagined her hair in a braid. She pulled the mirror up a second time and saw her hair in a braid, but it was the same boring brown.

"What's going on?" Mina asked. "Am I broken?"

"Hmm." Winona picked up a strand of Mina's hair and rubbed it between two fingers. "It seems you're already wearing a glamour, and a very strong one at that."

"What? That's not possible. I've looked like this my whole life. I have pictures to prove it."

"Yes, but remember that you're part-siren and part-human. Your siren side is being suppressed. Maybe concentrate on revealing your true self."

Doubt flooded Mina. She didn't know if she wanted anymore surprises. She wasn't ready to lose more of herself to the Fae world. Her appearance was the one thing that never changed. If she lost that, she'd see a stranger in the mirror. She couldn't do that.

But then she thought of someone *else* putting a glamour over her and changing the way she looked, making it so when she looked in the mirror, what she saw was a lie.

That infuriated her. How dare someone alter her, change her, do something to her without her consent? Mina let her anger boil over, felt the onslaught of power, and let it burn outward. She envisioned the lie burning away with siren fury.

The truth!

I want the truth, to see myself for who I truly am. She heard Winona gasp, and Mina looked up and wiped the stray angry tear out of her eye.

"What?"

"It worked." Winona's words made her shiver in fear.

"Is it bad?" She felt like a child asking.

Her grandmother covered her mouth, her own tears pouring forth. "No. You're beautiful."

Mina's skin was tinged with gold along her wrists, more obvious than the other sirens'. She raised the mirror, her hand shaking as she held it to see her reflection. Her skin was a pale white, her nose devoid of freckles. Her lips held more color, and her cheeks had a natural rosiness. Her nose and the shape of her mouth were the same, thank goodness.

But her eyes and hair!

Mina's boring brown hair was longer, fuller, with gold streaks. And her eyes were now filled with glowing flecks of gold. Even her grandmother's eyes weren't as bright as her own.

"Oh, how beautiful. Your mother had red accents and marks. But you're a gold siren—very rare. No wonder your power is so strong. It's a pity you can't shift. You'd have a gold tail. You are a gem, Mina. You're beautiful, and no one can tell you otherwise."

One more glance in the mirror made her cry in relief. She'd been worried that she'd be ugly. How absurd was that? But wasn't it a fear of all teenage girls who'd just been told they were part fish? Mina smiled at that.

"Now see if you can change it back," Winona said kindly.

Mina balked at the idea at first, but she knew it wasn't a demand. Her grandmother wanted to know if she could. It was so freeing to feel that heaviness and self-doubt gone that she didn't want to change. But she did it anyway—for her grandmother.

Mina closed her eyes and concentrated. She felt as if she was being suffocated as the glamour fell over her. How had she not noticed this before?

"Good, now don't be afraid. You can be yourself around us. It's just a useful tool to know when you go around the human plane."

It was such an odd conversation. Mina had been living on the human plane for seventeen years, and she was just *now* learning tools to survive it. She released the glamour and felt the cloying stickiness of it leave her.

Was this what it was like for Ever when she had to hide her wings? No wonder she only hid a part of herself. A glamour was not a comfortable thing to wear.

"Now, I think you have one last thing to work on."

"What's that?"

"Power of suggestion."

She shivered as she remembered the giant. "I'm not real fond of doing that."

"But you need to, so you can replicate it again." Winona called out over her shoulder. "Kino!"

Ternan heard his wife call and came over with Kino, who bounded up and paused as he laid eyes on Mina. "Oh, Mother of the Sea, please tell me I can marry her."

Mina blushed, and Ternan whacked Kino in the arm. "That's my granddaughter, you sea slug"

Kino blushed and tried to dodge another attack by Ternan.

"Kino, Mina has had a chance to get to know you, and I'd like your permission for her to try and control your mind."

Kino swallowed nervously. "But we haven't even courted yet."

"Kino." Ternan warned. "He's just teasing, Mina."

"Why Kino?" Mina asked them. "You said he was strong. Maybe I should start with someone else."

"*Because* he's strong," Winona said. "Ternan and I will be here to watch over the two of you."

"Okay." Mina looked up at Kino who ran his hands through his dreadlocks, making the water run from them. He crossed his arms and eyed her, challenging her to do her worst.

She looked into Kino's brown speckled eyes and glanced at the darker brown siren marks across his arms. She met his eyes and tried to command him to clap his hands.

She stared at him, and he just smirked.

"Nuh-uh, sea princess. I'm not so easily controlled."

That was right. Mina remembered. Giants were relatively dumb and hard to control. A virile young siren, one of the strongest, would be a little harder. She focused on what she wanted and thought she saw his hands flinch, but he just reached up and scratched his arm instead.

Oh bother.

"Have you gotten tired already? Am I too strong?" He flexed his muscles at her, and she grew irritated. "Maybe you need to go take a nap."

"Oh, go jump in the ocean!" Mina snapped.

She watched in surprise as the smile fell from his face. His eyes took on a hint of golden glow, he climbed the railing, and he jumped in.

"Uh, Mina, you need to tell him to swim out now. You can't give an order without clear directions."

"Oh right." She ran to the rail and saw that he'd sunk beneath the water. She couldn't see him. He was too far down.

"Swim! Come back to me," she demanded. A few seconds later, Kino's head popped above the surface, and he swam back and quickly crawled up the rope ladder.

Mina stepped away from him and had to break eye contact as she worked on releasing him. It took a few deep breaths before his eyes returned to their natural color.

"I could have killed you."

"Naw, I'm a siren. I can breathe underwater."

"But what if I told you not to?"

Kino's brown eyes went wide. "Well, um, yeah. Don't do that."

"I won't." Mina looked at the sky and saw that the sun was setting. "I probably need to go and wait at our spot in case Nan and Charlie get there."

"Don't let her go alone. We've been here too long in one spot. She'll need a guard." Ternan gave a look to Kino.

"Got it. I'll grab Reef and Genni." Kino took off, and a few minutes later returned with two more sirens, plus Nix and Ever. Reef was tall and slender with bright blue eyes and blue highlights and marks. Genni was short with red hair and warm honey-yellow eyes and marks, very catlike in appearance.

Ever and Nix had plenty to say about Mina's natural look, and, after a few barbs, they quieted their jokes. Their comments didn't faze her. Still, Mina worked to replace her glamour. It flowed over her easily. As she worked the illusion, so did the others. Genni's hair and eyes became dull, Reef's bright blue eyes turned a dark blue, and his highlights faded and disappeared. Their clothes shifted into casual shorts and plain shirts.

Mina led the way off the docks and down to the pier. It was weird to be flanked by her guard. With the addition of three extra guards, Ever and Nix seemed to be even more on edge. Ever was making sure she stayed on Mina's right to prove that she was serious in her duties as Godmother.

Mina slowed when they got to the meeting spot and stayed back, hanging out of the way as she watched the people coming and going. She had to tell Kino, Reef, and Genni to relax, because their serious facial expressions were too noticeable.

Kino relayed the plight of the animals in the aquarium, and Reef and Genni were appropriately appalled. Mina caught them whispering to each other and shooting looks in the direction of the aquarium. They were plotting something, but she didn't know what. Every part of her wanted to walk over and confront them, but now wasn't the time. Too many people were watching them.

"It could just be their natural good looks that shine through despite their glamour. Something about them still has that otherworldly feel," Ever whispered.

Even getting there early, Mina had them wait for an hour and a half. "I guess they aren't here yet. We'll come back tomorrow morning. I can't stay here any longer and draw more attention, or Teague will find me."

As they were walking back, the sun was finally setting, and Nix stopped to stare at the water. Ever noticed and asked him what was wrong.

"I don't know. I just feel unsettled."

"What do you mean?" Mina asked.

"Well, when I was a nixie, I could always tell when other water beings were around. It's sort of like that but different. I think it's that I'm on the human plane, and it feels different." He stopped and looked out across the water to stare at a stone building on an island. "I'm sure it's nothing, but that place is really giving me the heebie-jeebies."

Mina followed his gaze and realized he was pointing to the famous prison turned landmark.

Alcatraz.

Twenty-Nine

"Alcatraz." Mina pondered the word and eyed the prison again. It was surrounded by water. It would be the perfect hiding place for a sea witch. Especially one bold enough to change her name to an anagram of Alcatraz. It was her calling card. Anyone clever enough could find her.

Taz Clara resided on Alcatraz.

This time, it was Mina who stopped moving along the pier. Ever had to grab her arm and pull her along. Could it be? What were the chances that destiny would bring her to the doorstep of the very banished sprite? She couldn't let the opportunity pass her by, though she doubted that Winona or Ternan would let her go. They wouldn't risk losing her, so how else would she make it there if not on her own?

Back on the ship, the island wouldn't leave her mind. No matter what she did, she found her eyes straying to the water. When it was time to sleep, she continued to lie there with her eyes open, staring at the wall and the swaying hammocks.

She judged it to be around two a.m. when she slowly slid out of her hammock and tiptoed above deck. She paused and saw that there were two sirens on guard. Her palms were sweaty. She waited for the tall male siren to walk past and slowly stepped in front of him.

She pushed all of her will on him. "You never saw me. Go about your duty, but you don't see me."

She waited, holding her breath. After a moment, his eyes and face relaxed, and he walked past her. She sighed, slipped down the gangplank, and made her way over to the other side of the pier. Her plan was to try and steal a boat to make her way out to the prison, but she saw someone moving through the darkness on the pier. She froze until she recognized the silhouette.

It was Kino.

The way he was slinking made her suspicious, so she followed him. Sure enough, Kino made his way back to the aquarium, and two others joined him in the darkness— Reef and Genni. Kino went to the back door and, with a small inaudible bark, blasted the double doors off of the frames. Alarms rang out, and all three ran inside the building.

Mina rolled her eyes and went charging after them. Kino split off from the other two. Mina followed him as he went through the back storage areas and made it to the front of the exhibits.

"Don't worry, my friends, I'll have you free." Kino opened his mouth and a high pitch came forth making the closest exhibit explode. The saltwater flowed forth, bringing a school of jellyfish toward Mina's feet. She tried to get out of the way for fear of being stung.

"Kino, stop!" Mina called. "You can't do this."

The male siren turned to stare at her. His eyes were filled with pain. "I can't let them live like this. They need to be free. No one should live as a prisoner. No one." He whispered the last two words.

"I know this is hard for you. I understand, but this isn't your world. There are rules to follow. You can't just come into a place and start blowing it up." She tried to speak calmly, despite the blaring alarm.

Kino ignored her and moved over to the largest tank. Inside, she could see the sharks swimming in frenzied circles, upset by the sound and the vibration of the last blast. He laid his hands against the glass and placed his forehead against it. "They're so beautiful."

"And deadly. Please, step away from the glass. The police are on their way, and if we don't leave, we'll be arrested."

"I'd like to see them try. I'm too strong for them." He smirked. But when he faced her, his smile fell again. "Can you not hear their cries to be free?"

Mina tried to listen, but her head was pounding. "No, I don't hear anything."

"That's because you're not trying."

"I *am* trying."

He didn't seem to believe her and stepped away from the glass. More sharks came, now extremely interested in Kino's movements. Maybe he could hear them, but she couldn't let him continue.

Kino turned to the smaller aquariums, and he blasted out the glass. Small turtles and frogs fell to the floor. Mina didn't think Kino had a strategy, he was too emotional—endangering the creatures more than he was helping them. She was grateful that—at least—he was attacking in bursts, so he wouldn't bring the whole building down around them.

Mina had made it past the jellyfish and followed him down the hall until he stood inside the giant aquatic tube. He stared up in awe at the thousands of gallons of water surrounding him, confused at what he was walking through.

"Kino, stop right now. We have to leave."

"This isn't just a game anymore, Princess," he said. "I have a duty to let them free." He lifted his hands, and his mouth opened to let out a loud piercing shriek.

Mina covered her ears and fell to her knees in pain. She watched in horror as spider like cracks ran up the sides of the tubes. Pain wracked her brain, and she had to grit her teeth and force herself to get up and run toward Kino, but her equilibrium was off. She couldn't walk without stumbling. Rivulets of water ran down the tunnel and started to soak the carpet. How long before it gave out and crushed them? "You're being selfish, Kino. Please. Another day, another time, but you are jeopardizing the whole reason we came here, and that was to stay low and find my brother."

She could read all of the emotions plane as day across his face, and she knew he was struggling internally. She didn't blame him for his need to free the animals of the sea. She just faulted his methods and timing.

He released another almost inaudible yell, and her head throbbed.

The crack along the tube got longer. Her shoes were now soaked, and the carpet made squishing noises as she moved closer to him.

Mina pushed her panic aside and used her fury to thrust her will upon him. He didn't think she could do it again? Well, he was wrong. "You will stop!"

Kino stopped his piercing yell, and his hands fell to his sides. She could see the golden glow in his eyes. "Make your way back to the ship now, and wait below deck for Ternan and Winona. You will tell them what you've done."

He struggled against her. She watched as he tried to fight her power of suggestion. Before, he'd been willing to let her use it on him. This time it was a struggle, but she wasn't going to let up. She felt power rush to her, and she pushed everything she had into her words. "Obey me."

His back stiffened, and he turned and walked out of the room.

Mina collapsed on the ground and gently touched her ears. Small trails of blood had eked out, but it was worse than that.

Over the pain in her ears, Mina heard the distinct sound of cracking.

"Oh no!" She darted out of the tube just as it broke, and thousands of gallons of water filled the walkway behind her.

She ran down the hall, overcome with rushing water. She fought to get her head above water. Just as she regained her footing, something large knocked her into the wall. Mina screamed when she realized it was a shark, but the shark wasn't interested in her. It was going with the flow of water. Thankfully, she hadn't been directly under the aquarium when it broke. Still, while the water pulled at her feet and pushed her head forward, she wondered if she'd make it to the exit.

Chanda Hahn

She slipped, fell, and climbed back to her feet only to be knocked over again. Then the water picked her up and carried her right out the double doors. Mina found herself in the middle of the dock, looking up at the night sky, alit with flashing red and blue lights.

Someone picked Mina up by her forearms and dragged her through the water. Her brown hair was wrapped around her face, and she didn't fight the helping hands. Until she felt cold steel handcuffs placed around her wrists.

"What? No. I didn't do this." She tried to swing her head to brush the hair out of her eyes, but it clung to her face like tentacles. An uncaring female police officer shoved her forward.

The fire department and police rushed toward the building but stepped back when a shark made its appearance flipping and flopping along the deck. They had their hands full. Mina wasn't given a chance to explain as the female cop pushed her along, away from the others. *Hmm. Something feels off.*

When they walked past the cruisers and continued, that confirmed it. The woman kept silent, despite Mina's attempts at small talk. When they passed a store front window, she caught a glimpse of her captor, and her heart stopped in her chest. It was Claire.

"Claire! No, stop!" Mina reared back and fought the witch.

By now they were out of sight of help, and Claire turned, reaching for Mina's sopping wet head. "Should have known you were part Fae. Otherwise you'd never have beaten me." She laughed, and Mina felt herself start to suffocate.

258

How did they know she was Fae? She could breathe, but everything felt heavy, and her limbs wouldn't obey. She slid to the ground and noticed a dark form move out of the alley. Grey Tail.

"We have permission to kill her, right?" Grey Tail asked, his voice gruff. He still wore his black leather vest, and the wolf tattoo stood out as a taunt across his chest.

"Yes, we're supposed to kill her before he comes for her."

Wait. They're not here because of Teague?

"We need to move her farther away. There's enough Fae magic in the air, I can smell it for miles. It will attract unwanted attention." Grey Tail looked nervous and kept sniffing.

"You're right for once. We can't stay here." She pulled Mina roughly along.

The cuffs dug into her wrists, making her wince. As they walked, the police uniform slowly faded from Claire's form until she was in a skirt and her signature red heeled shoes. Her face was younger, proving she had been stealing the youth from others.

Mina tried to keep her head low as she gathered power to her. She had to try and control both of them *before* they caught on.

Grey Tail froze and looked at her, his nose sniffing the air, while Mina pushed at his mind, her arms tingling, the hair on the back of her neck telling her she was ready to attack. As She pushed toward Grey Tail, she felt Claire's hand on her head again. Her power was quickly siphoned off. Mina gasped for breath again, and she clutched at her chest.

"Keep it up, child. Grey Tail can smell magic, and you can't use it on me. All I have to do is keep draining you, and soon I'll drain you dead. You don't have a magic book this time. Let's see how you fare against me now."

If only Claire wasn't so close to her. If she could get away, maybe she'd have a fighting chance.

They kept hurrying her along the pier, and Mina only had one last idea. Maybe she could slowly pull enough power and not direct it at her captors but somewhere else, like a beacon for help.

Mina closed her eyes and felt the power tickle her fingers. She tried to keep it at bay and not let it rush to her. She pushed the power out and away from her with one intentional command.

Help me.

Claire and Grey Tail stopped by an abandoned building along the pier, far away from the flashing lights but still close to the water. Grey Tail ran his clawed hand along her cheek and tapped his nails against her skin.

"Very pretty. I can't wait to rip it to shreds."

Mina tried to stare him down and not show him how terrified she really was. Claire's phone beeped with an incoming text. Mina ignored Grey Tail and looked to Claire. She flipped her phone open and spoke in another language, quick and direct.

She turned with a scowl. "We have to wait. They want to be here to see her die."

"Who?" Mina asked, irritated that she couldn't face her enemy.

Was this the same person in the cloak who sent the trees to attack her? It certainly seemed, as she thought back, that there were some attempts on her life that had nothing to do with Teague. She was tired of playing hide–and-seek.

"Someone that you've ticked off. Apparently you stole something that belonged to them, and now you have to pay." Claire had leaned down to look her in her face. "Really, I was glad to take the job. You've been nothing but a problem for me since you walked into my factory. Now I'm free from one prison but stuck in another—servitude to the Fae Prince—but there's no reason I can't do a few odd jobs."

Claire's phone beeped, and she looked at the incoming text. Her face broke into a grin. "Never mind. The boss isn't coming, and the others don't care. We can kill you now."

Grey Tail made an excited snuffing noise, and Mina pushed out harder with her power, hoping someone would answer. But then Grey Tail's head cocked to the side, and he slowly turned toward her, eyes dilating.

"She's using magic again," he sneered.

Claire reached out and grabbed her arm roughly. "You think you're so smart? There's no one to save you now." Claire reached for Mina's head and began to drain her.

Horrible pain ran through her gut. This was what it had been like for Nan, although Nan was unconscious. Mina's head flopped to the side, and she called and called and called—weaker each time—in a final, desperate plea for help. Her eyes fell across the dock to the water, which was bubbling and moving.

Something large rose up out of the water. Riding the wave, it stepped onto the pier, its dark green hair braided. The light green skin almost glowed in the moonlight as the sea witch raised her hands and commanded the wave beneath her to rush over Claire, Mina, and Grey Tail. Mina had only a moment's notice. But that was time enough to prepare for the rush of water that flowed over her. She held her breath.

The wave moved like a living, breathing thing. It wrapped around Claire and Grey Tail and pulled them kicking and screaming back into the water as it receded into the ocean. Mina saw the green feet walk close to her face as she slowly closed her eyes for what she hoped wasn't the last time.

Thirty

Mina woke, surrounded by darkness and a very damp smell. It took a bit for her eyes to adjust, but she realized she lay on a makeshift bed in a cave. Soft glowing stones lined the wall, and Mina could make out a dark figure shucking oysters.

The sea witch. Mina watched her, wary but interested. There could only be one sea witch in the immediate area.

"Are you Taz Clara?"

The witch turned her black eyes on Mina. Her hair was just as dark as Nix's mother—the only other sea witch she'd ever run into.

Mina expected to feel intense hatred and anger roll off of her like it had with Nix's mother, but she didn't. Annoyance certainly, but she didn't feel in immediate danger.

"I am Taz Clara, and I don't like being compelled by anyone to do their bidding. Even if it's you, Mina Grimm."

"You know my name?" she said in disbelief.

"Of course I know your name. Do you not think I would know the person who started it all? I lost my position as a maidservant because I tried to save the prince's soul, and it didn't turn out the way the Fates wanted it. Still, it was my best work, and I'm proud of it. And here you are, wanting to undo it."

"I'm sorry. I didn't know."

"For great magic to work, there have to be rules set in place. Most everything done can be undone."

"Does that include the poisoned knife?"

Taz laughed. "Ah, now the real questions start. You could have called for the sirens to come and help you, but no… you had to raise Taz from her nice warm bed to be at your beck and call. And now you expect me to help you again? I think not."

"Thank you for coming to my rescue." Mina briefly wondered if Claire and Grey Tail had lived through it. But with Taz's mood, it didn't seem like the smartest idea to keep bringing up Teague, so Mina moved on to another line of questioning.

"How come you're not evil? I thought nixies become evil after they change, or do you prefer to be called a sprite?"

"You just found out you're Fae, and now you think you know everything."

"No, I realize how little I actually know, which is why I'm asking questions—so I can learn. I'm friends with a nixie, and he was scared of turning."

Taz's eyes took on a faraway look. "Yes, I faced the same dilemma: lose my connection with water and die or start killing and feeding on others. But I found a way around it. I don't have to kill and feed on lives; I can feed

on fears. I lived quite happily for a while. I even grew close
to the Fates. But after I couldn't save their son, I was
banished, and I came through the gate.

"Here on Alcatraz, there was enough fear, and
there were enough deaths to sustain me. When the prison
closed, I almost gave up and died, but I found the fear of
the tourists can sustain me. I don't go far because of the
danger of becoming hungry and hurting someone. So when
people need my help, they come to me."

"I need your help."

"No," Taz snapped. She moved away from Mina.

"You don't even know what I'm going to ask."

"Yes I do. You want me to help you split the prince
again, so you can be with the one called Jared."

Mina could feel her cheeks heating up.

"Have you not been listening? I was banished
because of you!"

"I fail to see how you being banished had anything
to do with me."

Taz turned her cat-like eyes on Mina, and her face
took on a look of fury. "The Fates came to me for help,
since *I* had succeeded in suppressing my dark nature. We
hoped I could cast the dark, poisoned side of him into an
object. They brought me his journal. How was I to know
that the journal had once been torn in two, and its twin was
on the human plane? That the one I held would mirror the
other?"

"You never meant to split them," Mina said aloud,
feeling as if her heart was breaking.

"No, it was an accident. But a terrible one. The
Fates let me take the blame for all of it. Prince Teague
wasn't as powerful without his other half, but I, still, had

failed in my intent. I don't plan on failing again, because I won't try. I especially will not help *you*. I don't want to be on the dark prince's radar."

"But you've helped so many other people… like my mother."

"And I've gained the anger of all the sirens in the world. I'm done with you and your kin. Be thankful that I helped you on the dock. That is the one and only boon you will ever get from me."

Mina's hands shook in anger. "Then what am I to do?"

"You could kill him," she said, as if it were nothing.

"That's what everyone says," Mina sighed irritably.

"Then why do you keep doubting yourself?"

"I don't want to lose him."

"If you don't, you will lose so much more." Taz spoke knowingly.

Mina's heart broke, and she started to cry. The sea witch came near her and cooed softly. The emotions she'd been holding back for so long poured out easily—her grief, anger, frustration. How dare everyone think that Teague's life didn't matter? Killing him now would be like killing off a part of her soul. She just couldn't do it.

She didn't know how long she'd been crying, but she knew that Taz had sat next to her and wrapped her arm gently around her. She let Mina cry.

"It's okay, my little Grimm Siren. It's okay," she said softly.

When Mina had cried herself out, she looked up and noticed a small tear in Taz Clara's eye. The sea witch wiped at it gently and sniffed. "Those were some of the most powerful emotions I've fed on in a long time."

Mina gasped, and Taz shook her head, tried to calm her down. "No, I didn't pull them from you. I only took what you were willing to give up. With the emotions of a siren and a Grimm, I will not have to feed for a very, very long time."

"Well, I'm sure that was worth something to you then," Mina said indignantly. She shouldn't have fed from her without asking.

The sea witch stood and waved at Mina in irritation. "Fine, I'll grant you a small favor of my choosing. But you must leave and never come back."

She beckoned with her hand and led Mina down a tunnel. Mina felt the press of power as they passed through a veil. They'd stepped out of a wall of rock that hid the entrance to Taz Clara's cave along the rocky shoreline.

It was morning, and fog rolled along the water, making it almost impossible to see anything beyond twenty feet. Somewhere in the distance, a fog horn sounded. The boat was coming closer.

"The morning tours will start soon. You should be able to make your way back on the ferry when they leave."

"Okay, thanks." Mina answered awkwardly and started up the path.

The sea witch's gaze followed her until she turned a corner. She ducked behind the rocks, staying low when the first ferry arrived. When the passengers disembarked and followed the tour guide, Mina tagged along for the two-hour tour. She snuck on the ferry with them at the end.

By the time she landed back at the pier, it was way past the agreed check-in time with Nan. Mina ran the whole way, knowing she would probably miss them, but also that her friends would be looking for her. Even when

Mina got a stitch in her side, she kept on running until she could see the Zoltar machine. A crowd had gathered in front of it, and Mina slowed to see if she could see what they were looking at.

Someone pulled on her arm.

"Hey," she cried, as Ever grabbed her and yanked her aside.

"Where have you been?" Ever yelled.

"Long story. Have you seen Charlie, Nan, and Brody?" Mina tried to pull away from Ever, but the pixie wouldn't let go.

"No, they didn't come," Ever answered. "Ternan and Winona are hysterical looking for you. Kino says something bad happened, and cops have been crawling all over the pier by the aquarium. Talk to me, Mina."

Mina pulled away from Ever and ran toward the machine. It was just a bunch of teenagers, putting money in and getting their fortune cards. She was about to turn away when she saw something that made her blood run cold.

"They were here." Mina jogged over to pick up the Superman action figure she'd shoved into Charlie's back pack. She flipped it over and saw C.G. written in black marker on the red boot.

"Charlie!" Mina rushed into the crowd, searching. "Charlie!"

Ever joined Mina, and they worked their way out in a circle, shouting. Mina spotted Nan's bug by a parking meter and checked out the car, but no one was in it. Just like she'd seen in her dream, though, Charlie's jacket and a bunch of comics covered the back seat.

"Ever, they have to be around here."

"I'll go this way." Ever pointed, taking off down the street and looking in boutiques. Mina ran back toward the gift shop and started to check the stores nearest their meeting point. Maybe they just got tired of waiting. Maybe they stopped for food.

Maybe they were kidnapped by Teague.

Oh, this was all her fault. If only she hadn't had snuck out. She caught a glimpse of a familiar form in the window and stopped. She looked over her shoulder.

No one was there.

Mina continued to search for her brother, but this time she didn't *imagine* seeing Teague. He didn't bother to hide his presence in the reflection of the mirror.

But she pretended she didn't see him and moved along the shops toward the end of the pier. When she got to the end, she waited until she felt the prickle of power. She closed her eyes and turned to face him.

He just stood there. His dark hair looked wet—it could have been gel—his jeans were well fitted, and he wore a homespun black shirt. His choice of clothes felt very Jared to her.

"You came." Mina spoke first. She wanted to try and reason with him, maybe find her friends.

"I did, because you left." His eyes lacked emotion.

Her fear-level rose, and she tried to squelch it. "Against my will."

"That's not what it looks like." He lifted his hands and gestured to the pier. "You seem quite frantic looking for your brother and friends. I wonder where they could have gone."

"Please, I would have stayed. It was my grandfather who took me. He thought he was rescuing me. He didn't understand, even though I tried to explain you'd blame me and try to hurt my brother."

"You're right. I do blame you." He stepped closer to her, his voice tapering off.

"Please, don't hurt them. I'll do anything," she begged.

Teague became irritated. "We've been here before, Mina. I already made a deal with you, and you broke it. I can't trust you."

"Yes, you can."

"You're a liar."

Mina closed her eyes and released the glamour, letting her siren side out. She wanted to see his face, his reaction when he saw her. She wasn't disappointed. He looked surprised, and she saw a hint of a smile at the corner of his mouth.

But what that smile meant was a mystery.

"I'm not lying or hiding anything anymore. You have my mirror. I can't hide from you, so why would I run when I know you'll find me?" This time she stepped toward him, closing the distance.

"Don't think you can use your power on me, because I won't be lured in by your tricks." She took another step closer to him and met his eyes. Finally, she could read the emotions. He was angry enough that he could hurt her, but the way he kept looking at her lips told her he still wanted to kiss her.

Mina had to be careful. She was playing one of the most dangerous games ever. And with the most dangerous opponent.

"Do you have them?" Mina asked softly again.

Teague turned his head and looked across the water, refusing to make eye contact. "Careful, or I'll destroy the whole pier. Shall I do what I did to your school here?"

Mina didn't take the bait. "I don't care about this place. I want to go back with you." She took another step forward and was almost face to face with him. His skin had turned yellowish, his veins dark blue. Annalora had to be right. The tip was working its way toward his heart. He was getting worse.

Now he smirked. "Trying to bargain with me again. That's not going to work. Maybe this will convince you I'm serious." The fog still made it hard to see, but she could hear something. Very loud creaking of metal followed by popping sounds. Horns honked, and then the creak echoed across the water again.

"What is that?"

"The gate. I came through the same one you did."

"But the sirens and the timing...how?"

"The sirens are gone. I had to move the stars and freeze the gate. My army must have finished coming through by now, so I imagine they are destroying it. Here, I'll show you."

Teague waved his hand, and the fog dissipated enough for Mina to see the Golden Gate Bridge bending and torquing as two stone golems attacked it. One worked on the base, bending and pushing the post, while the other stood in the middle of the road causing all of the cars to crash and veer dangerously as it snapped the cables.

"Stop it! People are going to get hurt." *What did he mean the sirens were gone?*

"It's too late for them, Mina. You can't save them all, just like you couldn't save your brother, friend, and boyfriend. But why should you? You always were selfish."

Mina watched as the destruction kept on. A stone golem picked up the nearest car and tossed it into the bay. The fog continued clearing, and she could make out more of his army, of Reapers, giants, and beasts roaming and bashing the hoods of the cars. A bright yellow school bus was trapped on the bridge.

Angry tears flowed, and she turned on him. The Fae power rushed to her—her hair whipped her face, and heat rose to her eyes as the power crackled off of her and she channeled all of it at Teague.

Teague stepped back startled. "Your eyes!" His hand moved to his heart in pain. "Stop it!"

"Call off your army!" she demanded.

"Never!" Teague yelled back, his angry blue eyes glowing with power. He lashed out with a blast and flung Mina against the railing. She lost her focus, the air momentarily knocked from her, and he retaliated again. Another blast of power had her spiraling through the air.

Onlookers screamed as she landed on the pier. Nearby people scattered. Teague roared, and the wood planks began to crack along the pier, separating her from anyone trying to help.

Mina got back up and tried to reach into Teague's mind. Searching, calling for him, for Jared. For the goodness that she knew was still inside of him. When Teague ran toward her, she stood her ground. She needed to get close to him.

Forever

"You are no match for me!" Teague stepped forward. With a wave of his hand, she slid across the pier and under the railing to fall into the bay.

She grabbed the post at the last minute and hung on, her fingers clawing at the post. Her feet dangled twenty feet above the water. Using every ounce of strength she had, she swung her body to the side and got her foot up. Slowly, she pulled herself back onto the pier.

"You're no match for my power, no match for my hate. You are weak," Teague taunted.

"That's where you're wrong." She stood up and wiped her hands on her pants. "You think hate makes you strong, and I understand. But love always wins," Mina answered back. "Jared!" Mina called to him. "I know you're in there."

Teague sneered, and she felt the squeezing pressure around her body as her feet slowly lifted off of the ground. Teague came forward, pulled out the poisoned dagger, and held it up in front of her. "You tried to kill yourself with this and rob me of my victory. I saved you. Now I will finish the job. Only I'll do better than *try*."

Mina struggled to look out across the bay. The golems continued to wreak havoc on the bridge. They were only a few cars away from the bus. *This has gone on too long. If I can't have Jared, I've just got to die and give Teague what he wants. It'll save everyone else.*

Just then, she heard a loud piercing shriek, and one of the stone golems burst into small pebbles. She saw the siren ship and recognized Kino at the bow attacking a third golem who'd appeared in the water. A giant wave surged up and over the bridge. As it passed, it deposited an army of very ticked off sirens. Cars began to rise up out of the water as if on lifts.

Mina knew Ternan and Winona would do their best to fight off Teague's army. But she also knew they were vastly outnumbered. There was only one way to stop this.

She couldn't feel her legs. They had gone numb from Teague's grip on her neck. But she had to fight against his power. As she hung in the air, she gathered all of the love she had—all the feelings and memories of Teague before he was poisoned—and she willed those images into his subconscious. Her memories of Ferah stabbing him, of Mina trying to save him, to close the wound in his chest.

He shook his head and shoved his hands into his hair. "Stop it. It's all lies." The pressure released from her neck, her feet touched the ground, and she sucked in a deep breath.

"No, only truth," she gasped out. "Love always prevails. Good always wins."

Teague turned and this time physically grabbed her by the throat. She slipped and fell backward onto the pier. He landed on top of her, and she tried to push against him, but he was too strong. The knife landed with a thud on the pier next to a piece of broken railing.

Mina used her right hand and scrabbled around trying to find the dagger. In a desperate attempt to stall, she closed her eyes and willed a piece of wood to morph into a decoy dagger. Then she made the dagger look like the broken railing stake. Jared had once shown her that very same trick on a beach.

She turned her head, frantic, and reached for the true dagger. Teague hadn't noticed her switch. He turned, grabbed the fake, and raised it above his head.

"I love you!" she choked out. "I always will."

It was about to come down toward her chest, when with a final lunge, her fingers reached her goal. She closed her eyes. The stake grew hot in her hand, and then it was gone. Disappeared. Morphed back into the dagger of Erjad.

Without hesitation, she thrust the blade upward into Teague's chest. He shuddered, his blue eyes opening wide in pain and then traveling to look at his closed hand. He opened his fist, and the wood shaft fell to the ground.

Mina sobbed as she shoved the knife deep, deeper, until it couldn't go anymore.

Teague's mouth opened and closed, and he reached down to gently touch her face. He didn't look angry. He didn't look full of hate. He looked… relieved.

"I knew you had it in you," he whispered and slowly fell forward.

Mina caught him and helped him onto his back. She leaned down and took his hand in hers. "I didn't want to. I never wanted to kill you. But you've hurt too many people, taken too many lives."

He tried to say something, but it was lost in a scream of pain as the blade, made entirely of hate, began to poison him again.

Desperate, Mina pushed more power into his mind. She searched and called and coaxed. He had to be in there. She imagined it like the dream, different mirrors with different reflections of Teague.

"Don't! Let me be. Let me die in peace," he said, trying to push her hand away.

Mina ignored it and kept holding onto him. "No, I won't give up on you. I won't."

Teague screamed at her, his eyes glowing with hate. He transformed, his mouth turning downward, his hands arching into claws. "Get away! I hate you." Blue veins appeared along his face as the dagger's hate-poison traveled through him, changed him. He gasped, and black blood bubbled up and poured slowly from the corner of his mouth. He grabbed at Mina's hand.

She gripped it tightly. His eyes opened again, and she watched the familiar blue slowly fade to gray.

"Mi…na," he mumbled. "You did what I didn't have the strength to. Thank…" He coughed, and more blood came up. He lost the battle with one last word, whispered across his lips."you."
Grieving, she eased her grip. His hand fell to the ground.

Thirty-One

"I'm sorry, Teague. I'm so sorry. I tried, and now I've lost you."

Mina felt the tingling of an approaching Fae and turned in time to see a wave rise up. The sea witch appeared.

"Aw, a death to feed on." Taz Clara stepped up onto the pier, her green skin slightly glowing, her dark green hair moving on its own.

"No, you can't feed on him," Mina spat. She stood.

The sea witch's face turned ugly. "You don't want to share? You're the one covered in his blood, not me."

"Go away!" Mina said.

"Listen, child, and listen well. Let me feed, and I'll see if I can save a part of him for you."

"You said you wouldn't help me with Teague."

"Not unless you killed him. I am a sea witch after all. I feed on the dead, the dying, and their fears."

"You can save just a part of him?"

"Did I stutter?" She smiled. "I am the most powerful after a death."

"Then save him!"

"How about a please?"

"Please," she added softly and kneeled back down next to Teague.

Taz Clara sighed. "I do owe you a boon after all." She smoothed out her sea green dress and kneeled on Teague's other side. Her mouth opened, and Mina caught a glimpse of sharp, pointy teeth. She almost changed her mind—but the sea witch-sprite didn't bite or tear into Teague. She began to sing.

It wasn't a happy song but a low-pitched song of mourning. Her voice carried across the bay. Time slowed as Mina listened to the haunting song and watched as the sirens battled the giants, ogres, and golems.

One of the giants picked up an abandoned truck and threw it at the ship. Kino blasted the truck mid-air. It exploded into smaller pieces, still hitting the ship but causing less damage. Mina saw someone or something flying along the bridge, leading a mass of people away from the army. Ever had revealed her wings to the world. Compared to the beasts behind them, she probably looked like a guardian angel.

The Coast Guard had shown up. They were trying to shoot the giants, but bullets kept bouncing off their thick skin. Another stone golem appeared out of the water, picked up a passing fishing boat, and launched it across the air. The crew on the US Coast guard ship dove overboard just as the boat crashed into their deck. An explosion followed, and Mina turned her head to protect her eyes from the blast.

Teague was dead. This should have stopped. Why were they still fighting? Mina had to do something. She looked over just as Taz stopped singing and lifted Teague's wrist, bending her mouth to it.

Mina couldn't stay and watch. She could do nothing more for Teague, but she could do something to help the others. She weighed her options, looked once more at Teague and Taz, and back to Ever at the bridge. Then, she took off running.

Mina had to tread carefully over the broken boards and walk along holding the handrails. When she got to the street, she waved down a passing car and leaned into the passenger window.

"I need to get to the bridge," Mina commanded. But when she saw a small child in the back, she quickly told the woman to go home by another route.

She waved down a white van. The driver was a heavyset guy, probably in his late forties. "I need to get to the bridge."

"That's where I'm headed. I hear there's a Godzilla-type-thing destroying it. Hop in."

She jumped in and held on as he drove crazily, weaving in and out of traffic. He ran two red lights as he made his way to the bridge. When he got as close as he could before being stopped by the police, he pulled over, jumped out, and opened up the back.

That was when Mina saw the camera gear and paid closer attention to the signage on the van. She'd gotten in a news cameraman's van.

"You can't video this," Mina begged.

"Are you kidding me? How can I not? This footage will be the start of a new career. I'll be famous."

She touched the camera and willed a flare of power into it. It sparked and caught fire.

"Ow, what'd you do?" He dropped the camera to the ground, reached in for a fire extinguisher.

"Sorry!" Mina called over her shoulder, as she ran past the police tape.

No one tried to stop her from going in, because the police were so busy rescuing people from the bridge.

Mina was exhausted, darting left and right of abandoned cars. She made it past the school bus, grateful to see it was finally deserted.

She found a metal pipe on the road and held it between her hands. Concentrating, she felt the power flare up. She turned it into a glowing sword just as a troll attacked.

Mina screamed and swung blindly at the troll's midsection. She let loose her power and—as she let the grief of Teague's death wash over her—the power eked through her skin.

She swung again at the troll. This time, he howled in pain and jumped off the bridge to avoid another onslaught from her. She turned to the next opponent— another smaller troll. On and on she fought, clearing a path until she got to the middle.

It seemed the advance charge from the sirens had stopped. Kino was on defense now, fighting off projectile attacks. Her grandparents and half the sirens were diving under water and doing their best to rescue people from the sunken cars.

Which were *still* being tossed from the bridge by one of the giants.

At the center, she realized there were too many. Fae were still pouring through the gate, more than just the strongest of Teague's army who had come through on small boats and vessels. This was a different army, more human-looking with tanned skin and angry eyes. Familiar, but Mina couldn't place who they were or why they would attack.

She had to stop the giants and the stone golem.

Ever waved and flew past her, knocking into a Fae wolf who looked a bit like Lonetree. He flailed and hit the water. He started to swim toward the land, but a siren pulled him beneath the water. Bubbles surfaced for a moment, then stopped.

Mina's stomach rolled. It would only get worse if she couldn't stop this.

"Mina!" Nix slid over the hood of a car to get to her. "Catch!" He tossed her journal to her, and Mina caught it mid-air. Her used-to-be notebook of Unaccomplishments and Epic Disasters. Now, leather bound and ready for action.

"Nix!" Mina looked down at her book and smiled.

"Yeah, I thought you might want that. If today isn't a day to use it, I don't know what is." He winked.

"Stand back." She waved them away.

"What's your plan?" Ever said as she flew around a nearby car.

"Ever, I thought I told you to get back!"

"And when have I ever listened to you?"

"I listen to her," Nix answered from the other side of Mina. "Just not this time. And yeah, what she said. What's the plan?"

"My plan is to not have a plan."

"I'm down with that." Nix pulled up short when they confronted the stone golem. "Except for now. Now, I think a plan would be dandy."

"Well, anyone know how to weaken a golem, so I can capture him in the Grimoire?" Mina asked.

"Water. No, fire… I think," Nix answered.

"Which is it?" Mina sang out as the golem turned and noticed the three teens standing below him on the bridge.

"Fire!" Nix yelled.

"Got it!" Mina turned the book into a large, flaming fireball, which she sent shooting directly at the golem's eyes. It roared in distress as it fell backward onto the cars, which rolled right off the broken bridge through the railings it had destroyed. The splash reached them on the bridge, soaking them.

Kino was there to meet the golem and introduce him to his powerful siren gift. A few seconds later, the golem was more debris littering the San Francisco Bay.

"One done, a hundred to go!" Nix marked an imaginary line in the air.

Ever rolled her eyes and said, "We can't take them on one at a time. Where are the Godmothers when you need them?"

"That's what you're for, remember?" Nix called out jokingly. "You always said you were worth a hundred Godmothers."

"You're right, Nix." Ever's shoulders went rigid as she took a deep breath. "I am."

She flew straight and true toward the mass of the army. Her fluttering wings created a wave of blue and purple in her wake. Above the army, she began to fly in circles. Round and round she flew, and blue pixie dust fell from her wings toward the army of Fae warriors climbing onto the bridge.

Mina waited, confused, as the first one playfully jabbed the second and laughed. Then the other one started laughing. One after another, the Fae stopped fighting and started rolling on the ground in hysterics.

Ever flew back, her face flushed with excitement. "Can you do anything now?"

"Yeah, the laughter is making them vulnerable." Mina rushed forward and held open her Grimoire.

The pages began to glow, and light burst from within, covering the Fae army in a gold aura. The book lifted out of Mina's hands, and she stepped back. The laughing army cried out in fear as they were dragged into the pages of the book. Trapped forever.

"Wow, Ever, who are you and where did you come from?" Nix looked amazed.

"I'm a pixie, you nitwit, and my gift just happens to be joy." She grumbled at him and punched him in the arm. "Don't you ever, ever tell *anyone*, or I swear I will send you to your grave."

He only grabbed her around the waist to bring her near. "So, Miss Pixie-of-Joy, am I going to die laughing?"

"Nix!" Ever growled and stomped on his toe.

"Ow, okay, okay. Your secret's safe with me," he mumbled as he jumped up and down on one foot. "If anyone asks, you're an irritable tyrant."

Nix covered his ears and looked around in panic. Mina didn't hear anything at first, and then her skin crawled as she heard the haunting whistle.

Just across the expanse of the gaping hole in the bridge, yards away, the Death Reaper with chin-length black hair stood beside the driver's door.

Mina's heart seized. The Reaper disappeared.

283

Then she heard the click of the omen's claws on the hood of a nearby Chevy Impala.

Mina stood there facing her doom. With Teague gone, she almost felt a sense of relief that it would all be over. But then she remembered Charlie.

"No!" Mina tried to send a full blast of her siren power at the dog. It phased right through him.

"You can't, Mina." Ever answered her question before she even spoke. "He's dead. Nothing can stop it. I don't even think the Grimoire can."

"Run!" Nix yelled. He tried to place himself in front of Mina to block the omen.

She didn't need any more prodding. She turned and ran, and she heard the sound of Nix screaming as the omen attacked.

"Nix!" Ever yelled.

"Get her out of here," Nix commanded. He tried to hold onto the dog.

Ever grabbed Mina under the arms and flew up in the air. Mina looked down and saw Nix lose his grip. He fell, struggling under the large black beast. He kept his arms up to protect his face, but its teeth and claws tore at his chest.

Come on. Come on. You want me not him. The farther away they could get, the sooner he'd give chase.

She heard a howl of pursuit, and the dog was after them again. She tried to look past her feet dangling in the air above the roofs of the cars, but was unable to see what had become of Nix. She prayed he was okay.

Something wet landed on her cheek, and Mina first thought it was rain, but then she looked up and saw Ever's face, wet with tears. Another one fell on Mina's shoulder.

They heard a growl beneath them, and Mina instinctively pulled her legs up. Ever tried to fly higher, but she was struggling with the added weight and getting tired. Ever couldn't keep up her pace. She was slowly flying lower and lower. Mina tried to reach into her bag for the Grimoire, but it was behind her.

She heard a howl and tried to scan the ground below her, but she couldn't see anything. The omen had disappeared. Ever whimpered, and her grip loosened. Mina's shoes brushed the top of a Toyota. She was too heavy for the sprite.

"Ever, stop. Put me down. It's fine," Mina said.

"No, I can't. I promised to protect you." She choked as more tears poured out of her eyes. "Even if we're doomed, I'll still protect you."

"Then fly over the water, and let's see how well he can swim."

Ever, too tired to answer, nodded and turned to fly Mina over the water. They had just cleared the railing when Ever cried out in pain.

The omen had pounced on her back.

"No you don't, you ugly beast!" Ever shouted as she turned on the invisible dog and tried to fight. She let go of Mina.

Mina plummeted from the bridge. "Ever!" she yelled, just before her body smacked against the water and everything went black.

Thirty-Two

"Wake up!" his warm voice demanded. Mina knew that voice, remembered it and sighed in contentment, knowing he was near.

"You have to wake up!"

"No, because if I wake up, you'll be dead," Mina answered. "In my dreams you're still alive."

Teague appeared in front of her, hair slicked back, wearing his royal robes, the same ones he'd worn when he greeted her on the steps for the Choosing Ceremony. His eyes weren't blue though. They were a comforting light gray. But that didn't matter like it had once upon a time. She knew now that she wanted to be with him, in any form.

"But sleep is not your destiny."

"Was it your destiny to die by my hand?"

"You freed me, and for that, I can never repay you." Teague's eyes were so full of love and understanding—the way they should have always been. He looked at her—not with accusation or contempt—but simple adoration and love. Seeing those emotions made her feel inadequate.

"I killed you! You can't possibly forgive me for that. Not when I don't forgive myself."

Teague came forward and wrapped his strong hands around her. "I forgave you the moment you stole my heart. A part of me will always live on." He pulled away just enough to touch her heart. "In here. Forever. But only if you wake up and fight for it."

"I want to stay here with you until I die."

"Which will be any minute. Don't waste your life feeling guilty. Because the thought of losing you will kill what's left of me for sure."

"I can't." She felt her lip tremble, and Teague leaned down, his lips gently brushing against hers in the softest of requests. Asking for her love in return. They brushed against her lips again, and she met him for the kiss. His hands wrapped gently around her face to hold her in place as he deepened the kiss.

She was drowning in the kiss. Losing herself to the feelings. Her lips started to tingle and go numb.

The kiss changed. Teague pressed his lips down and blew into her mouth, forcing her to breathe. Mina opened her eyes in surprise and gasped for breath before rolling over on the beach and emptying her lungs of water.

Her hair stuck to her face, and she peeled it away to take in her surroundings.

She was utterly alone on the beach—at the edge of a warzone. Her heart broke all over again, and fresh tears stung her eyes. Mina collapsed back onto the sand, trying to ignore the way it rubbed against her. And—was she sitting on something? Her bag! She tugged it out from underneath her hip and checked inside. Relief flooded her. She hadn't lost the Grimoire in the bay.

Fighter jets race overhead toward what was left of the Golden Gate Bridge. Helicopters whirred in the air. Everything was over—displayed on the news. The Fae were exposed. The siren ship lost its glamour, and the helicopter moved in, cameras homed in on the Fae ship. The world wouldn't understand that not all Fae were bad. The sirens were about to be attacked.

It appeared more than the Coast Guard had joined in the battle for the world. Humans in fatigues ducked in and out of the abandoned cars on the streets. More Fae army boats docked, and suddenly Mina knew who they were.

Gnomes. Gnomes and Reapers. Annalora was keeping her word. The gnomes and Reapers ran through the streets, targeting the human soldiers.

With legs like gelatin, Mina struggled to stand and make her way up the beach to the street. If she stayed still for too long, the omen would find her.

One foot in front of the other. Through pain and exhaustion, she moved, then walked, then jogged until she got up to the main road. She passed an abandoned vendor booth and grabbed a compact mirror from the display table. Had they run? Or were they too busy recording the battle on the Golden Gate Bridge?

Her side was aflame with pain. Mina pulled up her shirt to see a long black scratch on her stomach.

So Death had marked her after all.

Mina felt Death's presence and knew he was drawing near. Picking up her pace, she ran down another street and turned. Nothing looked even remotely familiar until she collapsed, hitting the pavement on her knees. Then, she remembered the vision she'd had the night she drank Winona's blue tea. She knew what was going to happen next, yet couldn't fight the curiosity.

She had lost. Charlie—Charlie!—and her friends were either dead or soon-to-be dead. She'd failed them. Teague was only a memory. What did she have to lose? She wasn't afraid to see her death coming.

"I'll be with you soon," she whispered, as she thought of both of her parents and Charlie, and of the one her heart lost. She opened the compact and scanned the area behind her.

Her mother was right. Only in hindsight can you see Death coming. Mina saw the omen's pale white eyes glowing behind her. It snarled and growled, saliva dripping from its canines as it tensed to attack.

Mina took off her bag, set it on the ground beside her and closed her eyes, waiting. She let the mirror fall from her hands, and it shattered on the pavement.

She heard the growls, but the attack never came. She looked over her shoulder, seeing nothing.

But she heard everything. Including his voice.

Mina snatched up the broken mirror and held it up, desperately trying to see in the only intact piece left in the frame.

"Come on." She turned and angled the mirror. And almost dropped it again.

Two of them appeared in the reflection, fighting to hold back her death. Her heart burst, and she couldn't control the tears. Jared and Teague. She turned, searching for them with her eyes but saw only an empty street. Was it because they were both dead? Was that the only way to hold back Death?

Jared cried out as the omen bit his shoulder, and he lost his grip on the dog. The dog rolled off and faced Teague, who stood directly in front of her. Shielding her with his body. He held his arms wide open like she'd seen her mom do, and he said in a loud voice, "Death, you've been trying to claim me for over a century. Take me instead. For I no longer fear you. I am free."

Jared yelled at his other half and dove for the dog, but the omen was too fast. He opened his mouth and lunged at Teague.

In a blast of black smoke, they both disappeared.

Mina screamed Teague's name and stood, but the parking lot was empty. Only a black circle remained on the ground where Death had claimed Teague.

"No, no, no." Mina stared at the blackened spot, vision blurring, and she clenched her hands. A tingle on her hand told her Jared was still there, although she couldn't seem him. She closed her eyes and opened her hand. His fingers slid between hers and gave a gentle squeeze.

"Please don't go. I can't lose you. I need you."

She felt another slight tingly sensation on her cheek and brought her hand up to touch the spot where Jared had kissed her. It felt like a goodbye kiss. This couldn't be happening.

How could he even be here? She was losing him *again*.

"Jared, how are you here?"

"They're here because of me," Taz Clara spoke. Her eyes glistened with power. "The power I gleaned feeding from you and from the prince's death afforded me enough strength to pull... memories from him as he died. What I learned surprised me. The prince, being separated for so long, created two distinct souls. They never fully fit together properly again. It was easy to sort through and find the largest group of memories. They came to me almost eagerly, so I took them with me. Strangely, both souls were attached to the memories, like they were a puzzle piece connecting the two princes."

"And the omen?"

"Well, you saved Teague. I suppose sacrificing his soul for you was his way of saying thank you. Don't be fooled, girl. Both souls loved you dearly. And you still have one part of him left, although I can't sustain him in this form very long."

The sprite who had once divided the prince waved her hand in front of Jared, and he became corporeal in front of Mina.

"Oh, Mina." He hugged her to him.

She took a deep breath and let the scent of Jared roll over her while the streets around them rumbled with dangerous activity.

"I never thought I would get to hold you again. I'm sorry for not telling you how I felt sooner... and for all the things that the poison of that hate blade did to me—to us. It lied and used our deepest insecurities against us."

"But the omen and my mother? You said you sent it, or Teague said that. I'm not sure what to believe anymore." She buried her head against his shoulder and felt him nuzzle the top of her head.

"No, that was a lie. I control the Fae Reapers, but the Death Reaper or omen is controlled by the one who has the bone whistle.

"Annalora."

"I believe so."

"How do we stop this?" Mina had been so wrapped up in her own near death and Teague's sacrifice and Jared's presence that she hadn't thought about the battle for a while. But it raged around them still. Annalora's gnome army was here.

"I don't know." He grimaced and flickered.

Mina looked to Taz in alarm. "What's happening?"

"His soul can't survive like this for long," she answered simply. "You destroyed his body beyond repair. I just saved a bit of his soul for you. I thought you'd be grateful."

"No, I am. I just don't want to lose him."

"Then don't," she challenged, as if it were nothing. "Do something about it."

"I don't know how. I can't lose them both."

"It's okay, Mina." The corner of Jared's mouth lifted, showing off his unbelievable grin. "You can let me go. I'm ready to leave."

Helicopters thwacked and thundered overhead.

"I *can't* let you go. Not now, not ever."

"You don't have to. I already told you, I will live on in here." He pointed to her heart.

"So that wasn't a dream?"

"No, we wouldn't let you give up on yourself."

"Then I'm not giving up on you. What can I do? I'm so sorry I caused all this in the first place, but I love you. I will fight for you."

Jared pressed his forehead to hers. "I know, but there's nothing I can do. It's Taz's power that's sustaining me now."

"The Grimoire!"

Mina reached into her bag and pulled out the Grimoire. "Taz split you before and bound your soul to a book. What if we did it again? What if we anchored your soul again?" He flickered, and urgency made her heart pound.

"To anchor my soul is to bind me eternally to you. And I can't do that, Mina. As much as I love you, I can never be a slave to another's whims again. Even if it's a very pretty whim." He kissed her nose sadly. "I don't want to be enslaved."

She pushed him away. "Why are you being so selfish? Why can't you think of anyone but yourself?" she yelled, instantly regretting her words. "I'm sorry," she whispered.

Taz Clara spoke. "We have a problem." She pointed to the tanks that rumbled past them.

Mina looked to Jared. Even as he flickered, his determination solidified. He nodded, and they began to run down the road after the tank. They were surprised when they met up with another Fae along the way. The young man had pointed ears and the bluest of blue eyes. He pulled a small sack of powder out of an ammo bag and tossed it on the tank's wheels, turning them to cement.

"Who are you?" Jared asked.

293

"Theo, of the SFGG." He saluted, then climbed up on top of the tank and used another bag of powder from his pouch to seal the door shut.

"The SFGG?" Mina asked.

"San Fran Godmother's Guild at your service. Constance and the others are already on the bridge trying to control the situation." He laughed and jumped down to run to another tank, disabling it just as fast. "Hey," he shouted from the top. "I think I know you. You're the Grimm."

"Yes," Mina answered.

"Then if you keep going forward," he gestured with his hand, you'll meet up with our leader. I think you'll be pleasantly surprised."

"Thank you," Jared answered pushing ahead.

"Are you going to disappear on me?" she asked him.

"I'll try not to." He looked over his shoulder. Taz had retreated and was following them along the water line. "She's taken back to the water. I think I'll last as long as she has the strength."

"I hope. I guess that's the best answer I'm going to get."

"Yep." He reached out and grabbed her hand, and they ran together. She stumbled once or twice, and he helped, pulling her along after him. "By the way, I like what you've done with your hair."

She blushed. "It's apparently a family trait."

"You should keep it."

"I think I have to."

He laughed and squeezed her hand again.

Theo was right. They soon met up with a large group of onlookers, who were really a group of Fae. It was easy to spot the one in charge. He was tall—impossibly tall—towering over seven feet, with a voice that carried easily. His arms and hands were like giant mallets, and he flung them around as he gave orders to his guild.

"It's Strong Arm," Jared said in surprise. "I thought I destroyed his guild long ago, but leave it to him to rebuild again. Think metallurgist—or, um, you would call them blacksmiths—but Fae."

To his side, she saw Constance. Next to Constance, she saw a face that made her cry out. "Charlie!" Mina ran forward, pushing through the crowd.

Charlie's eyes lit up. He flew off the podium and ran to jump into her arms.

"You're safe," she cooed, struggling under his weight. "And you've grown!" She laughed and put him down. Nan and Brody were on Charlie's heels, and Nan was the second to wrap her in a hug. "Oh, it was terrible. The Reapers grabbed us at the pier but..." Nan stopped talking when she saw Jared. "You!"

Brody leaped in front of her and grabbed Mina, pulling her behind him.

Jared's jaw ticked with anger, and he squared off in front of Brody. "Take your hands off of her, before you lose them."

"No," Brody growled, doing his best to be intimidating.

"Brody, wait." Mina looped her arm through his and met his eyes, pleading. When she turned to look at Jared next, she swallowed. His gaze was locked on her arm holding Brody's. He was about to let someone have it.

Mina quickly let go and stepped in front of Jared. "He's okay."

Now it was Jared's turn to pull her behind his back and keep her out of Brody's reach.

"I won't let you hurt her," Brody threatened. He crossed his arms over his muscular chest.

"I'm not going to… ever." Jared's voice dropped low.

"If you do, I'll kill you. Whatever it takes." Brody eyed Jared, and something passed between the two boys. A silent conversation.

Jared squinted.

Brody raised his chin.

A minute passed.

Mina sighed and rolled her eyes.

"Agreed." Jared laughed. "I can live with that."

Nan pushed past Brody. "Are you the evil one?" She jabbed him in the chest, and he stepped back with a look of chagrin. But it was clear he approved.

Mina couldn't help but smirk. "Evil never won."

She couldn't say anything else, because Strong Arm pointed at the gate. More boats and ships filled with warriors came through. A small dragon suddenly hovered over her shoulder, nodding to her.

Anders. Faithful through everything.

"I swear those are not my men," Jared answered.

"But how is it staying open so long?" Ever seemed miffed. "We only had window of a few seconds to get through."

"I froze the moment in which the gate opened." Jared shrugged like it was no big deal.

Forever

"They just keep coming," Nan said, her voice full of panic.

Mina looked at Jared and then back at the gate, her face filled with anger. "Then we have to finish what you started. We have to destroy the gate—even if it means we destroy the bridge. We can't let any more come through."

Jared seemed surprised at her answer. "There's that siren side of you!"

He ran up to speak with Strong Arm who agreed. He divided his and what was left of Constance's Godmothers, and they headed out toward the bridge.

Ternan's ship was still trying to retreat, under constant fire from the helicopters. A few of the Godmothers helped cloak it again, and it went invisible.

Kino rose up from the shoreline, limping, and shook the water from his hair. A boat of gnomes paddled furiously toward him.

"Godmothers!" Strong Arm pointed, and a few broke off to rush down to the shoreline to meet the oncoming hoard.

Kino crawled, barely able to get away from the gnomes. Brody rushed down and put Kino's arm around his neck. He half-dragged-half-carried Kino up to them.

"Siren." Strong Arm's voice only had one volume. "Are you still with us?"

Kino, visibly shaken, was covered in cuts and bruises. Mina didn't think he could fight anymore.

"Can you bring the bridge down?"

Kino followed his gaze to the Golden Gate Bridge and paled. "Not on my own I can't. I may be good, but I'm not that good."

Charlie rushed forward out of Nan's grasp and stood by Kino. He pointed his thumb toward his chest and back at the bridge.

"Charlie!" A strange mixture of pride and fear coursed through Mina. She'd seen him use the power of his siren gift—his heritage—before, but so much was at stake here. She just couldn't make herself believe he was safe. She ran to him and fell on her knees in front of him. "I love you, Charlie. Please be careful."

Charlie's lip quivered, and his eyes turned glassy. He gave Mina a thumbs up and grabbed Kino's hand.

"You protect him, Kino," Mina stated loudly. "Or I'll do more to you than make you jump overboard."

"Aye, aye, Princess." He swung Charlie's hand in his own and looked down. "Hey, little Prince, are you ready to see what a real siren call can do?"

Charlie just grinned crookedly at him. They turned and saw that Strong Arm's guild had incapacitated the boat of gnomes. One of the Fae gestured for Charlie and Kino to get in the boat. Taz rose out of the water and used a large wave to propel them toward the bridge.

"We need to clear the bridge." Constance said. Anders spun around excitedly above her head. "Warn any of our Fae to get away."

Anders darted through the air toward the bridge. Jared's hand slid into Mina's, and they watched as her little brother and Kino were thrust into the main battlefield, right into the stream of gnomes coming through. Her heart felt like it would stop beating any second.

Kino leaned down to whisper to Charlie. A few seconds later, a shriek ripped through the air, causing their own little boat to move backward in the water. A portion of the bridge crumbled.

Charlie and Kino let forth blast after blast and began to knock down the Golden Gate Bridge piece by piece. It crumbled and fell onto the gnome ships passing through, sinking them.

Fighter jets returned and started firing into the water at Charlie and Kino.

Mina screamed, but then Kino turned and directed a blast at the jet, sending it into a tailspin. The pilot ejected himself before the jet crashed into the water, where it skimmed the surface and took out another of the gnome ships.

Another fighter jet whizzed by, and Jared turned to Mina.

"Your turn." He flickered in and out.

"I can't see him. How can I control him?"

"You can." He placed his hand on her shoulder and gently lifted her hand up toward the jet. "I never wanted to admit it, but you are one of the most powerful Fae I've ever met. If you only believe." Mina couldn't pull her eyes away from Jared's. She searched for the lie but only saw truth. He believed in her.

Mina swallowed and turned her thoughts toward the jet. She felt the Fae power gather around her and channeled it to the approaching aircraft.

Jared growled when she hesitated. "You have to protect them!"

Kino was trying to fend off a helicopter, so Charlie focused on taking down the rest of the bridge by himself. She had to do it and do it now. The fighter jet fired it's guns, and a line of bullet spray ripped into the water to take them out.

She whispered to the pilot. "You can't see! Pull up." Immediately, the fighter jet veered to the left and peeled off. She breathed a sigh of relief as he missed her brother. That was easier than she'd expected. "Stay away," she told him.

Within minutes, the bridge was destroyed. Mina looked at the strangely empty skyline. Her heart grieved that the landmark had been annihilated.

She stared at the water, awed at all of the destruction that had happened because of her cursed life.

The Godmothers rushed to help any injured they found.

Even Brody and Nan left to help, unwilling to stay idle.

Mina, on the other hand, could barely stand without Jared's support. He held her close, as helicopters continued to zoom over them on their way to the bridge. Many were news copters. She could only imagine the stories that were being played out on screens across America. "It would take a miracle to erase the damage we've done."

"You're right," he admitted. "This is beyond altering the memories of a girl and her friends."

"Or school."

"Or school," he repeated.

"Then what can we do?"

"Who knows where Annalora is at the moment— or how many she's working with? For now, here, we try and protect the innocent Fae. We police our own and try to win the trust of the Fae that are here. Or we find another big enough gate and force them all back into the Fae world."

"That seems a little harsh."

"My reign of terror, followed by my parents' impaired judgment—that was harsh. I made all these Fae leave. I could force them to come back." He flickered again, and this time, she felt him disappear and come back.

She pulled from his embrace "Jared?" Mina grabbed for him, but her hands went right through him. He tried to speak, but she couldn't hear him, which meant Taz couldn't sustain him much longer.

One minute he was there—Mina felt a warmth encompass her body, and her heart burst with love in a final goodbye—and then he was gone.

Mina stared at the empty beach and the spot where Jared had stood. She wanted to scream her fury into the sky. She sat on the sand and looked back at the water. She waited. For what, she didn't know.

It was almost sunset when Nan and Brody found her. Ever and Nix came up behind her too. Both of them had been bandaged, and Nix complained about whoever had made the poultice for his wound. Mina felt relief at seeing her friends still alive, safe and sound. The omen hadn't taken them. But she could tell by the way Nix walked and Ever limped that they hadn't completely escape its fury.

Others gathered on the beach. It seemed that the worst of the war was over.

What was left of Teague's and Annalora's armies had run and were hiding in the hills. Apparently, with the destruction of the gate and without their leaders, they didn't know where to go. They would have to hunt them down another day.

Mina watched as Charlie met his grandparents, and he immediately hugged them, not letting them go. Ternan leaned down and lifted the boy up, holding him high in the air.

It seemed that everything would probably be alright for everyone. Except her.

Thirty-Three

"We did it! We won," Ever cheered as she came and stood by Mina. She didn't even attempt to hide her wings.

"If you call this winning," Mina answered. She looked across the Bay at the flashing lights and mob of rescue vehicles.

And Annalora was still out there, plotting.

"Well, we didn't die, so yeah," Ever glanced at Mina and her face turned solemn. "What's up?"

Taz Clara rose out of the Bay. Water trailed over her skin, dripping off in rivulets. She moved closer to the shore but didn't step onto the land. "I'm sorry. I held onto Jared for as long as I could, but he just slipped away from me."

"Ohhh," Ever whispered.

Every part of Mina wanted to scream and yell at her for not trying harder, but the sea witch did not deserve her temper. Taz hadn't plunged the knife into Teague's chest. Mina had. All Taz did was give her more time with him. She should have tried to bind him to the Grimoire despite his argument. But he would've ended up hating her in the end, because he'd once again be a prisoner. She couldn't bear to do that to him.

She felt adrift without him. It ached to admit it.

How could she ever smile again?

Until she heard it.

Thump... Thump... Thump.

And she remembered. Mina pressed her hand to her heart, and a tear slid down her cheek. He would never truly be gone, because she loved him.

Their small group on the beach started to grow in size as a meeting of the guilds and sirens coalesced on the shore.

"We have done all we can, for now." Strong Arm's voice rumbled deeply. "We must leave. It is no longer safe for us. Constance, your guild is welcome to join mine until yours is rebuilt."

Constance nodded her head in agreement. "Thank you for the offer, Strong Arm. I think we will take you up on it until this boils over."

She turned to Nan and Brody. "I think it's best if you two head home as soon as you can. Don't mention that you were anywhere near here. I'll send someone up to help smooth over your parents' memories, so you can try and slip back into your normal lives. I heard that with the school destroyed, you've been on a long break, so at least that bit should be easy enough."

Just hearing the news about her school being on break filled Mina with relief. She knew the Godmothers would take care of Nan and Brody. Their parents wouldn't even remember that Nan and Brody had disappeared. They had a chance at regaining their normal lives, and she was happy for them. As happy as she could feel with all these circumstances.

"Do we have to leave now? What will happen to Mina and Charlie?" Nan ran over to Mina and gave her best friend a hug. "I feel like I just got her back."

"They will be taken care of," Constance assured her.

"Will we see them again?" Nan asked.

"That will be up to them, but it might be better if you forgot all about them for the time being."

"No!" Brody and Nan answered together.

Mina was pleasantly surprised at her friends' determination.

"That will never happen," Brody looked over at Mina and smiled, his eyes crinkling ever so softly. Mina tried to offer a half-smile back.

Constance sighed. "Very well, but there's no time to waste. The sooner you leave, the better."

Nan reluctantly pulled away from Mina's side, and Brody came over to give her a hug. His embrace offered a familiar warmth and comfort. Mina sighed sadly as she struggled to keep her emotions at bay and her will from washing over him. Just because she was afraid of being alone didn't mean Brody was hers to keep.

He gave her another squeeze before he pulled away and reached for Nan's hand. Mina realized in that moment that maybe she was never meant to *have* a happily ever after.

Maybe, they didn't even exist.

Mina watched as Brody walked hand-in-hand with Nan up the shoreline and to the sidewalk before they took off at a jog for the car. She prayed they'd have a safe journey.

"Thank you, sea witch, for your help," Constance said.

Taz Clara remained, standing regally in the water. She smiled and brushed her hand in front of her in a mock bow. "I didn't help to gain the favor of the Godmothers, but of someone much more important."

Constance's lips pinched together, and Mina picked up on the tension between the two women. "I understand. I'm sure the effort will be repaid."

"I hope so," Taz said as she slowly sank into the bay and disappeared.

The siren ship Serenity pulled as close as they could, and Reef and Genni brought the ship's tender into the shore to pick them up and ferry them out. Nix, Ever, and Mina quickly sat down as the sirens swam them out to the ship. As soon as they were aboard, Ternan and Winona set sail.

Taz rose out of the water, her eyes black as night as she called forth a deep rolling fog to hide them. The sea witch raised her long green arm in a parting farewell. The sirens sailed out into the deep ocean, needing time to tend to their injured and find another way back to the Fae plane. The farther away they sailed, the less the damage seemed, until Mina could barely see San Francisco.

It all just felt like a horrible dream.

Charlie had been unwilling to leave Kino's side since the battle. Kino had already dubbed him the Sea Prince. Winona and Ternan struggled to hold their emotions in check as they stood before their grandson.

Winona's face was washed with tears, and Mina swore she saw Ternan's beard tremble with pride.

Charlie stared wide-eyed at the scars along his grandfather's arms. His mouth opened but then firmly shut.

Ternan kneeled down, his eyes shining bright. "There's no need to fear, my boy. You won't hurt me with your gift. As the siren king, I—" His words were cut off as Charlie tossed himself into his grandfather's arms.

Ternan held his hand out to the side, and her grandmother stepped into his arms and joined in the family reunion happening on deck. Mina met Winona's eyes and simply nodded.

Maybe she should have joined them, but something held her back. She couldn't have explained it, other than she felt too much was left undone.

She turned to look at the ocean and asked Ever, "When can we get back?"

"We just left. Why would you want to go back?"

"Not to the pier—to the Fae plane."

Ever bit her lip as she tried to think. "I'm not sure. We may be stuck here for a while."

"That can't be. We have to get back," Mina's heart told her something was wrong.

"There's another natural gate, but it may take a while to sail there," Kino answered as he came to stand by them. His face was covered with soot, and his arm had numerous cuts.

"Where?" Mina demanded.

"Well, the biggest one is the Bermuda Triangle." He rubbed the back of his head and winced when he brought his hand away with a bit of blood on it.

"We don't have that much time."

Annalora was out there somewhere, and Mina didn't know what else she had planned. But she would not let that stuck up gnome destroy everything.

"Well, you could always go yourself and use the seam ripper, but what's the hurry?"

"Annalora. I feel like I've missed something obvious. I don't like not knowing what's going on over there. There's... there's something big happening, and I can't tell what it is."

Ever faced Mina. "Let's use the seam ripper. I'll go with you. I trust your instincts."

Saying goodbye was difficult, but Mina knew her grandparents and Kino would watch over Charlie as they sailed toward the Bermuda Triangle.

None of them belonged here. She didn't even know if she belonged here, but they would all find each other again on the other side.

Ever and Nix stood directly behind Mina as she pulled out the seam ripper and opened the gate between worlds. But something *was* wrong. The gate didn't glow like it had before. It opened into a dark swirling vortex of wind, and sparks of lightning shot in and out of the gate.

"What's happening?" Ever yelled as she held up her hands to deflect the flying debris stirred up by the gate.

"This is what I've been feeling," Mina answered. "I think the gates are closing." She stared at the gate with mixed emotions. For a few years, this had been all she wanted, to close the gates between the worlds and to stop the Fae from coming over. Now, if it closed behind them, it would trap the sirens and her brother in the human plane forever. And it would also mean she'd never see her friends again.

"But why are they closing?" Nix yelled as he held onto Ever's shoulders to try and steady her.

Mina, unafraid of the wind and the vortex of darkness, walked toward it and listened. She let herself hear and feel what was coming through the gate. "There's not enough magic to keep them open anymore."

Mina took a step back before running toward the gate and jumping through. Coldness rushed through her body, followed by prickly pain. When she landed, she rolled through rough grass that scratched at her arms. Mina sat up and watched the gate close slowly. *Come on, guys.*

Ever and Nix came flying out at the last second.

The gate closed, and the wind stopped. They were left in utter silence.

Ever was the first one on her feet. Her mouth dropped open, and her hands flew to her mouth in horror. "Holy snickerdoodles on toast."

Mina got up and looked at the Fae plane. The trees were brown and withered, the grass had dried up to a crusty brown, the river beds were dried, and fish lay dead in the mud.

Nix turned away and covered his eyes. As far as they could see, the magic and life in their world was fading away.

"What's going on?" Ever cried out in despair.

Mina knew. She could feel it deep in her soul, and she answered. "The Fae plane is dying."

"How can that be?" Ever whispered. "We only just left."

"We have to get to the Fates and fast," Mina answered. "They were last in the swamps."

Nix looked around at their surroundings and ran up a small hill. He placed his hands on his hips and turned around to look at them. "I hate to tell you this, but I think we're *in* the swamps. Or what's left of them."

Mina turned full circle and then ran up to where Nix stood. Sure enough, he was right. The valley lay in the distance, and she recognized the mountains, so that meant the Fates should be here. She turned and spotted the large willow tree. And she took off running.

It was easier to cover the distance when the swamp was dry as a bone. She kicked up dust as she leaped over dried shrubs. She slowed when she came to the withered and dead willow tree. She should have been stopped. A guard or Reaper or *someone* should have tried to stop her, but there was no one. She reached forward and gently pushed the withered hanging branches to the side. She stepped under the boughs.

Her breath caught. Captain Plaith kneeled in front of the bodies of the Fates, who were laid out along the ground. Dried flower petals had been scattered across their formal outfits. The Captain of the Guard turned to look at Mina, his eyes red-rimmed and his face pale and covered in a fine coat of dust.

"Captain Plaith, what happened?" Mina asked, staying as far away as she could from the grieving man.

"How dare you enter here!" He spun on his knee and pulled a weapon out of his robes to attack.

Mina held up her hand in panic, and his blow froze mid-air. All she wanted him to do was stop, and he had.

His eyes looked about wildly, his teeth gnashed, and spit came flew out of his mouth. "I know you! I remember you from the maze, but you look different. How are you doing this? With the death of the Fates, there shouldn't be any magic left in our world."

"Well, maybe it's because I don't come from your world," she said coldly. "Now, I'm going to ask you again. What happened?"

"Poison," he said. "An offering came from the gnomes, and it was poisoned."

Mina closed her eyes and felt a pang of deep sorrow. It seemed that the all-powerful Fates were not immune after all. The whole family fell to poison. "What can we do?"

"There's nothing to do but prepare for the end," Captain Plaith answered. "The reason the Fates are so strong is because they are the conduits of all power that flows through our plane. That link has been broken. If Prince Teague were here, he could save us, but I fear he doesn't care about his people anymore."

"He's dead," Mina answered solemnly. She released Captain Plaith from her hold.

"Then I fear the worst." He put away his weapon.

"There has to be someone else."

"The strongest Fae have gone to the palace to see if they can restore the magic to our lands. Others are looking for ways to cross over to your world, since ours is doomed."

"Then we will go to the Fae palace," Mina said.

"Good luck. It's become quite the battleground. I'd stay very far away from there."

"Look, I didn't have to come back. I'm not even sure why I did, but if *I'm* not giving up on your world, then you better not either. Do you understand? That's an order."

Captain Plaith swallowed nervously, and a small smile crept onto his face. "Yes ma'am." He stood taller and gave her a bow before walking to the willows and pulling the branches aside so she could pass through.

On the other side, she met Nix and Ever. They nodded silently, as if they had overheard everything.

Captain Plaith pulled out a small flute and played a simple melody. A few minutes later, three centaurs came over the hills in a cloud of dust, all of them heavily armed. The dark-coated one had a long sword, a palomino female wore a long bow, and the tallest—with the whitest of coats—carried an axe.

"Thank you for coming Adrith, Basal, and Prase," Captain Plaith addressed them in order. "I think one has come who is able to save us. Can we count on your herd to escort us?"

The white centaur, Adrith, held up his axe and reared in challenge. "We do not fear battle. Your company will be safe with us."

"Then we must hurry," Captain Plaith answered. He gestured for Mina to mount Prase, the closest centaur, but Adrith stepped forward.

"I'll guard this one." He offered her his hand.

Mina placed her hand in his palm as he kneeled and helped her onto his back. Ever and Nix climbed upon Basal and Prase, while Captain Plaith readied his own Fae steed.

Adrith took off at a canter through what was left of the swamps. Mina's hair whipped around her face, and she tried to not let the darkness that was hopelessness envelope her. She had to have faith, even in the most difficult trials.

"I may not have been able to save you, but I will try to save your home," Mina whispered in promise to the air. Not a single tear fell from her eye. She doubted she had any left to shed.

When they came to the expansive bridge, Adrith pulled up short. The lake was still there, but barely. The palace was in full view, since the veil of magic that hid it was gone. Even from this distance, they could see a large group of Fae gathered on the other side of the bridge.

Basal sniffed the air and stomped his hooves in displeasure. "Reeks of gnome. Lots of them."

Prase shook her head in distaste, her white and brown hair flowing. "They're just thieves and scavengers. Coming to steal what's not rightfully theirs."

"Let them," Mina answered. "Things don't matter if we can't keep the world from dying."

"The girl is right," Adrith spoke. "We must restore the conduit of power."

"And does anyone know how to do that?" Ever asked.

"I do," Ferah spoke up. The elf walked up to them, her red hair falling in dirty clumps past her shoulders, her face streaked with tears. She turned to Mina, her shoulders slumped. "This is all my fault. This is what I saw, this is what was foretold. The death of our world. It's why I tried to kill the prince all those years ago. Now I've failed twice over."

Mina glared at Ferah but felt a twinge of sympathy. "Yes, this is your fault, but you don't carry the blame alone. That is too much a burden for any one of us. Now that you're here, you can prove yourself. Help us save the Fae world."

Ferah cupped her hands over her face and brushed fresh tears away. She sniffed and wiped her nose on her sleeve. Then she turned and looked at Mina with a gleam of determination. "If only I had seen it then. I would never have stood in your way."

A great rumbling began, and the centaurs shuffled in place as the ground quaked and shifted. In the middle of the lake, a fissure opened, and water rushed into the rift. The great stone bridge before them began to crumble, small stones falling into the remaining water.

"We must hurry." Ferah ran across the bridge before the earthquake finished.

Adrith yelled for Mina to hold on as the centaurs took off running toward the bridge. If they didn't hurry, they wouldn't make it across.

Mina's heart pounded in her chest as more stones fell away. Adrith was the first to cross, followed by the other centaurs. Prase's rear hooves just scraped the last stone before it dropped.

Mina turned and saw that Captain Plaith's horse had misjudged the distance. A cry ripped from her throat as the horse's hooves barely scraped the stone. Another rumble ripped through the plane, and more of the bridge fell away.

One second, the horse and captain were there.

The next they were gone over the ledge and lost to the deep chasm.

Thirty-Four

M ina stared at the edge of the bridge they'd barely made it across, until Ferah cried out in warning, "Go, go, go!"

The stones underneath her feet were cracking, and Basal neighed in fright. They couldn't afford to stop. Nix grabbed Ferah's hand and pulled her onto the mount with him, and the centaurs ran as if their lives depended on it, which they did.

They raced to outrun the ever-growing chasm that threatened to swallow them all.

Then it stopped. The middle of the lake was gone. Just an empty hole ending a few hundred feet from the end of the bridge.

They hurried on.

When they arrived at the doors of the palace, they were greeted by multiple Fae, old and young alike—all terrified. Some yelled, trying to assert their dominance over the group of frightened Fae. Mina and the others slid down from the centaurs and tried to hear what was going on.

"Settle down, settle down," a tall, broad shouldered gnome commanded. "We can solve this problem peacefully."

"Where are the Fates?" an angry dwarf yelled.

"Why are they not saving us?" an elderly elf asked.

The gnome leader seemed to be losing his patience. "They can't save our home anymore. A terrible accident has befallen them."

"We're doomed," the same elf cried out.

Mina and the group came along the outskirts of the Fae. Ferah motioned for Mina to follow her, so Nix and Ever said they'd stay and see what they could learn. Mina followed Ferah along the side path and around the palace until they arrived at the hedge maze.

"This wouldn't have happened if I had just stepped out of the way," she berated herself.

With the plants dead, it was easy to cross through the broken and dying bushes or step over them, until they came to the tower. The tower glass had been repaired, and something compelled Mina to hurry. She didn't need more prompting. She ran up the steps of the tower and came into the round observatory room.

"What now?" Mina asked as she stepped in and turned in a circle. A flood of memories rushed back to her as the former assassin joined her.

Ferah faced her. "I don't know. I only know that I was supposed to bring you here. All of the Fates have been chosen in this room. It's why the test ended here. Except…"

"Except what?" Mina asked, sensing her hesitation.

"I don't know. I feel like I've let you down. I don't know what else there is to do. I should leave you." Ferah looked around the tower once more and started back down the stairs.

Mina walked over to the large windows and saw how fast the Fae world was dying. So much had happened up here. The memories were equally sweet and painful. How she longed for the prince to be standing here with her.

The ground began to rumble again, and the tower swayed.

Mina tried to make sense of all this. She still felt like she was missing something. Captain Plaith said the Fates were a conduit of magic for the land, and with their deaths, the magic was gone.

"Again, you get in my way!" Annalora shrieked from behind Mina. The tower leaned, shifting with the quakes. Annalora stood in the stairwell, bracing the wall for support as the round of tremors passed. "How are you here? You should be dead! I've sacrificed too much for you to still be here."

"I guess I'm not so easy to kill."

Annalora placed a strange instrument—the bone whistle!—to her lips and blew. Mina instantly recognized that sound. She'd heard it the day her mother died.

Suddenly, the Death Reaper stood before her.

But not the same one.

This one wore a long black leather jacket. His head was bowed, and his dark hair fell loosely around his face, disguising him, but when he lifted his pale, white eyes and met her gaze, she wanted to cry.

Teague.

He had taken the place of the Death Reaper. In his hand, he held a black dagger.

"It's always come down to this," Annalora said. "We've waited centuries for the gnomes to have a chance to rule. We're the forgotten ones, the race that everyone overlooks. We're strong in our own right. Our armies have proven it. And our poison is the most deadly in the world. It's pure hate. It was perfect... until you came along. There could only be one of us in the end."

Annalora's laugh echoed through the tower. "I win." She pointed her finger and spoke a command.

Teague shifted into a black griffin with white eyes and lunged for Mina.

She didn't run, didn't move, but simply closed her eyes and opened her soul to him. There was a moment of shock as he passed through her. She expected the reaping of her soul to hurt, but instead, she opened her eyes to see that they were surrounded by darkness. Teague stood with his arms wrapped around her, his breathing ragged as he looked into her eyes.

"What happened?"

"I've taken you to the In Between. A place of purgatory for souls."

"So I'm dead?"

"No, you are very much alive," he whispered. "And I plan on keeping it that way."

"Teague, what happened to you?"

"A new omen has been chosen. I've become Death, a Reaper who will forever collect souls and bring them to the In Between."

"But how?"

"You saw that nothing can stop Death, except one who is dead or close to death. The omen brought my soul here, to the In Between. As soon as I stepped over, I challenged the Death Reaper and killed him, taking his place. It was the only way. I had to fight to get back to you. I won't abandon you again…ever."

"So you're here to take my soul?" Mina asked hesitantly.

"I'm here to collect a soul, but not yours," Teague spoke softly, touching his forehead to hers. "You have the other half of mine."

She inhaled in disbelief, but deep down, she knew it was the truth. How else could she have sensed such trouble on the Fae plane and the closing of the gates? Jared's side was still with her.

"Are you ready?" Teague asked, pulling away and holding out his hand to her.

She recognized the dagger he held and paused.

When he saw her hesitation, he quickly sheathed the dagger. "The weapon that kills the soul becomes the Reaper's weapon."

"I'm so sorry," she said again, her heart aching at what she had done.

"Don't be," Teague assured her. "You were the only one strong enough to do it. I've caused a lot of death over the years. I needed to be stopped, and this is truly a fitting punishment for me." He patted the hilt of the knife and smiled crookedly at her. "I'm just thankful you killed me with a bladed weapon instead of a rock." He chuckled, and she wanted to punch him in the arm.

In the darkness around her, she could hear the sounds of howling and gnashing of teeth. "What is that?" she asked fearfully.

"The lost souls. We can't stay here long, because you still have your soul, and there are those who hunger for it. They'll take it by force."

"It reminds me of the place in my dream, when I tried to save you and went into the mirror and found you in a dark prison."

Teague didn't miss a beat. "It is that place. You came here in your dream—to the In Between—and it remembers you. I have to take you out of here, but I wanted time to speak to you alone."

The sound of the shadows moving and the cold made her skin prickle. "Is my mom here?"

"Yes, I promise I'll find her and get her to the other side, but there's something you must understand, Mina." His voice sounded so earnest, she felt the bubble of worry start to overtake her.

"What?"

"Annalora's planned this all along. She has the bone whistle, the one item that can control me. I still have to take a soul, and I'll try and delay the reaping. But Mina, I can't touch her if she holds that whistle. When we go back, you *have* to get it from her and destroy it. Then we'll both be free of her. Can you do that?" He lifted his hand a second time to caress her face.

She swallowed and grabbed it, feeling the coldness of his skin against her warm cheek. "Yes, I can."

He nodded. "Good. Because if she commands me again, I'll have no choice but to take your soul. I'd promise to help you to the other side and not leave you in the In Between, but I'd rather not even have to go that far."

Mina didn't say anything else as black smoke surrounded them, and then they were back in the tower.

320

Forever

Annalora stood proud, full of herself, and oblivious, at the tower window chanting in a Fae language. Mina assumed she was celebrating. But as Mina moved toward her, Annalora turned, and her eyes went wide at seeing Mina still alive.

Mina lunged for the hand that held the whistle.

Annalora screeched and clawed at Mina's throat, but Mina pulled back her fist and punched the gnome girl in the face. Her head snapped back, and she dropped the whistle to the ground. Mina dove for it.

Annalora grabbed Mina's foot and dragged her along the floor and away from the bone whistle. Mina rolled over, summoned power, and shoved a blast of power into Annalora's chest, knocking her into a chair. She turned back over and watched as the whistle rolled to a stop at the top of the stairs.

In front of Ferah, who had stealthily returned.

Ferah bent down and picked up the whistle.

Annalora began to beg and cajole. "Ferah, give me the whistle, and I can make all of this go away. I just need to get rid of her."

The elf-girl stood up, still looking battle-weary and terrified. "I should never have told you of the prophecy which foretold the dark prince's reign and the end of our world."

"Grow up," Annalora snapped. "You and the Godmothers would never have been able to stop the prophecy. This is the end. Can't you see that?"

Mina got up from the floor and glanced around the room. She caught a reflection in the glass—Teague pacing in the corner of the room, unable to strike because the whistle was still in play. It seemed that none of the others could see him.

"You killed the Fates," Ferah cried out. Her hand holding the whistle shook in fury.

"Something you should have done long ago." Annalora tried to play it off as no big deal. "Now we can start fresh, build the Fae world anew. Just give me the whistle, and I'll end her. You can be head of the Royal Guard. I'll give you anything you want." She'd continued to walk and talk until she was only a foot from the elf.

Ferah shook her head. "No, this world will not be built on your darkness." She turned to look at Mina. "I see light when I look at you. I'll follow you till the end."

She reached out to hand the whistle to Mina, but Annalora grabbed one of Ferah's own daggers from her bandolier and stabbed the girl.

Ferah's eyes fluttered in disbelief. The whistle fell from her limp fingers followed by a trickle of blood. It dropped and bounced on the floor.

"*No!*" Mina let the fury she had been holding back burst forth.

The room erupted into a ball of light, and Annalora backed up, her arms in front of her face. Mina turned her anger on Annalora and did as Teague had done centuries ago. She blasted the girl through the glass tower window.

Annalora screamed, and then silence followed.

Ferah lay on the ground, unable to speak. She held up her hand, and Mina rushed to her side and grasped it between her own.

"I'm so sorry," she said in a pained whisper, "for betraying you over and over. Even in the Godmother's Guild, I tried to drown you. I never had enough faith. I'm sorry." She let out one last breath, and her head fell to the side.

"Teague," Mina screamed, but he didn't appear. She searched the floor in a blur of tears and picked up the bone whistle. She snapped it in two and threw it across the floor. Within seconds, he appeared by her side.

"Do something!" she begged.

"I can't, my love," Teague soothed. "Her soul has already passed to the In Between. I can meet her there and help her pass over and not be lost, but that is all."

Mina rocked back onto her heels and wiped at her eyes. Another earthquake erupted, and the jagged shards of remaining glass rained down beside them in colored pieces.

Teague helped her up. He led her to the empty windows, and they watched as the two yellow suns began to turn dark.

"What are we going to do?"

He reached for her hand, and she looked up into his white eyes. "We save our world."

"How?"

"When the worlds were first created, there was darkness. From that darkness, light came forth. There's a balance of light and dark. My mother the moon, my father the sun. I think it's safe to say that I'm darkness. And you, Mina, are light. I asked you once before if you would stay with me and rule by my side. I need you. I can't exist without you. So I ask again, will you stay with me?"

Mina turned and looked at their hands clasped together and over at the world that was crumbling and dying around them. She wouldn't let the circumstances pressure her into doing the wrong thing. She glanced into his eyes and still saw white. It didn't scare her. On him, it looked majestic and not deathly. Maybe because his eyes conveyed so much love.

In fact, there was so much love, so much honor, that she wasn't searching for them to change to blue or gray. The color didn't matter anymore. The soul did. The prince, as he stood before her, was both Teague and Jared, and she had a part of his soul.

Teague also possessed a bit of hers.

"Yes," she answered. "I'll stay." She felt a thrill as he smiled and bent to kiss her.

His lips claimed hers in a passionate kiss, and he whispered, "I've waited forever for you. Now I'm yours. Love me, rule with me. I'll love and protect you for eternity." The corner of his mouth lifted up in a smile as he reached up to caress her cheek.

"Eternity sounds perfect." Mina rose up on tiptoes to wrap her hands around his neck, and he laid a trail of kisses down her face until he kissed her mouth again.

"Then open your soul to me like you did before." He gently pulled away, and they turned to look out the tower across the land.

It was easy to do, to close her eyes and think of the love she had for him. She felt Teague do the same, and their minds touched.

He whispered, "Open your eyes."

She did, and she saw hundreds of lights rise up out of the land, and more come from the palace and flow to her. She didn't flinch or run away but felt the Fae magic flow through her and Teague, magnified like a prism. She and Teague began to glow together, and the Fae magic drew closer to them, uniting their souls.

Then, it shot out of them, across the sky, and into the Fae world.

She was a magnet—the conduit—for all the Fae power in the land. It flowed to them and through them. Mina understood now what the Fae lights were. There never had been anyone else in the palace. It was the magic that kept her company. She could see it, and it responded to her, just like when she was younger. It had always been attracted to her. It always seemed to come willingly to her.

It knew, just like Teague knew, they were meant to be together.

Mina felt no pain, only joy, as the Fae world slowly changed, grew and blossomed before her. The two suns brightened, the grass turned green, and the land healed itself. Water filled the lake again, but the magic wasn't done. The palace rebuilt itself, and the magnificent structure returned to its former glory.

But it didn't look the same. There were fewer towers, more rounded glass domes like observatories, and the river-paths flowed through the grounds.

Teague shifted into a black griffin as he turned toward Mina. This one had specks of white on the tips of his feathers, and his eyes stayed the same white as Teague's. Mina climbed onto his back as he jumped from the tower and flew across the palace and over the lake. For hours they flew, watching as the Fae world reknit itself and became even more beautiful. It was everything she ever dreamed of.

When everything seemed to be in order, they flew back to the palace and alit on the steps. Mina slipped off, and Teague shifted back. He stood by her side as hundreds of Fae pressed close, crying out in tears of joy and thankfulness.

Teague's face turned down, and she recognized his frustration. "What's the matter?" she whispered.

"I've only just got you, and I'm not in the mood to share," he grumbled as a Fae child ran up and hugged Mina around the waist. His frown turned to one of bewilderment as the same child, in turn, hugged him. He looked at a loss, and then his hand came down and gently patted the girl's head. "She can see me, and she's not scared of me."

"I think people can see you if they don't fear Death."

The little girl whispered, "Thank you."

At that moment, Teague must've appeared to others. They began to understand that it took two to save the world.

"All hail the Fates," Adrith called out from the crowd. "King of Darkness, Queen of Light."

"Alright!" Ever whooped.

Nix clapped eagerly. The Fae cheered on relentlessly, and the sound became deafening.

"Fate?" Mina asked as she looked to Teague.

He seemed a little confused. "What did you think I meant when I asked you to stay with me? It was a marriage proposal." He shrugged. "So maybe it wasn't the best one. Don't worry, the title of Queen won't come into effect until after the ceremony, but your fate's already tied to mine. We became the Fates when we saved the Fae plane."

"I guess I didn't expect to marry a Fate worse than Death."

Teague's eyes lit up as he picked Mina up and twirled her around to the encore of the crowd's cheers.

Forever

"I promise to love you forever," Teague said when he put her back down on the ground. He reached down and kissed her knuckles.

Mina smiled and spoke softly, "Forever isn't long enough."

Epilogue

The next few weeks were a whirlwind as the Fae planned her wedding to Teague and the coronation soon after. Teague kept his promise and returned to the In Between to help Ferah cross over. He also found her mother's soul, but he didn't just help her to the other side. He was able to do one better.

It seemed no one knew what to expect when a rogue prince who hardly played by the rules became the official Death Reaper. He was a Fate, and a Royal, and more powerful than any before him, so the rules became guidelines, and he bent them all.

Mina cried a river of tears when her father's spirit appeared to her in the Royal gardens. James was smiling, his short mustache wiggling over his teeth. A second later, her mother appeared by his side in her full siren glory, and her father didn't seem to mind. They both waved, and she watched as her father wrapped his arms around her mother before they slowly faded out. It was the best gift anyone could have given to her.

Her grandparents and brother finally made it back to the Fae plane, and Charlie seemed to be loving the siren life. He was wholly acclimated to the Fae world and customs. His clothes were covered in nets and shells, and he preferred to run around barefoot. He had even made friends with a younger siren boy.

Kino, Genni, and Reef frequently swam up the new networks of smaller streams in and around the new palace grounds, and Mina saw the reason the streams had been created. Because of her—for her family and friends. Nix loved to swim the streams too, and he would frequently pop out of the water and place shells and rocks along the sidewalks that lined the streams. Charlie planted his mother's remembrance seed in the palace gardens, and it sprouted into a beautiful and fitting red orchid, aptly named a ruby siren.

Everything seemed to be in place, except that she couldn't help but worry over her friends—the Godmothers, Nan, and Brody. The natural gates were still open, and there were hundreds of Fae that roamed the human plane—many evil ones who had been released when the Grimoire was destroyed the first time. She had some contact with the GMs, and it seemed like they had moved to a new location and were rebuilding, but no one was handling the rampant Fae.

Mina had wanted to go initially, but Teague said that was too dangerous for them all. If something happened to her, the Fae world would collapse again. She now understood the Fates' dilemma and the reason for sending the Grimm brothers after the Fae.

They'd done it out of desperation, and Mina was about to do the same.

Mina and Teague spent hours discussing it, and they agreed. Teague sent for Ever and Nix and had them brought to the throne room. They stood in front of the thrones on the floor, so they would be on the same level when Ever and Nix approached.

Their dear friends—and now subjects—looked nervous, because things had changed. Especially now that Mina wore royal Fae robes of gold and white, and Teague wore his own in shades of gray and black. Behind the two thrones, on the wall, mysteriously appeared the betrothal picture of her and Teague that she had been looking for in the storage room. Mina had a suspicion that Teague was the one who hid it and was also the one who made it reappear.

Teague and Mina laughed when Nix curtsied and Ever bowed.

When everyone's laughter died down, Mina asked them, "What are your plans for the future?"

Ever ran her fingers over her skirt and looked wary. "We're going to stay with you. Remember, I'm your Godmother," Ever answered.

Mina shook her head. "There's no need anymore. The curse is broken."

"Oh, yeah." Ever's wings slowly dipped in sadness.

Nix threw his arm over her shoulders and nudged her gently. "You can always be my guardian."

Ever gave a wry smile, but she was still sad. "I just thought that we make such a good team. It can't be over."

Mina turned and picked up the Grimoire from the throne behind her. "It's not. There are still hundreds of rogue Fae that can't be left to roam free on the human plane." She handed the book to Ever.

Forever

Ever's hands trembled as she held the book. "I can't take this. I'm not a Grimm."

"Grimm is just a title. Think of it as a job description," Teague said. "And as I've proven, those can be loosely followed. I think you'll do just fine. You'll make a phenomenal keeper of the Grimoire."

Ever ran her fingers over the gold lettering and opened up the pages. Her wings fluttered in anticipation. "I'm in, as long as you're sure you don't need me."

Mina smiled. "I've got my very own Reaper to protect me." She nudged Teague, who placed his arm around her waist in affirmation. "Although as a Grimm with the Grimoire, you may need a Godmother." Mina looked at Nix who seemed to balk at the idea.

"Nope, huh uh. I'm not going to do it if I have to be called a Godmother." He puffed out his cheeks and drawled in a thick accent. "You can call me the Godfather."

Ever rolled her eyes.

He grinned and winked.

Mina smiled. Her best friends were up for the challenge. She knew that Ever and Nix would look after Nan and Brody. The Godmothers, once they were reestablished, would help Ever as well. She hated that she was unable to help over there in the world she loved so much, but the Grimoire would be in very capable hands. Mina let out a deep breath. "I've waited so long to be free of the curse. And now that I am, I can't continue the quest. My story is done, but your story, Ever... is just beginning."

The End

331

Also by Chanda Hahn

Unfortunate Fairy Tale Series

UnEnchanted

Fairest

Fable

Reign

Forever

The Iron Butterfly Series

The Iron Butterfly

The Steele Wolf

The Silver Siren

Chanda Hahn is a New York Times and USA Today Bestselling Author. She uses experience as a children's pastor, children's librarian and bookseller to write compelling and popular fiction for teens. She was one of Amazon's top customer favorite authors of 2012 and is an ebook bestseller in five countries.

She was born in Seattle, Washington, grew up in Nebraska, and currently resides in Portland, Oregon with her husband and their twin children.

Visit Chanda Hahn's website to learn more about her other forthcoming books. www.chandahahn.com

Acknowledgements

A quick thank you to everyone who helped me with this book.

Thank you to everyone who has been apart of this journey. To my readers who have faithfully followed my books since I self-published UnEnchanted on New Years Eve in 2011. You've stuck with me through all of my unfortunate fairy tale endings and I hope that you are satisfied with the conclusion of Mina's story. But not all fairy tales have happily ever afters. Some just have afters. So we will have to wait and see if there are any more tales left to tell.

Thanks to my husband, Philip, who lost me to so many work related trips and signings and took care of the kids while I was away. He almost influenced me on changing the ending of the series, but I stuck to my guns. Sorry honey. To my kids, who had to constantly hear, "Shh Mom's writing."

To my editor Bethany Kaczmarek and her sister, Erynn Newman, who make me sound smarter than I really am. To my brother in law, Steve Hahn, who worked under my crazy deadlines to create my awesome covers.

And for everyone else that I've forgotten to mention above, let's insert your name here _____.

CPSIA information can be obtained at www.ICGtesting.com
Printed in the USA
LVOW11s2317131215

466546LV00001B/33/P